TIME'S ELLIPSE

By Frasier Armitage

For Lunarbelle and the boy

You are my world and my star

CONTENTS

TIME'S ELLIPSE

DOCTOR ROLANDS

I

April 2047

Time stopped in the bunker. Bodies crammed into the tight space, pressing against me, but not as much as the darkness which seeped into everything, stilling the seconds while the storm raged above.

Hurricanes unleashed a throaty growl, overwhelming the sound-proof shielding in the ceiling. Hail blasted the roof louder than machine gun fire. Or it could've been swarming sand clouds. Either way, maintenance would need to replace the paneling. Again. Too many dents. There were always too many dents.

I crossed my fingers that the antenna which connected us to Wifi didn't snap, if a lightning blast hadn't already melted it. Without Wifi, we were alone with our thoughts. Which is the last place I wanted to be.

"So here's a question that should help us pass the time," I said to no one in particular, raising my voice above the storm's shriek. "Are we moving through time, or is time moving through us?"

"Another conundrum, Doctor? Really?" The voice came from among the huddle. Hard to tell exactly which of the sharp-suited business execs had finally lost their patience. "Haven't we spent enough time playing games when we should be talking about the launch?"

"We spent two hours in that conference room before the storm hit," I continued, ignoring him. "And time felt like it zipped by. But down here, the past two hours have felt like a million eternities. Isn't that strange? It's like time is speeding up and slowing down just for us."

"I'm sure you've got a theory for it, Doctor. But I've got a theory of my own. I think the reason you insist on raising these hypotheticals has nothing to do with keeping us occupied, and everything to do with avoiding the real issue. It's time for you to make a decision."

Grumbles of agreement could roughly be translated as *we wouldn't even be in here if you hadn't already kept us waiting.* They were right. It was my fault we were down here. My fault we'd delayed. But it was also my fault we even had a decision to make in the first place. 'The Great Doctor Emily Rolands.' If I'd never opened my mouth, and had kept my theories to myself, I wouldn't be standing where I am today. And neither would the rest of them. Maybe some of them would have preferred that. But maybes weren't going to save us. They were no use to anyone.

"How can any of us sanction the launch?" I asked. "Knowing what we know — there has to be another way."

Another voice from the dark. "Speaking frankly, how can we *not* sanction it, Doctor? Would any of us be here if it wasn't necessary?"

I shook my head. "Those are six people you're asking me to condemn to an early grave. Do any of you want that on your conscience?"

"Emily. Just listen for a moment. Really listen." Everything stilled in the bunker as the thudding on the roof grew louder. Louder.

"I'm listening," I said.

"We're only hearing that storm now, but you heard it first, didn't you? You heard every storm before it arrived. Before any of us. You predicted all of this. The tornadoes, tsunamis, the sun boiling us in our filth. Isn't that why you started Orbicon in the first place? And it's exactly *because* you listened all those years ago that we even have a chance. Just listen one more time. Can't you hear it? The world is condemned already. What are six more lives?"

I could've corrected them — told them I founded Orbicon all those years ago because I was too young to know the difference between a good idea and a bad one. Too young to resist being carried away by the lure of hubris. But what good was nitpicking over details when these sharks were right anyway? The planet had died long before any of us figured it out. Even me.

"I know you want to make this into an equation," I said. "Normally, I would too. Math is simple. Beautiful. It's the foundation of logic and you can use that logic to make yourself feel like you've done the right thing. Or convince yourself that this is a binary choice. Wrong or right. Live or die. But we're not talking about pitting billions of lives against six. We're talking about asking six people to come forward on a hunch. To send them to their deaths for the hope of maybe saving what's left of the rest of us. Maybe. The only guarantee for you to rationalize with logic is that six people are going to die. And *that's* what you're asking me to sanction."

"We're all guaranteed to die, Doctor. But it would be nice to have a choice about the how and when, don't you think?"

Was that a real question or just a sales technique? I couldn't tell anymore. I used to be able to know the difference.

A panel rippled under the force of the tornado. Everyone held their breath. But after a few seconds, it settled. The panel didn't buckle. Not yet.

That was too close.

How did we get to here? I remembered the first time I'd sat in front of these same businessmen, each of them wearing inhumanly pristine smiles to match their neckties. I could always spot the difference between a SpaceGen money-man and a scientist by their smile alone.

Back then, the execs were excited about the fortune my theories could gain for the company. AKA, for them. Every conversation ended in how the 'orbital constant' would make us all rich. How 'gravitational wave propulsion' would revolutionize our industry. Now, the lights were off. The smiles gone. And they were the ones lecturing me on the ethics of survival.

I knew what Chrissie would say if she was still here. She'd say *look how far we've come. Look how far your theories have taken us.* Yeah. How far backwards.

Poor Chrissie. She was so bright-eyed. So hopeful. How many of these businessmen and women — so concerned about preserving life — even remembered her? Could they describe the color of her curls? Her eyes? The way the tsunami took her? What did they know about life?

"There has to be another way," I said.

"How many times have we been over this, Emily? We can't send machines, can we?"

"No. Asking machines to do the job would be like trying to program an AI to interpret how to love, or how to be angry. To a robot, a second is a second, just like gravity is gravity. We need to send people who understand more than just the mechanics of the situation. We need to send people who can understand the implications. Machines aren't an option."

"So that means sending humans to Trappist-1E. You can't get around it, Doctor."

I shrugged. "Or we could focus on Mars."

"After what happened with the lander? You know the only way we're getting to Mars is by going through Trappist."

I hated admitting that he was right. It used to be that Mars was the obvious solution. If we made a refuge off-world, it didn't matter if the planet died. There'd be somewhere we could hide. Somewhere to hunker down, to colonize. But figuring out how to land a spacecraft in the paper-thin gravity of Mars was like trying to slow down a bullet before it killed you.

It was no wonder the lander failed. No wonder the public turned on SpaceGen and NASA — accused them of wasting too many resources when the problem was at home. No wonder 'space' became a dirty word. And it didn't help when temperatures started rising and people stopped going outside. A whole generation of insiders — to them, space wasn't just dirty, it was a monster. The outside was a killer. If Chrissie hadn't persuaded so many celebrities to take a trip to Orbicon's Space Collider back in the day, there wouldn't be a space program right now.

We wouldn't be here in this bunker with at least an option on the table. We'd all just be in here wondering how much longer the toilet would keep flushing.

Too many dents. It was the same with the planet. There was no fixing it. We needed a new one. And that meant leaving.

"Doctor Rolands." Another voice in the dark. "I was looking over your proposal from years ago, when you argued that the Trappist system is our best shot at testing OCT. Has anything changed?"

Yeah. I grew up. "Nothing has changed. It's still the best site to confirm Orbital Constant Theory."

"So what's the problem in sanctioning a flight there? There's a cost to every experiment — didn't you say that once?"

"Yes, but—"

"Well, then. If the cost of keeping humanity alive is six volunteers, isn't that a price that's worth paying?"

Trappist-1E — it sounded ridiculous that an exoplanet I'd learned about on a YouTube video thirty years ago could potentially save humanity. Landing there wouldn't be a problem. The atmosphere was Earth-like enough to support life. And if my Orbital Constant Theory was proved right, it would change everything. Give us another shot at Mars. Or somewhere else. Somewhere we hadn't found yet. The solution to every problem was already out there, just waiting to be discovered. This was no different.

I hated admitting all of this. I hated that to save the world, we had to change its mind. We had to make space palatable again. This wasn't what scientists were supposed to do with their lives. We weren't a clergy. We weren't meant to shepherd the masses. How did we ever stray so far?

"Alright," I huffed. "Trappist-1E is a potential stepping stone. I'll agree on that. But you all know what happens when they land there. You all know that Trappist isn't the solution."

"But it's a start."

"We can make a start from here. Why do we have to send anyone? Telescopes could still present us with the answer. We might be able to find somewhere eventually. Another planet. Just look at everything we've discovered in the skies over the last century, all while keeping our feet on the ground."

"We don't have another century, Emily. It's time. There aren't any other options. Now what's it going to be? You know we can't sustain the Space Collider forever with our budgets. Look. If you approve the launch date, there are still a few months until then. We'll still need to do the recruiting and the training of the six who'll actually fly there. What if you said yes today, and then kept searching in the meantime? We can abort if you find another habitable world. But this sets the ball in motion. It keeps us alive a little while longer. And isn't that the whole point of Orbicon?"

Nobody could have heard me sigh above the gail that threatened to rip the bunker apart, and us with it. Pressure pushed against my chest like a pneumatic drill, and yet, I barely felt it.

"What good is saving humanity," I said, "if it means sacrificing people to do it? We'd be giving up everything that makes us human. And you want me to say yes, like it's the obvious solution. But there's no solution which keeps us human. Only one that keeps us alive." I stifled a sob and rubbed my eyes, grateful that the lights were off.

"Mom." Henry's voice echoed beside me. "It's okay. It's going to be okay. You don't have to choose who lives and who dies. I can handle the recruitment. It's enough that *someone* lives, right?"

Henry was never meant to be a part of this. Never meant to be sweeping up my mess. He was supposed to be like Halley. She wanted nothing to do with Orbicon, and I was proud of her for that. But now, my little boy was telling me he'd handle it. That he'd take responsibility for the lives I would destroy.

Oh, Henry. Why couldn't you have wasted your life playing video games?

And in this bunker. Of all places. The same bunker where Halley had drawn the O on her dusty bunk which had become the Orbicon symbol ever since. The same bunker where Henry had begged me to allow him to enroll in the company. Where Chrissie and I would talk long into the nights about how we'd get our next funding from the bigwigs at SpaceGen who'd say yes to anything if she asked them in her little red dress. Where the designs for the space collider had been approved. Where the wind had ripped the outer door open and Chrissie had been the one to seal it. Where the tornado had taken the shielding, and then it took her too. And now it was taking my little boy. Making him an accomplice to my crime.

This same bunker. In the darkness of this tomb. The same darkness that still consumed us after all these years. Of course it was here where the fate of our species was being decided by a few business execs in stuffy shirts. And me. Where else would it be?

Henry. I wish I could've saved you from what we were all about to become. But what other choice did we have?

"Fine." I whimpered the word, hoping nobody would hear it above the storm. Hoping that I could still take it back.

"Is that a yes?" More voices from the dark. They didn't wait for an answer. They knew.

"You've made the right decision, Mom." Henry squeezed my arm. The same way he used to when he didn't want to go to bed, and he thought a cuddle would keep him up a few more minutes. Now, he was about to choose who Orbicon would launch thirty-nine lightyears into space using gravitational wave propulsion, to the most distant grave in the universe. I'd just killed six people. And worse, I'd given my boy the job of choosing the victims in this little quest to save the world.

And all I could hear was Chrissie's voice. *Look at how far we've come.*

II

August 2047

Backstage at the auditorium, reinforced walls deadened the sound from beyond. I wished they'd do the same for my nerves.

I checked my phone for the thousandth time. Not looking at anything besides the wallpaper of my screen. But it was enough to remind me that I should've prepared more.

FRASIER ARMITAGE

'Just make sure you're offline by 11.' My last message to Halley. She should have been here instead of gallivanting online. Why did I agree to do this?

My earpiece received an announcement from the auditorium's microphone. Henry's voice filtered through static.

"May I introduce the head and founder of Orbicon — Dr. Emily Rolands."

That was my cue.

A spattering of applause rippled through the conference hall as I entered and edged up to the podium. Empty seats jeered at me, broken up by fourteen young faces. There was Henry, his assistant — I forget her name — and the twelve astronauts that made up the primary crew and the backup team.

I locked eyes with the captain of the primaries. He was a strong, handsome man of about twenty five, with dark hair and brown eyes. A dead man who seemed invincible.

I smiled at him. I didn't know why. And then my eyes passed to the woman next to him. Deliberately. I'd already decided that I wasn't going to begin until I'd looked every single one of them in the eye. They deserved that much.

The woman had beautiful skin, a lovely figure and a broad smile. The pilot.

Beside her, a shy-looking pale girl shivered, probably the youngest of the bunch — blonde, pony-tailed, with blue eyes. Must be the Doctor.

A curvy redhead who reminded me of Chrissie sat forward intently, focused, intelligent and alert. The Biologist. I liked her. A pit gnawed at my stomach, groaning open as I began sinking into it. But I closed my eyes, exhaled and moved on to the row in front of them.

The other two men who made up the last of the primary crew sat side by side. One was similar to the captain — strong, muscular. He was from Asia, what little of it was left after the floods. The Astrophysicist.

Next to him was a thin, frail, bearded man of about thirty, sat with his arms folded, frowning. He stood out like a sore thumb — the only one who seemed disinterested in being here. He yawned. Of all the astronauts, he was the one who looked most like a scientist. His scruffy hair gave him away. The Mathematician.

I'd stopped thinking about them as people after Henry had brought them on board, and more as jobs. Pilot. Biologist. That sort of thing. But now I'd laid eyes on them, their faces were inescapable. This was the crew I'd be sentencing to death with a pat on the back.

The backup crew were a similar mix, but this speech wasn't for them. It was for the ones launching in less than three months.

"Good afternoon," I said. "I'd like to thank you for being here today. As you know, I'm Dr. Emily Rolands, Chief of Orbicon. It's been my mandate for the past thirty years to achieve interstellar travel, and after decades of hard work, because of the diligence of thousands, it's my pleasure to be addressing you, the first humans that will reap the fruits of all that we've achieved. Make no mistake that your mission is historic by its nature. Succeed or fail, in three months time you will make history. Millions will applaud your bravery and sacrifice in choosing this mission, but I would like to be the first."

I stopped talking and clapped. They all joined in. So far, so good.

"The sacrifice you make in this historic venture requires courage. It's your courage that will be remembered, along with your names, for all time. There are many hazards — many unknowns — but I'm not here to brief you on the 'what-ifs'. What I'm here to talk to you about are the risks we *know* this mission will hold. The purpose of your voyage is to prove *Rolands' theory of the orbital constant.* I'm sure you all know it very well, but let me remind you of what it means."

I paused, sipping the water left for me behind the podium, my hands shaking.

Pull yourself together, Emily. It's just a speech.

"As you know, time is linked to gravity. And gravity is linked to orbit. That means the way we interact with time is connected to our orbit of the sun. One orbit equals one year, whether you're on Earth, or Mars, or anywhere else orbiting a star. Simple, yes?"

I mean, it was a lot more complicated. There's a reason the equations had earned me enough to set up this company. But this was as simple as it needed to be for these astronauts.

One orbit equaled one year. I wondered if they believed it. If that factored into why they'd accepted the mission. Or whether they'd even made the link until they were sitting here listening to me dance around the one thing I knew I had to say, but didn't want to.

"Initially, when I first set up Orbicon, it was with the idea that we could prove 'orbital locking' was more than just a theory, but a fact. Our information could then aid the Mars Project, which SpaceGen has tirelessly developed these past years. Each day, we hear they're getting closer to cracking the problem of landing a shuttle on Mars."

I coughed. How long had they been saying that?

"But if we could prove Orbital Constant Theory, then we'd know for sure that landing on Mars would extend the lifespan of the human race. It would give us much needed hope. If time is fixed to orbit, then a year on Mars would be almost twice as long as a year on Earth. Mars takes 687 days to orbit the sun. Humans would experience those 687 days as one year. Every year of your life would effectively double. Imagine experiencing all that extra time, and devoting it to research and study — the things we would learn. Imagine expanding our life expectancy overnight. Imagine the world's greatest minds having twice as long to invent and discover. Isn't that a reason for hope?"

If hope had any meaning anymore. I'd parroted these lines so many times over the years, they were just words now. Just sounds that came out of my mouth. But it was what had brought me to this podium — the promise of Orbicon. The promise of hope.

"The situation today is more bleak and urgent than we could have anticipated when we first set out on this grand scheme. If we can't land on Mars, then our only hope is interstellar travel. It's the key to our future. For that reason, Orbicon has become synonymous with hope. Which is why my lecture today is such unfamiliar territory to me. I've made so many speeches about building a better future, that it seems odd to brief you on what is the very opposite — the very sobering reality of your mission."

Faces in the audience twisted, contorting into grimaces as eyes searched for the meaning in my words — as any good explorer's would. All except for the thin, disgruntled man, who appeared unmoved and sat stiffly with his arms folded. I swallowed hard, trying to remember what I was here to say.

"We've been determined to reach Trappist-1 since Orbicon was founded. But since the space collider was completed last year, we've delayed the launch for as long as possible. We invested in telescopes to try and find some other, more promising destination to send you, rather than Trappist-1E, the fourth planet in the Trappist-1 system. But we've found nothing, and we can delay no longer. The future is at stake, and we must act now, or face the consequences of inaction."

Another gulp of water. I shook my head.

"The reason we've delayed in sending you to Trappist-1E until now, is because of the implications of what 'Rolands theory of the orbital constant' would mean for you when you arrive on the planet. You see, if time and orbit are linked in the way that I've predicted, you will age one year for every orbit that Trappist-1E makes of its sun. Could we put the projection up on the screen, please?"

Behind me, the wall lit up with the graphic showing the Trappist-1 system and the exoplanets' rate of orbit around their sun. Little circles dashed around the large red sphere in the center.

"Here, you can see the rate at which the planets of the Trappist-1 system orbit their red sun. Trappist-1E is the planet with your best chance of survival. It's perfectly placed in the goldilocks zone, and by all known tests, will be habitable to sustain human life. But for how long? That is the question I am here to answer for you today. That is what this graphic shows, and what I must prepare you for."

Their eyes fixed on the image of the planets, widening as they intuited my meaning. They stared back at me in disbelief and horror, even disgust. I glanced down at the podium. There were no notes, but I couldn't meet their judgmental eyes.

"One orbit of Trappist-1E is the equivalent of six Earth days. Owing to the principle of orbital locking, even if you arrive safely on Trappist-1E with no complications, your life expectancy of thirty years translates on Trappist-1E into thirty orbits."

"What are you trying to say?" the sprightly redhead interrupted, shouting from her seat, aghast.

"I'm saying that your total life expectancy, according to our projections, is—"

"180 days. Call it six months", the unkempt man with folded arms called out. I was grateful for his interruption. I hadn't wanted to say it out loud.

"Are you asking us to sacrifice thirty years of life on Earth for six months of life on Trappist-1E?" the redhead continued, shocked at what the implication of their mission would mean.

I glanced back up and met her eyes. I was just a kid when I'd blurted out Trappist-1 as the future of Orbicon all those decades ago, more interested in proving myself right than I was in things like responsibility and consequences. Accountability is something learned with age. Had I known then that I'd wind up facing this group of twelve people, six of whom I'd be asking to give up their chance of growing old, I'd like to think I'd have at least hesitated a little.

"Yes, it would mean trading thirty years for six months," I said. "Thirty years on Earth, for six months on a new planet, untouched, unexplored, holding the answers to questions we don't even know to ask. You'd be the first people to travel to another part of the galaxy. You'd be the first people to land on another world. You'd be the first people to extend the reach of the human race. You'd be trading your own future here on Earth for the future of everyone else stuck here on Earth. It's a one way trip. You've known that from the start. But what a way to go."

Silence settled in the room. The prospect of everything this mission entailed settled with it. A hopeless glaze of acceptance washed over their eyes. As it did, part of me wanted them to fight it. I wanted them to resist. To make it harder than it was. It was my choice to send them away. It shouldn't have been this easy.

"How can we agree to such a thing?" the redhead said, the last of them to let go of the horror of what I'd asked them to do.

"How can we not?" the bearded man with folded arms replied.

"It's alright for you," she blurted out quickly, and instantly regretted her words. Her eyes filled with guilt, dousing her fire, before she too glassed over, just like the rest of them.

And then it was over. I didn't say anything more. I just left the podium, walking away, letting the graphic play out and the exoplanets of the Trappist-1 system spin and spin, as my own head spun.

I rushed through the offices as fast as I could, up to my room, and banged on Halley's door. She opened and let me in, annoyed that her connection online had been interrupted.

I didn't say anything, but held her in my arms, dowsing her top in my tears.

What had I done?

III

November 2047

Was it really a week ago that the shuttle docked at the space collider? The night of the launch had come round so fast. What was I thinking — letting Henry talk me into appearing on all the late night shows, being interviewed over and over about the very thing I wanted to avoid. But at least I wasn't there — Mission Control — having to look at the faces of the crew on the Icarus One.

That night, lounging on the family couch, I watched the show — the interview we'd recorded earlier in the afternoon. From the other side of his desk, some young, interesting comedian scrutinized my every move. Lights blared down on me and an audience applauded everything I said. Even watching it now made me uncomfortable. Henry had insisted on tagging along. He was a good kid, and I was grateful for having him with me. He sat next to me on the couch, both on the screen and in the living room as we watched it play out.

"So, Dr. Rolands, how does it feel to be the most famous scientific mind alive today?" the host asked.

"I didn't think I was that famous," Henry said. "Oh, you were talking to my Mom. Sorry, my mistake." He was always good at talking — just like his Dad.

"I don't feel famous," I said, "so I guess it's much the same as anyone in the audience feels."

"Brilliant, and modest. Will you marry me?" the comedian joked. The spectators laughed, and I smiled, trying to see the compliment in it.

"I think your wife might have something to say about that," Henry said quickly, protectively.

The host turned to the screen. "Honey, I love you." More applause. Then he swiveled his chair back to me. "But seriously, Dr. Rolands, you've pioneered this project from day one at Orbicon. The whole reason we're launching later this evening is because of you. It's your greatest achievement." More like my greatest folly. "Time magazine listed you in the top five most influential minds in the whole of scientific history. You've got to be feeling pretty smart, right?"

"Smarts have little to do with it. Physics isn't just about brains. It's about discovery. You think of names like Newton, Einstein, Hawking. They're only famous because of what they *found*. Scientists are just like archaeologists, only we don't dig up the past, we dig up the future. Every scientist has the potential to strike gold. I'm just one of the lucky ones."

"Yeah, but for years you were the only one digging. I mean, it's not like there are hundreds of companies like Orbicon out there. I mean, just look at the space collider. Who else besides you could've built a hadron collider in space?"

I shrugged. "In the past, landmarks in space travel involved competition. Landing on the moon, for example. When I started in this business, I was told it moved fast. That I was entering a space race. But if what we were doing was a race, then Orbicon was the only one running it. The advantage of not having to compete with anyone is that I've had the privilege of working with the finest minds this planet has to offer. All the talent came to us. They're the ones with the real smarts. The launch tonight is not my success, it's theirs. Or should I say, it's *ours*."

I'd rehearsed that line especially for the program. Henry sat back and nodded. The crowd applauded. But listening to my voice as I said the words onscreen made me wince.

"Okay, so let's talk about the launch," the host said. "What exactly is the mission for these astronauts?"

"The mission is to land on Trappist-1E, which is an exoplanet roughly 39.6 lightyears from Earth."

"Exoplanet?"

"That's a term which describes a planet outside our solar system."

"Gotcha. I almost forgot I was talking to a scientist. Sounds like a long way."

"They'll cross that distance in a matter of moments, propelled by the gravitational waves we'll generate with the space collider. Then the real work begins. The crew will land on the planet and set up their camp, arranging telescopes on the surface. They'll point them in every direction, and communicate the results back to us."

"Why's that important?"

"It sounds crazy, because a lot of people think of space as this big, vast, open expanse. But in reality, space is full of little corners and pockets we just can't see around. If we're going to find a future home, we need to see the whole picture. And that's what this mission will mean. We'll be able to effectively map out all those nooks and crannies, like casting a torch into the universe. Who knows what we'll find?"

"Probably a Starbucks," Henry answered, and everyone laughed again.

"There's one on every corner on this planet, so why would it be any different in space?" The host continued the joke. I didn't care much for coffee. "We all found out about this mission just recently, but you've been living with this for the past thirty years. How do you get your head around that? Around the *gravity* of it all?"

And there it was — the same joke about gravity everybody had made for the past three decades. "The answer is there's simply no other choice. It's why six brave men and women are sitting tonight in the cockpit of that shuttle, ready to sacrifice everything. If there was any other way, we'd have found it by now." I said the words, hoping they'd bring me some comfort, hoping I'd eventually believe them. 'No other choice' was a platitude of the guilt-ridden. Wasn't there always a choice? Mine had been to send six people in a shuttlecraft to an early grave. Why? Because I had 'no other choice.'

"I understand that you first got your idea from a late-night chat show. So, universe, on behalf of late night chat show hosts, can I just say, you're welcome. How did that come abo—"

I clicked the remote and switched the TV off. Both Henry and Halley blurted out protestations.

"Come on, Mom. I was just about to get the biggest laugh of the night," Henry said.

"Why are you turning it off?" Halley asked.

I couldn't watch any more. The longer it stayed on, the more I was reminded of the thing I was trying to forget. "Let's see what else is on."

"There's nothing else on. Only broadcasts of the launch. That late night show is the last thing which doesn't have anything to do with Icarus One, and I didn't think you wanted to watch the launch?" Halley said.

"You're right. Let's not watch anything, eh? Let's talk for a bit."

"Talk about what?"

"Anything. Something. Nothing. Pick one." The phone rang. 'Hank Carter' flashed across the screen. "I've got to take this," I said, and left the room. The TV went straight back on behind me, and I closed the kitchen door to block out the noise. "Hello?"

"May I speak with Emily Rolands?"

"Quit playing around, Hank."

"Congratulations, my dear. You've done it. How do you feel?" His voice was as smooth as ever.

"Honestly? I can't stand it. I wish it was me in that shuttle, and not those poor kids."

"You don't mean that. Not really. Once it's over, you'll start feeling better. Our boy looks good on TV, doesn't he?"

"Yeah, he does."

"So do you."

"Don't start, Hank. Not tonight."

"As you wish. I just wanted to say congratulations. Feel happy, Em. You did it. I'll give you a ring tomorrow. Ciao."

He hung up, and I was left alone, the noise of the TV from the other room muffled as it drifted through the door. My phone buzzed on the table — alerts from HQ updating me on how the launch was going. It vibrated every few minutes, then every few seconds. I turned it off, poured a glass of wine and sat there in the dark, propped on the bar stool, sipping red, swallowing guilt.

Then, through the window, a flash of light scorched a path through the sky, and a fantastic shot of black ripped across the stars. Starlight faded for an instant before returning, the briefest interruption to its shimmering meadow.

So long, Icarus One.

Down went another glass of red.

I always knew that discovery would take me somewhere, that I'd soar on the wings of the secrets I'd uncover. And it had. My discovery had taken me to where I was today — alone, at the bottom of a wine bottle.

Look at how far we've come.

Look at how far we were going. Thirty-nine lightyears, riding the crest of a gravitational wave, all so we could roll the dice. All so that one day in the future, a comedian will get to tell a joke about it and the whole planet will laugh.

"Are we moving through time, or is time moving through us?" I asked out loud to no-one. And then I reached for another bottle of wine.

Next stop, Trappist1-E.

KIRK

I

"I give you about eighteen months," the doctor told me as he held onto his clipboard like it made all the difference. What would happen if he dropped it? Would he give me another six months out of embarrassment? I don't know why he looked so depressed. It wasn't like I was the one telling him that he only had five hundred and forty days left to live before he'd snuff it. It wasn't me grappling with the clipboard and watching him struggle to take in the pronouncement of death. Smile, doctor, you've got plenty of things to be happy about. You don't have a sell-by-date. Eighteen months and I'd be off the shelf.

What a great start to the day.

Of course, I did the dutiful thing that everyone's supposed to do, and I questioned his prognosis.

"Are you sure?" I asked. What a stupid thing to say. Of course he was sure. What was the probability of him changing his mind? Who in their right mind would go around telling people they only had eighteen months to live unless they were absolutely sure of it? What was I expecting?

'Let me double check . . . what's this? We thought it was an impossible to pronounce, terminal illness, but it

31

turns out that you've actually just got a heavy cold. Take some hot lemon and you'll feel right as rain.'

What else was he going to say? What was I hoping for? That he'd mixed up the clipboards?

"I'm afraid so," he said. "The good news is that your quality of life shouldn't deteriorate until the final weeks of the illness, when it'll become rapid. Until then, you'll be able to do anything you like. Live life to the full."

Oh, thank you, doctor. Marvelous news. It's so nice to know I'll be able to pass for a normal human being until I suddenly croak. What did he anticipate I'd be doing over the next eighteen months? Scale Everest? Become an astronaut?

"Thank you, doctor," I murmured. Maybe if he'd seen how crestfallen I looked, he'd have taken pity and given me an extra month free of charge. But he just sidled off and placed the clipboard in its holder on the wall, where all the charts were stored.

I laid on the uncomfortable hospital bed. The words refused to sink in.

Eighteen months. A multiple of nine, six, three, and two. Not a bad number. Quite elegant really.

Eighteen months. It could've been worse. Could've been seventeen months.

Wait, was I actually looking for a positive in this? I was twenty eight years old and had just found out I wouldn't make it to thirty. That's insane. I wanted a sports car. I wanted a yacht. I wanted a wild night out on the town and a swimwear-model girlfriend. Was I having a midlife crisis? No, I was thirteen years too late to be having a midlife crisis. But one thing was for sure — I was definitely growing a beard. Goodbye shaving. I didn't have time for you anymore. There'd probably be a lot of things I wouldn't have time for. Moping certainly wasn't one of them, though. Plenty of time for moping. A whole eighteen months.

When the nurse finally came around, she talked about discharging me. After all, I was taking up a precious bed for someone who might need it to die on. Me — I'd have a nice, long stint before I'd need it again.

I left the hospital and returned home, picking up my post and the voicemails I'd missed, having spent the past six days on the ward.

Most of the messages were just sales companies. There was one from my mum telling me how worried she was for me. She knew I was in hospital, but she'd rung all the same. Did she think I was going to answer? Yes, Mum, I'm over fifty miles away from the phone, but don't you worry, I'll pick up if you call. Still, it broke up the voices of salesmen. *'Reinforced windows to prevent storm damage.'* *'Extra-strength brickwork coating to stop floodwater from entering the home.'* *'Hurricane-proof doors.'* *'Foundation reconditioning so your house won't tip over in an earthquake.'* Natural disasters — who knew they'd make such good business opportunities? Then an unusual message played.

"Hello. This is a message for Kirk. My name's Henry Rolands. I'm calling from Orbicon, trying to make contact with potential recruits. We're putting together a team for a special mission and I need a mathematician. Your name has come to my attention and I'd like to meet with you to discuss it further. Give me a call on this number."

Orbicon? Maybe I was going to be an astronaut after all.

No. Don't be daft.

As soon as they learned about my condition, they'd lose interest in whatever it was they wanted me for. I'd just give them a call and tell them about it, and that would be that.

"Hello, you've reached Orbicon. How may I help you?" a voice chimed down the phone.

"Yeah, I'm returning a call from Henry Rolands."

"Name?"

"Kirk MacIntosh."

"Ah, yes. Mr. Rolands is currently away from his desk at the moment. But he's asked if you'd be willing to fly out to Houston in order to meet with him, to discuss his proposal?"

"Well. That's very nice of him. But I'm afraid now's not exactly the best time."

"I'm sorry to hear that. Could I ask why?"

"Well, I've just been told I've only got eighteen months left." Silence filled the other end of the phone. Did she already know my sell-by-date or something? "So I suppose Mr. Rolands will want to reconsider my involvement in whatever he's planning."

"I'm sorry to hear your news, but Mr. Rolands was very specific. If you're able to get the next flight out to Houston, we'd be happy to pick up the bill."

Seriously? "Sure. Why not? Could be fun."

"If you need any of the funds in advance, don't hesitate to call, and we'll provide them."

The line cut out, and I rang Mum.

"You're not going to believe this, Mum, but Orbicon want to meet with me. How good is that? . . . I don't know what it's about, but it's exciting, isn't it? . . . Oh, and before I forget, the Doctor says I've only got eighteen months left to live."

She burst into tears, inconsolable and wild. Maybe I should have put it a little gentler.

Where was a clipboard when you needed it?

II

"A physicist, an engineer, a biologist, a pilot, a psychiatrist, and a mathematician?"

"That's it," Henry Rolands replied, through that ridiculous perma-grin of his.

"It sounds like the start of a joke," I said.

How was it possible that he could smile more? Was this guy even human? "We send you into space," he said. "Launch you from the space collider and the next thing you know, you're almost forty lightyears away, landing on Trappist-1E."

Henry Rolands was a smug child. He knew how every word sounded — enticing, stimulating, preposterous, but in a good way. I could imagine the advert. *'Don't miss your chance to get away from it all. Travel to an untouched part of the universe. Be the first to experience life on another planet. And if you sign up today, we'll throw in a place in the history books for free.'* He didn't need to sell it to me. What choice did I have? Live out my last 536 days here on Earth with nothing to do but sulk about it, or do something meaningful with the time I had left?

Ah, who was I kidding? I just liked the idea of free food and a trip to space.

Like every responsible salesman, Henry's youthful, brimming, arrogant little face sobered for a moment, and his mouth formed the immortal shape of the word that would signify the catch to this whole scheme. I'd been waiting patiently for it, waiting for the 'but'. And then it came.

"*But* it's very much a one way trip. We've got the collider on this side, nothing on the other. Once you get to Trappist-1E, there's no way to come back. You'd live out your remaining days on the exoplanet."

He emphasized the word 'days' for some reason. Wasn't sure why. But if that was the catch, it didn't sound so bad. How would Mum take it?

'Hi, Mum. Good news and bad news. Good news is I'm doing something worthwhile with the time I've got left. Bad news is I'll be thirty-nine lightyears away. See ya!' I'd have to start carrying a handkerchief around so that I could at least do something with my hands when she cried.

"I know this will be the third time I've mentioned it," I said. "But with stakes like this, why would you want someone on the mission who you know is going to snuff it? Why are you interested in a dying mathematician when you could have your pick of anyone?"

That arrogant grin which made him look about twelve years old filled his awful little face. Note to self: never trust a man who smiles too much.

"I've spoken to your doctors," he said. "I'm confident you're the perfect fit for this mission." The *perfect fit.* He made me sound like a tuxedo. "So what do you say, Kirk?"

I shrugged. "Ah, go on then. Why not, eh?"

It wasn't until my clock had ticked down to 508 days to go, that they'd finished recruiting the other five brilliant people who would be joining me on this little soiree, 39.6 lightyears into space.

The engineer was our captain — Max. We met in a corridor.

"You must be Kirk." Bingo. He shook my hand with the kind of grip that would put a pro-footballer to shame. "I'm Max. So . . . what brings a guy like you to a place like this?"

I shrugged. "Oh, nothing much. Just saving the world. What about you?"

He laughed. "Same. Sounds like fun, right? It's good to have you on the team." He winked and strode ahead at a hundred miles-per-hour to find the next recruit.

Right from that first moment, I hated how perfect Max was. Even his teeth looked attractive and strong. His height was perfect. His hair was perfect. His name was perfect. But even worse – he was as charming as he was perfect. It took a lot of effort to hate someone who was genuinely charming. But until I found a flaw, I was determined to put the effort in to dislike him.

At the end of the corridor, a room had been outfitted as a little 'getting to know you' area. In other words, there was cheesy music and a punch bowl, and the desks were pushed up to the wall. Otherwise, it was a typical meeting room.

The other man on the team was the physicist. Harold Wang. He lingered by the punch bowl. I'd read his file, and already knew it would take some practice before I could say the words 'Doctor Wang' with a straight face. I approached.

"I'm Kirk. You must be Doctor . . .?"

"Wang. But you can call me Harold." What a relief.

"Is it good?" I nodded to the punch.

"I don't know. Haven't tried it. I just figured I couldn't back out of meeting people if I stood here."

"Are you nervous, Harold?"

"We're heading lightyears into space. What's there to be nervous about?"

I smiled. "Fancy a glass? I will if you will."

He poured us a glass each and he raised his. "To lightyears," he said. "For being the perfect way to explain that space and time are interconnected. It's a distance that we measure in a time format. Simple. Elegant. Fascinating, wouldn't you agree?" The 'teacher vibes' were strong with this one. But aside from the fact that he might come out with something interesting every now and then, I didn't really have anything to hold against him.

I downed the punch and glanced around the room. In the corner, Captain Max was flexing his best lines on the pilot. Sonja. She was Caribbean, with a beautiful face and drop-dead-gorgeous figure. And when she smiled, she lit up the room. I could tell by the way she laughed that everything about her was fun and intoxicating. She was like rum in human form. And Captain Max was making her laugh. A lot. But that was hardly a surprise. The two of them together resembled bookends, with the rest of the human race falling somewhere in between. In mathematical terms, the chances of Sonja spending a great amount of time with anyone else besides Max on this mission equated to exactly one more reason to dislike him.

In the other corner, the remaining two crew members chatted. Well, I say chatted. But it was more like a one-way tirade.

The psychiatrist was a timid, pale girl by the name of June. She was blonde, and constantly putting her hair behind her ear. Maybe she was deliberately quiet? After all, it would be hard to be objective about the crew unless there was a bit of distance between us. She had that air of someone who was holding themselves back. My future doctor. Poor thing.

And then there was Cassandra. Auburn haired. Curves. Fiery. Her mouth going at the speed of light, trying to talk June into spiking the punch, from what I could glean. She was the biologist, and I could see why. If there was anyone in this room who seemed ready to roll up their sleeves and get their hands dirty, it was Cassandra. Or Cass, as she was telling June she liked to be called.

We eventually mingled, each saying an awkward hello to the other. Cass never did get round to spiking the punch. Which was a shame. With a few units of booze, we might've actually said how we felt about being there.

One thing was absolutely clear, though. If Henry goody-two-shoes, smug, sycophantic Rolands exceeded in anything, it was that he recruited well. He'd gathered a textbook crew. Five perfect specimens, and me. Five fit, intelligent, talented, model, dexterous fingers — plus one sore thumb. So why me? What unique thing about me was it that made me the *perfect fit* alongside these five others? Was it my beard?

420 days to go, and I finally got my answer.

***

After three months of training, the whole crew was summoned into a conference room for a lecture from our great and illustrious leader. Henry stood behind a podium, and we sat together. Across from us, the backup team lingered. They were training alongside us, but we never saw one another. It was like being back at school, in two different classes.

Henry prattled on about something or other, welcoming us, thanking us for being there, yadda yadda yadda.

"May I introduce the head and founder of Orbicon, Dr. Emily Rolands," he said. We leaned in expectantly, waiting to catch our first glimpse of the ice queen. She'd never looked in on us once — the great mind behind the mission. Like the wizard of Oz, in the background, never seen, but there was a mystique about her. Although, in the flesh, she was a lot taller than the wizard was. And much more attractive. Slender in body, her wrinkles hid behind thick spectacles. The gray in her hair suited her. She didn't look like the ice queen she was reputed to be. That's if you could see past her frown.

Dr. Rolands gazed out at us. She thanked us for our sacrifice in accepting the mission, we all clapped, and then she lectured us on 'orbital constant theory.' A graphic flashed up on the wall, showing the exoplanets orbiting the red sun, and how many days each took to complete one full orbit.

"One orbit of Trappist-1E is the equivalent of six Earth days," she said. "Owing to the principle of orbital locking, even if you arrive safely on Trappist-1E with no complications, your life expectancy of thirty years translates on Trappist-1E into thirty orbits."

So that was what made me the *perfect fit.* 420 days and counting until I croaked. It wasn't so much to sacrifice, certainly not compared to the rest of them.

"What are you trying to say?" Cass blurted out. Trust Cass to be the one to interrupt. Dr. Rolands just stared back at her sternly.

"I'm saying that your total life expectancy, according to our projections, in days is . . ."

"180 days. Call it six months," I shouted. I wasn't going to let Cass have all the fun. Besides, I'd done the math. If we're talking about six days being the equivalent of 365, then the ratio was about 1:60, so we'd be shortening our lives by sixty times what they would've been if we stayed on Earth. Well, I say *we,* but I was hardly in the same boat as the rest of them.

"Are you asking us to sacrifice thirty years of life on Earth for six months of life on Trappist-1E?" Cass called out again. She was shocked, and rightly so. Note to self: you were right. You can never trust a person who smiles too much.

Dr. Rolands stood like a statue, unmoved by the whole thing. Maybe she was as hard as people said she was?

"Yes, it would mean trading thirty years for six months," she said, and then she quoted the same pitch we'd heard over and again, the one that had got us here in the first place. The one that told us we'd be the first to explore a part of the universe untouched by humans, and that extending the reach of the human race didn't seem like such a bad way to go.

I hadn't given much credence to the greater good. It wasn't the reason I was here. Free food and space travel — that was enough for me. The future of the species was a bonus. But as for the rest of them, did they actually believe that whole 'you can change the world' line?

"How can we agree to such a thing?" Cass refused to budge.

"How can we not?" I replied. It was my best impression of a 'believer.'

"It's alright for you." Cass frowned at me. And then it must have sunk in, what she'd said. But she was right. It was different for me. I wasn't trading thirty years for six months. I'd be losing about a hundred days, give or take. Still, three months or thirty years — sacrificing any amount of time was hard enough.

Leaving us dumbstruck in the conference room, the illustrious Dr. Rolands stepped away from the podium. She'd said everything she wanted to. 'You'll all die young. Bye.' She'd have been much better doing it with a clipboard.

After a while of just sitting in silence, Max gave a big speech about the advantages of the mission and the benefits it would bring, the sacrifice being worth it, and all that. He knew exactly what to say to calm everyone down and keep them level headed. When I'd been given my prognosis, I'd grown a beard in protest. He'd been told that he'd have six months post-launch to live, and had almost immediately made an eloquent, motivational speech. Pretentious swine. Great captain, though.

The rest of them left one by one to think it over. But it didn't change anything. We were all still going to Trappist-1E, regardless. I walked straight to Henry's office.

"Perfect fit?" I bellowed at him. "How long do I get up there? Six days? Less?"

He sat behind his desk with that same toothy grin. "Your doctors assure me that your condition won't be affected by the orbital locking. You'll have just as much time as everyone else. Think about it, Kirk. On this mission, you'll actually be gaining time, if you look at it that way. Your lifespan will equate to the same lifespan of a thirty-year-old. I think the expression is, you're welcome."

I didn't thank him.

Gaining time — what a ridiculous notion. The thought of it made my skin crawl. But what wound me up more than anything was that I couldn't tell him he was wrong.

III

295 days to go.

It's been said that, in space, no-one can hear you scream. Not true. We'd been in space for a week, and every day, I screamed, and every day, someone told me to pack it in. What would be more accurate is, 'In space, nobody who screams is very popular.'

Super-Max designed the ship. It was cold and jagged and we were always floating into one sharp edge or another. Hardly the ideal place to do zero-gravity somersaults. Thanks for that, Max.

The collider's small shell was surrounded by huge sails made from a clear alloy to catch the gravitational waves like a glider catches the air. The whole thing would come apart when we landed, so we could rebuild it into some sort of base camp. The captain assured me it wouldn't break up before then. But I kept on asking him, just to be sure.

In about an hour, we'd be on the other side of the galaxy. Odd thought, really, that we should be so close to somewhere so far away.

"Nervous?" I asked Harold as we suited up together.

He shrugged. "Not really. Either we make it, or we don't. It's an equation with two variables. So I have just as much reason to expect us to succeed as I do that we'll fail."

"Pack it in, Harold. You don't need to play 'physicist' with me."

"Okay, I'm nervous. You happy now?"

"Very." I smiled. "See, that wasn't so hard, was it?"

"He's not making you nervous, is he?" Cass called through to Harold.

"How long have you been lurking?" I asked.

"Long enough to get a peek at you before that suit covers you up for good." She drifted through the corridor towards us.

"Pervert," I said.

She didn't argue. She just laughed.

The suits were cumbersome, even without gravity, and I dreaded the weight of them on the other side. Whoever designed the space suit must have got the idea from staring too long at a marshmallow. That's what we all looked like once we were suited up — big marshmallows with helmets on. Good job I wasn't hungry. If people wondered why astronauts in the movies were always getting eaten by the aliens they encountered, that's the reason. What did they expect if they kept dressing us up as food?

The hour passed quickly enough, and we took turns dialing the last calls we were going to make to anyone outside of Mission Control. I called Mum. She didn't answer. Typical. I left a message.

"Bye, Mum. I've left you a box of hankies. When you look up at the stars, think of me, won't you? Thanks for everything. Oh, this is Kirk, by the way."

After I hung up, it dawned on me that I should have said 'I love you.' Oh well. Nobody's perfect. Except for Captain Max. I bet he'd remember to tell his Mum he loves her. That's if he even has a Mum, and he isn't some kind of laboratory experiment — the perfect specimen.

I shouldn't have eavesdropped on the others making their calls, but it wasn't like I had anything else to be getting on with. Twiddling my thumbs in the marshmallow suit was harder than it sounded. There were lots of tears. Too many for my taste. Then, after a few minutes in the cockpit, we all composed ourselves, and readied for launch.

"Take a look at the stars, people," Harold said. "It's the last time we'll see these constellations."

"They're amazing," Sonja said.

Silence overcame them as they sat in wonder at the heavens.

"Let's not get sentimental about some twinkling lights in the sky," I said. If they were going to get this nostalgic about stars, what would happen if they looked down and spotted the moon, or worse still, the Earth, now just a swirling blue crescent on the lip of a black globe beneath us? It was enough to make people get weepy. And I wasn't in the mood for that kind of thing. Not twice in the space of an hour. It'd be better to just get on with it, travel faster than light, arrive at this new exoplanet and get our tent pitched for the night.

"Nice, Kirk. Way to embrace the moment," Cass said.

I grinned at her through my helmet.

Sonja took to the radio. "Mission Control, this is Icarus One. Flight checks all normal."

She let Max say his big line.

"We are a go for launch."

Grammar in the space program was so stupid. 'We are a go for launch' made absolutely no sense whatsoever. I knew it was tradition, and everything. But how could a linguist ever hold down a job in space? It was bad enough for me, and I was a mathematician.

"Roger that, Icarus One. We are starting the collider now. Prepare for launch in t-minus one minute."

T-minus — the start of an equation. Now that was more like my kind of talk.

Sixty seconds remained until we'd find out whether faster-than-light travel was going to rip our bodies to shreds. I was half-tempted to start a conversation with Harold about it, but decided I'd best not. If my observation about the stars had been less than well received, it was hardly going to win me any brownie points. Did Mum pick up my message?

'T-minus 10 . . . 9 . . .' a voice counted down.

There was nothing like the sound of numbers to soothe the mind. Familiar. Dependable. Safe. What would we do without them?

'3 . . . 2 . . . 1' crackled over the radio.

A burst of light shone behind us where the collider threw mass together. It lit up like a star and for a moment we were swathed in light on all sides.

Then came the incredible force that pulled us along with it. A gravity wave formed, rippling space, and us with it.

And everything went black.

Light couldn't keep up with us. It lagged behind. We were beyond it. Stuck in that impossible void. Every move was a move I'd already made and was about to make all at the same time. I couldn't hear anything, or taste anything, or touch anything, but I was touching, hearing, and tasting everything at once. Every sense was bombarded by its displacement. As I realized what was about to happen, I caught hold of the thought as if it were a memory.

I remembered laughing, and then I laughed. I remembered blinking, and then I blinked. It was impossible, but it went on for how long, who could say? A second, or a million years? It was both and neither, and the next thing I knew, I was opening my eyes to a blur of unfamiliar lights and a faint red glow.

"Where are we?" Cass's exhausted voice popped into my ears.

Then came Sonja's. "If I'm not mistaken, we're looking at Trappist-1."

IV

Day 1 on Trappist-1E = T-minus 179 days.

Hard rock crunched against the ship's landing gears, thunking through my suit to jolt me upright. Sonja flicked a switch and the roar of engines quieted, cycling down. As the fans slowed, so did the trembling of my seat until everything was still. Shame really. I quite liked the judders. Made me feel like a kid in a fairground. All I needed now was some cotton candy and a paper bag of piping hot doughnuts to burn my fingers.

We'd parked in the 'dark zone.' The border where light met dark. Trappist-1E may have been Earth-sized, but it was hardly similar. It didn't even spin. And spinning was very important, apparently. When Earth rotated, it resulted in day and night. But here, the planet was tidally locked, meaning it didn't rotate. At all. One half faced the red sun and the other half never saw light or heat. It was like being on the waltzers without having some guy to send it twirling. How boring.

On the plus side, you got the 'dark zone,' a strip of condensation wrapping around the whole planet. It was the edge where sunlight stopped and darkness took over. And then kept taking over for half the world. The difference in temperature between sun and shade bathed the crest of rocky hills in perpetual fog. Meaning water. And it was somewhere in this misty halfway house where we landed.

As the cabin door whooshed open, a veil of mist crept into the ship, blanketing everyone and everything. Moisture droplets formed on my helmet instantaneously. These helmets didn't come with screen-wipers, and after the third time of my glove wiping away the water, the whole experience had already worn a little thin.

Max teetered on the edge of the gangway, poised to be the first person in history to plant their foot on another world, and fully aware of the 'significance' of it all.

"This first step marks the start of our journey to a better future," he said.

Please. What utter tripe. Why not just say what we're all thinking? Something along the lines of, 'How cool is this?', or 'On your marks, get set, go.' Why's everything gotta be so historic?

We each took it in turns to make history. I was last out. Take that, Max! You'll never be the 'last' person to ever step on another planet, will you?

Kirk 1 – Max 0. But who's counting?

The rocks we trod over were regular rocks. Ahead of me, five silhouettes tiptoed as though they walked on a high wire. Did they think their footsteps were tarnishing some scientific marvel? They were just rocks, guys. No big deal. Unless the crew's brains were fried in transit and they'd forgotten what rocks looked like.

"Okay, let's get started dismantling," Max said. He assigned me to disassemble the rear panels.

Step one, unscrew the fixing. Step two, lift the metallic frame. Step three, unfold the panel into a wall for our new base camp like some rudimentary precursor to the Transformers.

I blinked through the blur of water clouding my visor, and the gray screw and silver panel meshed into one. Nothing was ever easy, was it? After a half-hour of twiddling blindly in the haze, I'd finally accomplished all three steps. One panel down. Fifteen to go.

"It's beautiful isn't it?" Harold gawped. His voice crackled through my earpiece.

Beautiful? What was beautiful? Being soaked in a suit that weighed more than an obese rhino? Having to stop what I was doing every few minutes to wipe my helmet just so I could glimpse the slightest trace of what my hands were doing before the screen misted up again? Or being forced to spend the first thirty minutes of my time on an alien world toying with screws on a metal plate? Which of these many joyful aspects of life thus far on Trappist-1E could possibly answer to the charge of 'beautiful'?

"Yeah, I know what you mean," Cass answered.

Was I on the wrong exoplanet or something?

"What do you see?" I asked, hoping to get clued into the big joke.

"Look up, Kirk," June said. It must've been good to have moved June to speech.

I craned my neck upwards through the mist. Heaven was covered in an ethereal cloak. The red sun hung dim in the same part of the sky, never moving while we did our merry dance around it. Its light was so faint I could stare at it without squinting. Across its surface were two black dots. Other exoplanets, maybe? They could've been circling the sun at a closer distance than we were.

In the sky, around the deep crimson orb, three huge planet-sized baubles dangled. They resembled the moon, only two-and-a-half times as big and not as bright, with more colors and more detail than a pair of eyes can process. That just about gives the sum of it.

Was it beautiful? I don't know. All I saw was a cosmic battery. The sails of our ship which had harnessed gravitational waves to bring us here weren't simply decorative. Once we'd converted them into Solar Sails, we'd generate enough solar power to keep a city going. Mathematically speaking, the unchanging red sun and planets suspended motionless in the sky like a celestial painting amounted to no more than the microwaved meals of the future.

"Did nobody ever tell you that looking at the sun will damage your eyes?" I said into my helmet.

"I could stare at this all day," Harold replied, fascinated by the heavens, as any physicist would have been.

I let him gawp. He would come around, eventually. There was only so long a person could look at a painting before they tired of it.

Two hours later, and everyone, even Harold, was back to the grind.

That's the thing about another planet – at the end of the day, it's still a planet. Sure, I was on another world. An alien rock. One of six humans to ever step foot in the orbit of a different star. But all it looked like was a bunch of rocks that went out in every direction with a few spots of water collecting in their shadows. Grayish brown as far as the horizon, which was itself a shadow. The dark zone – a gloom beyond the mist. Why had I been expecting purple crystals or red weed? I guess the air had a pinky tint to it, but apart from that, it was Planet Crag. Stony McStoneface.

Yawn.

The cockpit of the ship was the last thing to be dismantled, so for the next few days, we used it as a sort of communal bedroom, until the structure of the main hub was up and airtight. A large dome. Of course, it was Max's design, so every panel slotted in perfectly. The one time I didn't mind his flawlessness.

The next day, Cass skipped into the hub. "It works! It actually works!" she said.

"What does?"

"Don't you notice anything different about me?"

That was a dangerous question at the best of times. On a world with no hiding places, it could've been deadly. "Was I supposed to?"

"You're looking at a girl who's just stepped out of the bath."

"The water catcher?"

"Works like a charm."

"Cass, I could kiss you."

"Easy, tiger." She winked. Fitted on the shelter's skin, the water-catcher trapped mist, extracted moisture from the condensing vapor, purified it and converted it into water we could drink and bathe in. My first shower on Trappist-1E was five days in. If ever there was a moment for a historic speech, it was then.

"It's one small wash for man, one giant relief for mankind." Something like that.

It hadn't felt like five days. Without night or day, there was no real way for the body to measure time. Sundials were less than useless, stuck in the constant glow of a crimson sun. We knew how long it took the other planets to orbit the sun, so by observing them, we could get some idea. But in all the time we'd been here, they'd not moved an inch.

"Harold, why aren't the planets moving?" I asked.

He spluttered out some physics lingo which must have sounded as confusing to him as it did to me, and it took him about ten minutes to say what basically amounted to 'I don't know.'

Some time later, we gathered with the others in the hub.

"Three, two, one." Max plunged the button. The clink of gears reverberated through the wall. Voices cheered. A spatter of applause echoed through the finished dome, bouncing off the window. "Congratulations everyone. We did it. But now's no time to slack off. There's work to do, so I, for one, am heading for an early night."

One by one, they disappeared to their rooms, leaving me alone to celebrate. Two weeks. That's how long it had taken to build. Half the dome was transparent aluminum — a huge window from which we could observe the solar system and the surface of the planet. The other half of it was a solid wall of solar panels, set to spin so the whole shelter would rotate once every twenty-four hours. We got the sun through the window while it was day, and then it went dark when the wall stopped the red hue from reaching the inside of our little compound. We had restored night and day, and I, for one, felt like a titan.

Finally, it was time for a long overdue proper night's sleep.

***

T-minus 155.

It had been ten days since we'd finished the shelter before the motor spinning it broke.

The breakage was the first thing to go wrong, so we all took a great interest in what had happened. The 3D printer produced a diagnostic tool for Max to analyze the broken pieces.

'Burnout. Overheating,' the device read.

"That should only happen if the motor is being overused," he said.

"But it hasn't been," Sonja replied.

"I don't understand it."

"Me neither. What do you want to do?"

The motor was designed to spin every twenty-four hours by none other than Captain Max himself. And that's exactly what it had done. It was unthinkable for it to have broken down.

Before another hour passed, Max printed out another motor and fitted it, and we all forgot about it. Until ten days later, when it broke again.

We boiled it down to a design flaw. Sweet relief. A flaw. At last, proof that Max was fallible. A weight was lifted. Something he'd done was less than perfect. I could finally start to endear myself towards him, begin to overlook his supermodel face and abundant charm. That is, if he hadn't been so stupid in designing a shelter that broke every ten days. And the fact that we no longer had day or night, that we'd be constantly stuck in the dim red glow of the crimson sun until our last day, gave me even more reason to dislike him. I guess there was no winning with some people.

"All done." Harold stepped away from the last of his telescopes.

"Took you long enough," I said.

"These things are precise. One slip and the whole point of our being here would be moot."

"Don't worry, I'm not going to mess with them."

"Music to my ears."

I stared at the sky. "It's kind of sad really, isn't it?"

"What is?"

"The fact we've been sent all this way just for you to look through some telescopes."

"You should see June if you're feeling sad, Kirk."

"I think I'll check in with comms first. Give myself something to do."

Max had set up the communication system in an antechamber. He was broadcasting when I entered.

"Yes, Kirk?"

"Just wondering if we'd heard anything from the other side?"

He sighed. "Nothing yet."

"You sure it's working?"

"Of course." He tapped the console impatiently.

"I'll let you get back to it." I left him to make his reports. Who knew if our messages were even going through?

'We've landed successfully.'

'We've built the shelter.'

'We've finished the telescopes.'

'We've analyzed the surface rock and it's mainly hard stone and iron, as we thought.'

That was Cass's job. She took to studying the topography straight away, which was barren for the most part, like rocks on a beach.

I went rock-pooling once when I was a kid, while the oceans were still cool enough back on Earth, before they started boiling. Everything was so sharp and jagged. The rough rock's edges sliced my feet, and inside the murky pools, weird green stuff grew everywhere. That was how it looked from the window of the shelter. One giant, flat expanse of rock-pools, as far as we could see, all the way to the horizon.

I was hardly excited about it, but Cass was over the moon. Or should I say, she was in a merry orbit? She was on the far side of the sun? No moon here to speak of, so she could hardly be over it. Idioms — another reason why space travel was not for the linguist. Every day, she went out rock-pooling, with her net and bucket and the widest, sincerest smile, like a kid hoping to catch a crab or something. Space crabs — delightful thought, but not my cup of tea. We still had tea, thankfully, so that one still made sense.

For the most part, I assisted Harold with the telescopes. Sonja and Max tinkered with the sails to maximize efficiency. June was always in the background making little notes, observations on our behavior, no doubt.

It wasn't like I had anything else to be getting on with. The computers were working, which made me obsolete. I was brought here as a backup calculator in case the equipment failed. A contingency. But so far, the closest thing to a failure on this planet – besides Max's motor – was me.

***

T-minus 50.

Not much had changed. We'd all adjusted to the atmosphere pretty well, although we still couldn't go outside without our helmets on. There wasn't much difference in gravity. It was different to the moon, where a person would float around. Quite boring really. The atmosphere was thick enough for us to breathe, but the snag was that the combination of gasses didn't give enough oxygen to our lungs and after a few minutes, we started to suffocate. Cass had been working on an inhaler we could use to explore the surface without the need for a mask, in between her experiments crushing the ground into powder to extract minerals which she could use as soil. She was almost always in her spacesuit, conducting some kind of experiment.

The sails were up, catching the light from the sun. Plenty of power. Although there's nothing to do with all that energy. It wasn't like we could sit and binge our favorite TV show. The nearest channel was broadcasting thirty-nine lightyears away, so even if they patched us in, it'd be some time before we'd get any kind of a picture.

June saw us more and more these days. She was still timid, but her heart was in the right place. She was probably trying to get us to open up about how we felt, knowing we only had fifty days left to go. I guessed she just didn't want us to go crazy and rip a hole in the shelter.

I kept telling her my biggest regret was not smuggling a crate of whiskey on board the Icarus One. She thought I was joking to alleviate the stress of the situation. Funny girl. She'd be a lot less melancholic after a few shots of whiskey.

Harold made for good company, when he wasn't puzzling over his telescopes.

"It doesn't make sense," was his go-to line these days. Asking him what exactly it was that didn't make sense got me an hour-long lecture, which helped pass the time. He could be quite amusing when he was befuddled.

In all this time, we'd still received no communication from Earth. But Max kept broadcasting all the same. June suggested we record messages to our loved ones in case the broadcasts were being received at the other end. I started writing mine.

'Dear Mum, I'm getting a fantastic sun tan. At least I think I am. Everything looks red, including my skin, but that's because the sun's red here. It's been pretty much what I expected. Free food — we've got twice as many rations as we need, although I'm getting a bit sick of the fish pie. No aliens yet to speak of. But you never know. I wonder what little green men would look like underneath a red sun. Anyway, I love you, Mum. Will you send my best to Aunt Mavis?'

It was a bit long, and too sentimental for my taste. I'd maybe give it a few days before working out the kinks.

I asked Max if I could take a light and see what was out there in the dark zone, but he flat out refused. He didn't just refuse. He flat out refused. Which meant a massive telling off followed by an even more massive speech on how we all had to stay together for the sake of the mission and how none of us should go anywhere to jeopardize the safety of our crew and bla bla bla. It was like he'd made a rule in his head about not being allowed to explore beyond the mist, and he'd applied it to all of us.

Note to self: if I want a lecture, get it from Harold.

"Do you feel any different from when we landed?" I asked Cass, after she returned from her daily forage.

"What do you mean?"

"I don't know . . . Older?"

"Are you trying to insult me, Kirk?"

She was carrying a trowel. I didn't like the way this was heading. "With the aging, I mean?"

She raised an eyebrow. "Go on."

"Well, if a year is about six days, then with how long we've been here, we should have aged almost twenty-two years by now. Do you feel like a fifty-year-old?"

"I feel just the same."

"No complaints, and no wrinkles."

"Thanks for noticing." She tossed her hair back and winked.

"Don't you think it's odd?"

"What would you prefer? To be decrepit?"

"It just doesn't add up."

"You're the mathematician, Kirk. I'm sure you'll figure it out."

***

T-minus 10.

We decided to have a party. To go out in style. But the whole thing was too somber, and too sober. What were we celebrating? Nothing. Who was going to be the first to go? I guessed it'd be me. Although I hoped it was Max.

It was a shame really, because we'd finally got everything set up just right. Apart from the motor breaking, things had gone pretty well, and the shelter was actually starting to feel like home. Still, we had ten days left to enjoy our little slice of luxury on Trappist-1E.

***

T-minus 5.

I sent my message to Mum. I hadn't bothered changing it. If I'd learnt anything in my last six months of life on an alien world, it's that eponymous last words weren't really my specialty.

V

T-plus 30.

It'd been a month since we were supposed to have died.

But everything kept ticking over, much the same. Good job we'd brought extra rations, otherwise we'd have starved by now. Cass worked on the soil and made that her priority, although I didn't know why. Any day could've been our last. Maybe she wanted to hope that we'd outlive our rations? Although, outliving our six months had been bad enough.

Everyone had become a lot less interesting now that we were in 'unknown' territory. They were all studying what's going on, and it made things so much less fun. Take Harold. He was always good for a lecture every now and then. But if I tried to pin him down to a five minute conversation, he'd tell me he's got too much work to do with the telescopes to sit and chat.

Then there was Cass. All she talked about was soil, soil, soil. Minerals and soil. Climate and soil. 'Do you think we could make a greenhouse?'

'Why do you say that, Cass? Thinking of growing tomatoes?'

'It might be good for making soil'.

'Soil, what a surprise that you mention soil. Do you know, Cass, I'd completely forgotten that you were working on harvesting soil for us to grow real food in. It's not like you mention it every five minutes.'

Max let her make a greenhouse. Another dome. It was humid in there, and the floor was brown. I dreaded what Cass has used as fertilizer to make it brown.

Then there were Sonja and Max – always busy on one thing or another. They squirreled themselves away in a room, and in between printing some new mechanical oddity out of the 3D printer every so often, all they did was laugh together. When I eventually found where they'd been hiding, I tried to join in, but everything just got a bit awkward. They jogged around the compound at the same time every day, and exercised together to keep their figures athletic. Let's just say that unless I became a fitness fanatic, or a mechanical engineer, there wasn't a great deal to chat about.

That left June, who, ironically, seemed ill-prepared for the fact we weren't dead. She must've gotten her head around the countdown, but now that we were no longer ticking the days off, it was like she struggled to cope. She sat with Harold a lot, working as his assistant. The two of them never spoke, they just sat there in silence, watching the telescopes.

And in all that time, none of us dared mention the end. It was like a spell that nobody wanted to break. Everyone had their projects – their own way of trying to figure it out. But stray too close to a question about it, and it was like straying near to the dark zone. And the last thing we needed was another hour from Max about sticking together.

Still, an extra month of tedium was probably better than an extra month of being dead. Probably.

Although – total honesty – I was kind of starting to look forward to it all being over.

***

T-plus 100.

Still alive.

Max called a meeting. He'd decided that we were going to finally break the silence and figure this out, which meant – and I quote – *coordinated communication and cooperation*. Could've been a line directly out of the SpaceGen Captain's Manual For How To Be A Pain In The Butt. But at least it would give us all something to do.

"Why aren't we dead?" he asked the room. "June, you're the doctor. Is there any medical reason why we would survive for longer than anticipated?"

She shook her head. "I've been monitoring our vitals regularly. There's no indication that our bodies are undergoing anything unusual. All the readings look normal."

"So we can dismiss any ideas of a physical anomaly that would explain it?"

"I think so," she answered, uncertainly.

"Yes or no, June."

"Leave it alone, Max. She said there was nothing wrong with us physically," Harold said. Good for you, Harold. Sock it to Mr. Perfect Teeth.

"Okay. Sorry, June. So if we discount medical reasons for why we're still alive, what else could explain it?"

Everyone went quiet for a while. It was fun getting together and standing in silence. We should have been doing it more often.

"Look," Harold said, "I don't know if it helps or not, but the information I'm getting from the telescopes has been confusing to say the least."

"What do you mean?" Max asked.

"Just look out the window at the planets in the sky."

We all craned our necks. Same old view. Same old baubles hanging motionless.

"What of it, Harold?"

"We're orbiting around the sun at a rate of one orbit every six days. Take those two spots on the sun. Those planets are orbiting the sun at a rate of one orbit every two or three days, which means that we should see them traveling across the sun, appearing and disappearing almost every single day. But they don't. They just hang there."

Some brows furrowed, but mine remained where they were. So the planets weren't moving. Hooray for them.

"I thought it was some trick of the atmosphere at first," Harold continued. "But I didn't really have time to examine it with the telescopes, because I needed to point the equipment into space and send the readings back to Mission Control. But even that was confusing. I'd be looking at a star in the sky, plotting how fast it was traveling and predicting where it would be the next day, then I'd examine that region of space and it would be empty."

"Empty?" Max said. "What do you mean, empty?"

"There's no other way to put it. I was losing stars and planets and nebulas almost every time I moved the telescope. But when I went back to check the initial position of them, I'd find them again. It was like they weren't moving. And it's the same with those planets. They're not moving. Nothing's moving. It's like space is standing still."

That was. It. He'd cracked. Harold had gone bananas.

The funny thing about space was that, no matter what anybody said, it was *always* moving. One of the constants in the universe. And it didn't just move, its motion was like the inside of a clock — precise, predictable, complex, possessing a certain finesse. A complicated mechanism with some part always ticking. The mathematics of it is literally breathtaking. What Harold suggested was that the universe had stopped its relentless motion, that the hands of the clock had stopped ticking. And if that were true, then goodbye cruel world, we'd all be dead anyway. So he couldn't be right, and he knew it. But that didn't explain the data from his telescope.

"Any theories as to why this is happening?" Max asked.

Harold shook his head, stuck for words and ideas.

"Anyone else got any explanations?" Max looked at the rest of us.

Who else could explain the motion of the universe better than the physicist? If Harold had gone bananas, then the rest of us didn't even make it to the fruit bowl. We stood no chance. But we stood all the same, looking at one another in silence, trying to fathom out a solution.

I started cataloging every anomaly we'd hit upon since arriving. After all, I couldn't formulate an equation unless I took into account all the factors and variables.

Then I remembered the motor. It had burnt out — overheating. Max's one flaw. And suddenly, it all came clear.

"What if Dr. Rolands was right and wrong at the same time?" I suggested.

"What do you mean, Kirk?"

Everyone stared at me expectantly. It seemed like the ideal moment to stroke my beard, looking thoughtful and meditative. After all, what good was a beard if I couldn't use it for dramatic effect at moments like this one?

"'Rolands theory of the orbital constant' equates one orbit with one year," I said. "We had every reason to believe that the orbit would be the factor in the equation which would remain constant, and our rate of aging would alter around it. But what if it was the other way around? What if the way we interacted with time and orbit was flipped? What if, instead of one year being six days, our six days around the sun was the equivalent of one year? It explains everything."

They all looked a little baffled. Maybe I'd overworked the beard a bit.

"It's like this," I continued, "the chances of the entire universe coming to a standstill are so remote that you might as well call it impossible. But the chances of us interacting with the universe at a slower rate because of orbital locking are far more likely. The motor is the key to this whole thing."

I suddenly realized what I was about to tell them, and it almost pained me to do so. What I was about to suggest would make Max perfect again, which was a thought that galled me so much, I almost didn't say anything.

"Go on," Sonja urged me.

I sighed. "You remember the motor? It burnt out after ten days both times, right? Design flaw. That's what we put it down to. But what if it wasn't? What if it really was overheating?"

"How could it be overheating? It was spinning once every twenty-four hours?" Cass interrupted.

"Yeah, once every twenty-four hours as far as we were concerned. But let's say we're spinning around the sun once every six days, and those six days to us are the equivalent of one year — 365 days back on Earth. That would mean we're interacting with the universe 60 times slower than when we were back on Earth. The mechanics of our lives here and life on Earth are out of alignment."

"Slower, instead of faster?" Harold asked.

"You got it. Twenty-four hours to us would be the same as twenty-four minutes on Earth. So we'd set the motor to spin once every twenty-four hours, but in actual fact, it'd be spinning once every twenty-four minutes. If the machines were operating on the same mechanics as Earth time, it's no wonder it burnt out. You see, to us, the planets seem to be hung in space. But they're not. They're spinning at the same rate that they've always spun. It's just that orbital locking means that we're experiencing that spin 60 times slower than it's actually happening."

They tried to take it in. Harold was the first to twig.

"So our thirty year life-expectancy isn't six months after all," he said.

"Yes and no. It's six months on Earth. But that's thirty years here."

"That would explain why our telescopes are telling us that we've not yet completed a full rotation of the sun." His eyes lit up. "Do you know Kirk, I think you might be right."

The others weren't quite as quick to catch up.

"What are you saying?" Cass asked, trying to get her head around things.

"I'm saying that you'd better get to work on fixing that soil. We're going to need it."

Eventually, Max printed a white-board and some markers, and between me and Harold, we got it through to them. Dr. Rolands had been right about orbital locking, but had completely misunderstood its implications. She'd thought that getting to Trappist-1E would shorten our lifespan, when in actual fact, it would do the opposite. In six months on Earth, we would live thirty years on Trappist-1E.

We'd been on Trappist-1E for about 280 days, thinking that had been the equivalent of about 46 years. When in actual fact, we'd only been on Trappist-1E for close to five days. We just perceived it differently because of orbital locking. That meant our T-plus 100 was in actual fact, T-minus 29 years and 85 days. And we only had about seventy more days of rations left.

We all started sounding like Cass. What we needed was food, and that meant one thing.

Soil, soil, soil.

VI

T-plus 101.

We partied hard last night. Well, I say 'we'. I didn't party very hard at the best of times. But the realization that we'd have at least twenty-nine more years before we reached six months on Trappist-1E made everyone else euphoric. And I didn't want to be the one that dampened the mood, so I played along for the most part.

Without alcohol, it was difficult to celebrate anything. But June figured out a way of mixing some of the medicines from the supply of chemicals she'd brought to simulate the effects of alcohol. Shy, timid June. People used to tell me, 'you've got to watch the quiet ones.' Maybe there was something in that.

While she was mixing the solution, Max and Sonja worked out a new motor design. Now they knew the speed of rotation, getting a fix on it was easy enough. The 3D printer produced the part, and the hub was spinning again before June's cocktail was ready.

When the spin blocked the sun from reaching the interior, the lights came on. LEDs. Sonja set them so they flashed with the atmosphere of a rave. June had brought a drive with her favorite tunes, which we printed out some speakers for, and got to listen to her playlist. Hardcore dance music interspersed with vintage pop. Who'd have guessed that our psychiatrist was a closet diva?

Once we'd imbibed the cocktails and started dancing, the rest of them unleashed the stress of the last six months. But it was a bit too gaudy for my tastes. So after a couple of hours spent throwing shapes — very odd, awkward and unsightly shapes — I took a seat on the sofa and turned into a casual observer. This cocktail of June's worked wonders though. I was seeing double before I'd noticed Cass had joined me on the sofa.

"Come and dance," she pleaded.

But I shook my head. "Come and talk."

She took a seat next to me. "June should have made this stuff a long time ago." Her red hair seemed very bright to me all of a sudden.

"Agreed. Where did everybody go?" I asked.

"They've all disappeared. I think my moves were a bit too intimidating for them. It's just been you and me for the past half-hour."

I hadn't even noticed.

"Congratulations by the way," she slurred.

"What for?"

"For figuring it out. I bet you never thought you'd get an extra thirty years."

I frowned. "What do you mean?"

"You know what I mean," she said. "You're not daft, Kirk. I'm happy for you."

The thing was, I knew exactly what she meant, but I was hardly happy about it.

While the others had been thrilled at the prospect of having more time, I was numb about the whole thing. My head went back to that hospital bed, and the doctor with the magic clipboard. Eighteen months, he'd said. Back then, I'd have given anything for more time.

I thought I'd come to terms with it. Eighteen months was plenty, I'd told myself. Look what I've achieved in eighteen months. I was on an alien planet. I'd traveled 39.6 lightyears from Earth. That was enough, wasn't it? What else was there left for me to do?

Free food, that's why I'd taken this mission. It had nothing to do with running away from dying. That's not why I'd agreed to come. If I'd been running away, then the news of getting more time should have made me ecstatic. But I wasn't ecstatic. I didn't know how to feel about it. When had I started accepting that eighteen months was enough? Was it when we got here? Was it when we'd built the shelter? Was it when I realized that the last 200 meals of our rations were all fish pie? Or was it that day in Henry Rolands' office when he'd told me I was gaining time?

Gaining time. All I could see was that little twerp's smug face. What had he said? 'You're welcome.' It didn't seem right then, and it didn't seem right now. It wasn't fair somehow. The other five had given up thirty years in coming here. I'd gained thirty years. It didn't equate properly. Unless . . .

"You're right, Cass. I never thought I'd get thirty years. But what about you?"

"What do you mean, Kirk? What about me?"

"Exactly. What about you?"

My head spun, and the red hair that hung around her freckled cheeks kept distracting me from the epiphany I was undergoing.

"Are you going to tell me or not?" she said.

"I'll tell you. Let's see. They were wrong about the effects of orbital locking. We know that for certain. What if they were wrong about the aging too?"

She looked more puzzled than a thousand piece jigsaw. June's cocktail didn't make absorbing complex theoretical spacetime equations any easier.

"Spit it out, Kirk, before my head explodes." She giggled, swaying her head to the music still playing loud through the speakers.

"Well, they said that we'd age at an accelerated rate as we traveled around Trappist-1E, right?"

"I'm with you so far."

"What if our rate of aging doesn't change, and we keep aging at the same rate as we would if we were on Earth?"

"You lost me."

"Okay, think of it this way. Six days on Earth is like 365 days for us here. The orbital thingy has seen to that. In that time, we're supposed to age the equivalent of one year. What if we don't? What if we only age six days, like we would on Earth? That would mean you'd live 60 times longer on Trappist-1E."

"Meaning?"

"Meaning someone with a predicted lifespan of 30 years might end up living 60 times longer here. Call it 1,800 years."

"I don't have a clue what you're saying. Come on, Kirk, let's dance."

I didn't argue with her anymore. Her red curls had won in the battle for my attention. I got up on the dance floor, and pounded out my best moves until I passed out.

***

The crimson rays of the spinning sun brought the morning, and brought me round. Cass was laid out on the sofa.

"Morning," I said.

She stirred. "Just five more minutes," she groaned, not opening her eyes. "Why is it so bright?"

"I think we need to ask Max about printing out some curtains."

By the time she'd woken properly, I'd fixed us both a drink. I didn't think she remembered our conversation last night, but I did.

Gaining time. It was a ridiculous notion. I wasn't happy about it, but that could have been as much to do with the headache as the actual situation. Maybe I'd get my head around it in time.

We'd set out for Trappist-1E with six months left to live. Now we had to start thinking about the prospect of living years here. For the rest of them, who knew how long they'd live on this rock? Was it really possible that these five unsuspecting dopes could end up existing here for hundreds of years? Maybe thousands?

Having more time — it was all well and good. But was there such a thing as having too much?

I knew I'd have to tell them eventually. I couldn't just keep this kind of news to myself. So when everyone had stumbled in, bleary-eyed for their morning tea, I called a meeting to start in ten minutes and rushed down to the 3D printer.

It took about that long for me to print out a clipboard. I was hardly going to deliver news like this without one.

HAROLD

Dawn was hard to come by on a planet that never spun.

My first glimpse of the sun the day we arrived on Trappist-1E would likely be the final dawn I'd ever live to see. If that turned out to be true, it was worth it.

Every day of my life on Earth was a day I spent in the stars. That's what it meant to be an astrophysicist. But until we landed here, I'd never been anywhere close to a real star. The sun wasn't exactly close to Earth. It was more like a bulb than a star.

Sure, I'd curated enough planetariums to stand side by side with any gas giant I cared to load into the projector. Simulations. Virtual Reality. But it was all so distant. Like a picture behind a glass frame. No matter how close I got, there was always a barrier between me and the canvas. However hard I stared, I'd never see it for what it truly was. I'd only ever experience it from the other side. The far side.

Not like Trappist-1E. Here, I could look at the sun with my own eyes. My *own* eyes. I didn't need a telescope or an instrument to mediate. No translation required in this conversation. It was just me and the star, a crimson flame flickering in heaven's hearth.

From the moment I raised my head to gaze at that red sun, the gloves had been ripped off. I'd touched the universe for the first time. And it felt — how can I put it? — it was like that moment when winter was replaced by the first glimpse of spring. Dew trapped on snowdrops. Frost banished. Except, the moment didn't pass. I'd been reborn in perpetual springtime. The light was like water, gushing from a fountain, bathing us clean.

Life. Trappist is life.

"Are you alright?" June wrapped her hand around my arm.

"Sorry, darling. Was I mumbling again?"

"You always get so lost when you're stargazing."

I shrugged. "Occupational hazard."

She nuzzled her head on my shoulder. Her blonde hair whispered on my neck. "Tell me what you see."

"Same as you, darling."

"All I see is the sky."

"I know. Amazing, isn't it?"

She scowled. "Well it's big, I'll give you that."

"Naturally."

"It's just so . . ." she shrugged.

"So what?"

"So . . . empty."

I laughed. "Empty? That's a good one. I'll have to remember that."

"What's funny?"

"Look again," I said. "Only a little harder. The sky isn't empty, June. It's full."

"Yeah, right. Full of dead rocks zipping around space maybe."

I shook my head. "The sky is the most living thing there is, darling. Think of how it moves. Graceful, yet powerful, like a ballet dancer with sledgehammers for legs and a butterfly's finesse. It never stops growing, expanding with every second that ticks by, giving birth to countless new stars. Have you ever known something to reproduce so voraciously? It feeds. It opens its many mouths, and gigantic black holes consume everything they touch. It speaks in waves and radiation that flood it like a cosmic reservoir. And it breathes. Give me your hand. Can you feel it breathing on your skin?"

"You're crazy, Harold. You know that?"

"Is that your official diagnosis, doctor?"

"I'm afraid so. I'll get Max to send off my report. Dr. Harold Wang, rotten fruitcake fit for the loony bin."

"Takes one to know one."

"Hey." She punched my arm, playful but firm. Those skinny limbs didn't half pack a wallop.

"Alright." I lifted my hands to surrender. "I give up. I'm sorry."

She folded her arms and smirked. "That's more like it."

"Trust you to call me crazy and then have me apologize for it."

"See, I told you. You're nuts."

"But that's why you love me. Right? You just can't get enough of this whacko-nut-job and his crazy sky-talk."

"Occupational hazard." She clasped my hand and wove her fingers through mine.

We sat in silence staring at the sun. The star. The dim light that swathed us in its majesty. With June in my arms and the heavens in full bloom, maybe the next few thousand years might not be so bad? If Kirk was right, of course. And why wouldn't he be? The sky didn't lie. I trusted it. Ever since we'd landed, that trust had only deepened.

On Earth, the horizon had been the barrier between man and what lay above. We could never fully give ourselves over to it. Always tied to the ground. Not so here.

On Trappist-1E, there was no seam. I reached out and embraced the universe and every time I delved further into the expanse, the exhilaration tingled sharper. Pins and needles. I was alive. Connected to everything at once. To June. To the stars.

My lungs filled with the breath of untold eons. I could taste the millennia that awaited us, and it tickled my tongue. Everywhere I looked, there was life. So much of it. And more beauty than a thousand sunrises. I guess it was a fair trade. If we were going to be stuck circling the same view of the heavens for the next few centuries, the view might as well be this one.

"I think you're wrong about the sky," June said, snapping me out of myself again. She turned her neck and gazed at me with those intent, blue eyes.

"Really, darling? What bit did I get wrong?"

"The part about it being the most living thing in the universe." She dragged my hand to her belly and pushed my palm on her stomach.

"You don't mean—?"

"Harold. I'm pregnant."

What do you know? Another dawn.

PENELOPE

I

My first color was red.

R is for Red, like the sun and the ground and the light and the air and my blanket. Most things are red. That's why it was my first. I learnt all the other colors after a while, but I didn't need to. The only reason I wanted to learn them is because of all the stories Mummy and Daddy told me about the place that's far away from here — too far for me to see. They talk about *green* hills and *blue* seas and *yellow* sand and I didn't really understand it. I could picture sand — it's like powdered rock. And I could see hills sometimes if I closed my eyes and thought really hard. It was just so weird to imagine them as being anything apart from red.

"Then one day, a horse rode up to the forest."

"What's a horse Mummy?" I asked.

She stopped the story and smiled. Mummy was so pretty when she smiled. Her hair was yellow, so I tried to think about Mummy's hair being like sand sometimes.

"It's an animal back on Earth," she told me.

"An animal?"

"Yes, you remember? We've talked about animals before?"

"Are they like Oscar?" Oscar was the boy I'd marry one day.

"No, Oscar's a boy. Animals are different to boys."

"If you say so, Mummy."

"Well, almost," she whispered, and she giggled to herself. "Don't say that in front of Daddy though," she warned me. She'd told me once before that Auntie Cassandra was the best person to ask about animals, but I never did get to ask her about them. Maybe I would. Auntie Cassandra's hair was red, and I liked red the best.

"What's a forest, Mummy?" I asked.

She wrinkled up her nose to think hard. "It's mainly green. Do you know green?"

That's why I'd decided to learn my colors. It helped me understand what Mummy wanted me to know. She never got very far into her stories until I'd learnt my colors.

***

The next day, I played with Oscar. He had more toys than I did. There was one with a weird shape on it.

"What's that?" I asked.

"It's an animal."

'So *that's* an animal,' I thought. It was small, soft and cuddly, and stuffed with fluffy things, and it gave good hugs.

"A horse is an animal," I told him. He didn't believe me at first.

"Hoss," he tried to repeat me.

"Ho*r*se."

"Horse."

Much better. He could be so silly sometimes, but then again, it wasn't his fault. He couldn't help being two years younger than me. 'One year and four months' he protested, but I kept telling him it's two.

"Mummy, I saw a horse today." I ran in and told her.

"Really?" she said, excited. "What did it look like?"

"It had a tail at one end."

"Very good."

"And a mouth at the other."

"Excellent."

"And two fins."

Mummy looked confused. "Are you sure it was a horse?"

"Yes, of course it was. Oscar said it was an animal, and a horse is an animal."

"One of Oscar's toys?"

"Yes."

"It could have been a seahorse," Daddy said from across the room.

"Very funny, Harold," Mummy said, although she didn't laugh. Usually, Mummy laughed if she thought something was very funny. But not this time. "Sweetheart, a toy is not the same as an animal. A toy is just a toy."

"What do you mean?"

"Well, do you remember in our story, the horse rode up to the forest? Toys don't move by themselves. They're not alive, like we are. But animals can move on their own. They've got life in them."

"So I was right. They *are* the same as boys."

"What have you been teaching her, June?" Daddy asked Mummy. This time Mummy laughed.

"Oh, Penelope. You can be funny sometimes, even if it gets us in trouble."

"I'll show you how much like animals boys can be," Daddy said, and he dropped the charts he was looking at and chased Mummy with his 'tickle fingers.' She ran off, batting him away with a towel and Daddy roared. It was a good game while it lasted.

I didn't quite understand what Mummy was saying about animals moving on their own. But it sounded exciting. When Daddy had 'gobbled' Mummy up with his tickle fingers, he sat down again to look at his charts.

"Are there animals here that we can play with?" I asked.

"There may be, in the unexplored regions of the planet," Daddy said. "There's water here, and that means life. So we can't discount that possibility." Daddy was using words I didn't understand.

Mummy was good at helping him to make sense. I think that's why she was a doctor, because she helped things make sense. "There might be animals somewhere, but we don't know for sure," she said.

"Where?" I asked.

"Maybe somewhere that we haven't ever been before."

"Somewhere like in Daddy's telescopes? Like where it's dark?"

Mummy stopped and put on her 'cross' face. "What have we told you about the dark zone? What's the rule?" she said sternly.

"The rule is to never go where it's dark," I repeated, like always.

"Good," she said, then sent me to bed. I wondered what it would be like to find an animal somewhere. I bet Oscar would like to see one.

***

The next day, I went out with Oscar to search for an animal. We wandered outside, and were both wearing our special boots that made the rocks less sharp on our feet. Oscar wanted to look for animals in the pools of water between rocks, but I wouldn't let him. We'd never seen them in the pools when we looked from the window, so if there were animals around, they must be far away.

"Come on, Oscar. Don't dawdle." I'd heard Auntie Sonja say it to him once, and thought it sounded good. Auntie Sonja was Oscar's Mummy, and she knew how to handle him much better than I did. I was going to have a lot of work to do with Oscar if I was going to marry him. I'd got him to the point where he always did what I suggested to him, but it was always such a lot of effort. When we were married, he'd have to be a lot quicker about doing what I told him.

We were almost out of sight from the shelter. The mist was thin today, and made my face wet. Behind us, fog covered our tracks. We'd walked so far into it, I couldn't even see the shelter anymore.

"Where are we going?" He panted.

"We're hunting for animals, Oscar. Now keep a lookout."

He was tired. We'd walked a long way. He took a whiff of his inhaler and he stopped panting after that.

My chest hurt a little and I started coughing, so I reached into my pocket for my inhaler. But it wasn't there. I must have left it in the pocket of my other trousers. "Oh no."

"What's wrong?"

"I don't have my inhaler."

He crossed his arms. "Well you can't have mine."

"Why not?"

"I don't want your mouth on my inhaler. There's germs on girls."

"What does it matter?" I said. "We're going to be married one day. You'll have to get used to my germs then."

"Don't remind me." He shuddered a little bit. Five-and-a-half year olds can be so immature.

My chest tightened and I coughed harder.

"Where did you leave it?" he asked.

"What?"

"Your inhaler."

"It's in my other trouser pocket," I told him, though it hurt to speak.

He thought about it for a moment. "Wait here," he said. "I'll run back and get it for you."

Away he went, running across the rocks into the mist as fast as he could until he disappeared. I coughed so much, I had to sit down. Then I had to lie down. My chest was hurting more than ever, and I tried to breathe slowly, like Mummy had shown me when I was little, but it didn't help. She'd told me to always carry my inhaler if I went outside. It was one of the rules, like not going into the dark. She said that I wouldn't be able to breathe very well without it. She was right. I guess Mummies were always right. How long was Oscar going to be? Would he even be able to find me again?

I grew woozy. Eyes heavy. I held back a yawn and the pain in my chest got worse.

Was that Mummy's voice I could hear? It was shouting my name.

"Penelope! Penelope, where are you?"

But I was hurting too much to call back. I just had to go to sleep. I closed my eyes, but it didn't go black. Everything around me turned the prettiest red I'd ever seen.

II

"Why have you got to be such a brute Oscar?" I told him but he just laughed in response.

"Oh come on, Pen. Don't tell me you didn't find it a little bit funny?"

It wasn't much of a defense, but I forgave him anyway. Why was I always so quick to forgive him?

It seemed like a lifetime ago since Oscar had asked me to take a walk with him. Probably not since we were kids playing in rock pools. It was nice to be alone with him for a change. But why had he asked me? Was it explicitly so that he could push me into the nearest pool and ruin my brand new printed walking boots? Boys!

I gritted my teeth, feigning a smile as he held out his hand, helping me stumble out of the water. Grotesque one moment, gallant the next. His sudden turns made me dizzy, but at least he wasn't boring. Still, he wasn't exactly being his usual self. Was he nervous or something?

We walked on in silence for a while. The mist cleared a little, and we looked up at the sky. Years ago, Mum had told me about romantic walks. She said that on Earth there was this thing called a sunset, which turned the sky red in long rays of color as the sun disappeared beyond the horizon. That was when it was most romantic, apparently. I couldn't understand how the sun might disappear. It was always there. Hung in the same spot. And it was always that deep, crimson-red color. Mum said it's like a constant sunset here — that we might very well be on the most romantic planet in the universe. That's when Oscar reached over for my hand and intertwined his fingers through mine.

"It's so pretty, don't you think?" I asked.

"What is?"

"The sky, dummy." I rolled my eyes.

"Yeah, but I can think of prettier things."

"Such as?"

"You, for a start," he almost whispered through an anxious smile.

My cheeks flushed hot. I was grateful for the red sun, so Oscar wouldn't see the color on my face. We still had a whole year before we were to be married. It wasn't like he needed to flatter me or anything.

We didn't speak again for a few minutes. We just swung our arms together until we reached the edge of the plateau. The rock dropped away so suddenly and so far that it scared me, and instinctively, I slowed down as we neared the edge. At the bottom of the cliff, a large pool of water collected, much larger than the ones we had up here, and more of the same sharp rocky undulations stretched into the distance.

Oscar perched on the cliff top, swinging his legs over the precipice. My chest thumped but I joined him, resting my head on his shoulder. We stayed that way for ages. Time slowed until it stopped altogether. There was nothing else around us or above us. There was just the two of us, the only things that moved and breathed, and everything else became a backdrop to our whims. He tipped his head towards mine, nestling me into him.

"I know that we don't have much of a choice about it," he whispered, "but even if I did, I wouldn't choose to marry anyone but you."

I twisted my head, looking up into his eyes. "Do you mean that?"

"Is the sun red?"

I thought about it for a moment. "I think I'd choose you too," I whispered back.

He leaned towards me, and I didn't pull away. His lips curled into an awkward shape, and I felt mine do the same. Then they touched, soft and gentle at first, until we pressed them hard together and closed our eyes. For a moment, I was floating. It was like we'd fallen from our perch to soar through the skies. We leaned back until we laid out on the rock, and its jagged points jabbed hard beneath me.

Our first kiss couldn't have been more perfect. After a while, our lips parted, and I opened my eyes, staring into his. We lay that way for a long time, our bodies touching, and I rested my head on his shoulder, squeezing my arm around him. We gazed up at the sun, and I made a wish on it, that forever would be like this, that Oscar and I would always feel this way.

He propped himself on his elbows as he reached into his pocket and took his inhaler. He offered it to me and I breathed in a whiff, the air filling my lungs and my head, blood pulsing through my veins, renewed.

"I brought something with me." He yanked a small hammer and chisel from his pocket.

"What's that for?"

"I'll show you." He knelt up and aimed the chisel on the rock, knocking it with the hammer, moving it around so as to carve a word. Every bang from the swing of his wrist was a mixture of a dull thud and a harsh twang, echoing down the cliff side. He kept engraving the stone where we'd laid out together until he'd spelt it out in full. OSCAR, it read.

Then he handed the tools to me.

"What should I do?" I asked.

"It's so you can write your name together with mine, and then, when I wake up tomorrow, I'll take a walk and come out here, and I'll know I wasn't dreaming."

I smiled, and awkwardly did my best to strike PENNY into the rock beneath his name.

Once it was done, he leaned in and we shared another short kiss before we started back home.

Mum was waiting up for me, despite it being the middle of the night inside the dome. Sure, it was always light outside. But we'd stayed out too late, and the dome had spun to night, blocking the sun from shining through the atrium.

I rushed in and told her all about it. We hardly ever got to spend time alone together. The other kids were always tugging at one of us, taking us away from each other. Either that, or Mum was busy counseling in her clinic. It was nice to be able to talk with her like we used to, while everyone else slept.

"My little girl's all grown up." She lifted a hand to my cheek. As she looked at me, I wondered if I'd ever stay as pretty as Mum was. "It's all going so fast," she said.

I didn't really grasp what she meant. "I wish it would hurry up and I could marry Oscar right away."

"Trust me, when you get to be as old as I am — older, in fact — you'll feel just the opposite."

I'd only have a few more years left of being younger than Mum. She didn't want things to change, I guess. She wouldn't change, so why should everything else?

We eventually called it a night, but I couldn't sleep, re-living that kiss over and over. I'd never been so conscious of my lips before. It was like I was feeling them for the first time.

Oscar would often take me for walks to our spot, where our names were scratched as a monument to one another. It would be the spot where he'd propose with that ruby engagement ring he'd printed out, knowing how much I loved the color of ruby. That view — it never changed, although our chiseled names began to fade, just a little, the closer we came to the wedding.

III

"Push, Penny. You're doing great. Breathe. One last push, and it'll all be over."

I shrieked in agony through the heaving, and threw my entire being into the pain. It rushed at me, and I fought to ignore the wrenching, sweating, clenching, intensity of the ordeal, and just push. With Oscar in one hand, and Mum in the other, I squeezed them as hard as I could, convinced I was going to burst. My heart pounded. One last release.

I screamed so hard I shook from head to toe, until the pressure faded, and the sound of another scream came to my ears. A child's scream.

My child.

Was it all over at last? The answer, of course, was no. It was only just beginning.

Tears of joy flooded my cheeks, intermingled with tears of pain. Contentment surged through my chest and into my arms as I held my baby girl for the first time, as well as an awful throbbing weakness as I struggled to keep her steady.

"You did it," Oscar whispered.

"I'm so proud of you, darling," Mum said.

All I could do was cry. I couldn't tell if it was the pain or the happiness, the trauma of the ordeal or the relief of it being over, or just the sheer magnitude of looking at my beautiful girl in the face for the first time. I wondered if I'd ever lose that feeling of awe as I stared at her delicate, gorgeous features, and introduced myself.

"Hey there, baby. It's me. It's your Mum."

***

The next year passed by like it was all one big dream, and before I knew it, she was eating food and I was teaching her to walk.

"That's it, Ruby. You can do it!" I beckoned to her with my arms outstretched, as she took her first few steps towards them. She fell over so many times, but I was always there to catch her.

Every night, I'd sit with Ruby and tell stories, just like Mum did with me. Until we were expecting our second, and I needed the extra sleep. Then her bedtime tales turned into sentences. One or two at most. Poems were short. I liked poems for that. Mum came in and picked up whatever I couldn't manage, just as I'd done for her since I was a little girl. She was tireless about it, and I was always grateful.

One night, I overheard Mum telling Ruby one of her stories, indulging her in one of the longer yarns.

"What's a horse?" Ruby asked, and I chuckled.

"She takes after me," I whispered to Oscar, cradling my bump.

"Who does?" he said.

"Ruby."

He smiled at me. "Yeah, she's beautiful. Just like her Mum," he whispered back. It might have been the hormones, but I yanked him by the arm and pushed him into the bedroom, locking the door behind us. What did he expect, bestowing compliments on a pregnant woman?

We made sure that Ruby always played with Chris, as the two of them would marry when they got old enough, like me and Oscar had. And the same with Charlie — he was always put to play with Isabel.

So many kids, it made me feel old, and I finally understood what Mum had once told me about wanting everything to slow down. Never was that more true than the first time Lori — our third, still learning to talk — looked up at Mum, pointed, and said, "Mama."

"I'm not your Mummy. I'm your Nanna June," Mum said. "*That's* your Mummy." She pointed at me.

Creases crumpled Lori's forehead as she glanced across at me, shook her head, looked back at Mum and repeated, "Mama."

Mum said she was sorry about it, but I didn't mind. I could hardly blame Lori. Mum and I could easily have passed for sisters, with her looking like the younger of the two of us. It wasn't her fault. It wasn't anybody's fault. But it made me feel old, and I just wanted everything to stop, to give me a chance to take it in and absorb it, instead of rushing by so fast that I'd miss it before it began.

***

When Ruby was ten, I took her out to the spot where Oscar had first kissed me. The view hadn't changed a bit. I struggled to find the carving on the rock. It had faded so much over the years, but I could still make out the words. I handed her a chisel and hammer.

"Where, Mummy?" she asked.

"Just there, next to where it says 'Penny'." I pointed.

"What's Penny?"

"That's Mummy's name."

She pretended to understand, and shook her blonde hair back over her shoulders. It was the same color as Mum's hair, and reminded me of the sand I'd imagined when I was a kid. My hair was much the same, although it had started fading, and the few gray hairs I found had made it pale.

Ruby took the chisel and hammer in her two firm hands, stooped down, and carved out a rough version of her name.

OSCAR
PENNY
RUBY

We admired her craftsmanship, and walked back home, puffing on our inhalers and stopping at every rock pool to inspect the empty contents, just in case anything had changed.

When we got back, I walked into the middle of a frenzy. Toys flew across the room. Tears stained the floor. Bombs did less damage. What could possibly have caused such havoc in the couple of hours I'd taken Ruby out to carve her name? Charlie, that's what.

After the air settled and the screaming calmed, I took Charlie to one side.

"It wasn't like that Mummy, I—"

"No, Charlie. You know the rules."

"But I didn't mean to hurt her," he said indignantly, as if it wasn't fair, him being punished for what had happened.

"You printed it out, and then you hit her with it. Poor Isabel. She's been crying for hours now. Is that any way to treat your future wife? Do you really think she'll *want* to marry you after this?"

"But, it was an accident. I didn't mean it."

"I don't care if it was an accident or not. You know the rules. What's the rule, Charlie?" I lectured him through an angry frown.

"Never go where it's dark," he recited arrogantly, knowing that wasn't what I meant, but thinking himself so clever for saying it anyway.

"No. Not that one. What's the rule?" I repeated.

He sighed. "No weapons, no harm," he said.

"Yes. And do you understand why we don't print things out that can be used as weapons after what you did to Isabel?"

His head hung in shame. "Yes, Mummy."

"Good. Now what do you say?"

"I'm sorry, Mummy," he said quietly, so I knew it was sincere.

"Now go and say sorry to Isabel."

His head drooped and he left the room in a slump.

Ruby stopped what she was doing with Mum and looked across at me. "Boys!" she gasped, and rolled her eyes.

I caught Mum's glance and we both laughed. "Remind you of anyone?" Mum asked.

She did. But more and more, Ruby was reminding me of Mum. At one time, Mum and I could have passed for sisters, but as each year passed, Ruby looked more like Mum, rather than me, and their similarity grew uncanny. So it was nice to hear Ruby say something every now and then that wasn't a lightyear away from what I used to sound like.

That night, I stared at my face in the mirror, at the tired lines etched into my skin. I was the oldest of us in the shelter. There were so many kids, but none of them were older than me. Not even Aunt Cassandra had wrinkles. Not like these. I'd never seen an old person before, and it scared me.

Oscar came and wrapped his arms around me, kissing my neck. Our eyes met in the mirror's reflection.

"Do you think I'm still as pretty as the sun?" I asked him. "Even with these wrinkles?"

He smiled at me. "Always," he said. Turning my face away from the mirror, he forced me to meet his eyes. His own face had started to wrinkle, the same as mine, but those gorgeous eyes looked just the same as ever. The same little boy I'd always known was still there, staring back at me.

"Listen to me," he said. "No matter what happens, no matter how many orbits we pass through, you will always be the most beautiful thing in the universe."

His eyes may have been sincere, but something nagged at me. "You don't think my Mum is prettier?" I asked. "She looks more like me than I do these days."

He laughed and shook his head. "I've known your Mum since I was a baby, and she hasn't aged a day. You and me — what we share goes beyond that. It's more than superficial. We're growing old together. Who else here can say that?" He leaned in and kissed me on my cheek.

"Come on, you old thing. Let's be teenagers again, one last time." I pulled him towards me and smothered his lips with mine.

IV

How many months had we been planning Ruby's wedding?

Oscar had been working with his Dad to design a new dome for Ruby that would meet her requirements, and it had given him more than one headache over these past weeks. But Max was a great help to Oscar. He was like a rock. 'No problem is without a solution,' he reminded us when it all started getting a bit much. Oscar's solution was to cancel the wedding, but that was hardly an option. So, instead, he figured out a way to make Ruby's new dome spin in the opposite direction to the main shelter, replace the transparent aluminum with glass, and fit natural stone into the external structure, however crazy it sounded.

Fortunately for Ruby, Oscar had inherited his Dad's practical mind, even if he hadn't inherited much patience.

When they showed me the structure, I searched for a tissue to wipe my eyes. Whether Ruby would appreciate everything Oscar had done for her or not, it was worth it just to see the thing built. Of course, Ruby would have to wait until the big day. It was bad luck for her to see the dome before her wedding day.

Chris was not all that interested in where the ceremony was going to take place. Typical groom. But Ruby had decided it should be outside, which meant more printing, and more building. I told her she'd wear out the printer before they'd even started married life, but she didn't seem concerned.

"Dad can fix anything," was her stock reply.

I wondered if her tastes would have been so extravagant had I been married into a scientist's family instead of an engineer's.

Eventually, everything was printed and positioned exactly where she'd imagined. The chairs, the decorations, and Aunt Cassandra had even managed to grow a bouquet of flowers from the stalks of the potatoes she'd been harvesting. They were beautiful. Even the drabbest flowers were rare at the best of times, but I'd never seen so pretty a sprig in all my years.

The night before the big day, I fixed the dress she'd wear. My old dress. Lace. White. Mum had sewn it for me before I was a bride, and now I was altering it for Ruby. My fingers weren't as flexible as they used to be. Tinkering to get the perfect fit ached my joints. My eyesight was on the blink. I kept losing the thread. And the spectacles that Mum had printed out for me were getting their share of use.

Why couldn't I work faster? I never used to be this slow. Mum and Ruby laughed in the other room while I was busying away at the machine. I wanted to be there, soaking up every minute with them.

When it was finally ready, I called Ruby in to try a fitting, and it couldn't have looked better on her. "You look beautiful, sweetheart," I said.

"Do you really think so?"

I choked up, nodding.

"What do you think, Nanna June?" Ruby asked.

"Your mother's right. You look beautiful, Ruby."

Ruby twirled in the gown, her smile adorning her more perfectly than any fabric.

"Let's get you dressed too, Mum," I said.

"Me?"

"I want to see what you look like together."

Mum was going to be the bridesmaid. It didn't take her more than a minute to throw on her dress, and when they stood beside one another, she and Ruby sparkled like sisters. They could have been twins. Two petite blondes without a blemish between them. No wonder I felt like the odd one out.

Then it came — that feeling in my chest. A dull pounding. I'd noticed it before, more and more recently. Mum had looked me over in her clinic, but found nothing to be the matter. 'It's just the stress,' I told myself. Stress of the big day. That's all it was. And I sipped some water until it went away.

We all stayed up talking until the dome's spin took the sun away. I tired long before Mum and Ruby, and went to bed early, leaving them both too excited to sleep.

The night passed fast, and I wondered if someone had sped up the shelter's motor. Ruby made Oscar's patience look virtuous, and I wouldn't have put it past her to pull a stunt like that. I remembered feeling the same, about wanting to speed things up. 'She'll learn,' I chuckled to myself.

Before the shelter spun past its first crescent, everyone was gathered outside. Lori looked adorable, and Charlie had even turned out smart. He sat with Isabel, planning their own wedding day.

Oscar and I helped to look after Mum's two little ones. Two and four years old. Dad couldn't handle both of them at the same time, and Mum had her bridesmaid's duties to perform. I wore my favorite shade of red. I'd printed out a hat specially for the event. My one extravagance.

Chris stood statuesque, waiting beneath the arch we'd put up, and he formed a handsome silhouette against the sun. His dark suit was sheathed in crimson as the light shone radiantly across the plateau.

Mum walked through the aisle of chairs, and stood beside Chris. Ruby followed. She walked faster than she'd practiced. No surprise there.

Chris said his vows first. Ruby cried through hers. My chest swelled with pride at my little girl.

"As long as the sun is in the sky, I am yours and you are mine." The vows always finished that way. I'd said the same thing to Oscar. How many years ago?

The kids behaved brilliantly, and after the vows, it was all over with a kiss. Max announced they were wed, the same way he'd done with everyone, and that we could now bestow on them their new dome. Chris and Ruby led the way through the shelter to their new home, where Aunt Cassandra and her eldest two had laid out a wonderful spread from the greenhouse. We sat and ate and laughed, and before long, the music pumped through speakers and the dancing began. Ruby's third dance was with Oscar. It was my turn to dance with Dad. Mum was more than a match for the two little ones, and Dad relished the chance to get on the dance floor and show his stuff.

It was a slow dance, and he took me by the hand and waist with those same old firm hands of his.

"Tell me if I'm going too fast," he whispered to me, through a smile.

"I may be old, but I'm not *that* old, Dad!" I said.

"You know, I remember your wedding day just like it was yesterday." He chuckled as we swayed together.

"It seems like so long ago now."

"Children are a fascinating experiment in relativity," he started, as if he were lecturing in that same old wistful way of his — always the physicist. "The days are interminably long, but the months and years fly by so fast. I wonder if there's an equation for that?"

"If there is, I'm sure you'll find it."

He looked into my eyes and his smile widened. There wasn't a line on his face. It was the same smile he'd had for as long as I could remember.

"I'm glad we got this chance to throw some shapes," he said. "I've been meaning to thank you, and I think this is the perfect time."

"Thank me? Whatever for?"

"I've been trying to figure out a means of expressing it to you which makes sense. But I realized a long time ago that you could only really understand it as a parent. I've been wanting to thank you, because the happiness you feel today for Ruby is the same happiness you've given us your whole life. They equate to the same value, and it surpasses any quantifiable integer," he said.

There wasn't any need for words. I just rested my head on his strong, firm chest, and looked over his broad shoulder across at my little girl, dancing with Oscar. I wondered what Oscar was telling her. Probably something similar, I hoped. He looked so old. A real sugar daddy — that's what Sonja called him these days.

I closed my eyes, and in Dad's arms, I felt like I was twenty again. The way he cradled me in his chest was just the same as it had always been. Then I opened my eyes and saw the wrinkles on my hand as it fit snug into his youthful, perfect grip, unchanged after all these years. The pain in my chest returned, pounding a little, but it passed quickly.

We swayed for a few more minutes, until the song ended, and Dad asked me if I was up to another. But I was tired, and needed to sit down, and he said he understood.

I sought out Oscar, and we set up camp at a table, watching the youngsters party while the dome slowly turned until the sun was shut out behind the natural stone wall. Then we shuffled back to our dome.

Lori and Charlie were still at the party. For the first time since we'd welcomed Ruby into our shelter, the place was empty. It was so quiet. Too quiet.

Oscar sidled around, making us something to drink, and I reclined, my back aching and my legs numb. He passed me my hot mug, and we sipped it together, talking about the day and how it had gone.

"I don't think Ruby will ever forgive you," he said.

"What are you talking about, you old thing?"

"For upstaging her, of course. That hat of yours. You were the most beautiful thing there by an orbit and a half."

I smiled back at him, and shook my head. "She looked stunning, didn't she?"

"Yeah. It brought back memories. Seeing her in your dress."

"Look how much we've changed since then."

"Improved, you mean?" He winked.

"Is that what you call it?" I reached for my spectacles to stare at him over their lids. "I remember dancing well into the night in that dress. Now, look at us. My hat's already in the cupboard. And if it wasn't for this hot mug, I'd have dozed off by now."

Oscar stopped for a minute, and then put his mug down. He stood and offered me his hand. "Care to join me, Penny, for a quick jig?"

I laughed. "You're not serious?"

"That I am. We can't let these youngsters have all the fun now, can we?"

Despite the pain in my muscles, I took his hand and rose to my feet. We stood in each other's arms swaying and I nuzzled my head on his chest. It didn't feel solid, like Dad's. It felt flat and weak, and our hands shook as they clasped together.

"See? What did I tell you? Our dancing's never been better. We've improved, and here's the proof."

"Whatever you say, old man." I leaned in slowly to give him a peck on his familiar lips.

We were still on our feet when Lori and Charlie walked through the door, and the spinning shelter brought a slither of the first red light of morning.

"Mum, Dad! You should be in bed," Charlie said.

"What's the matter, Charlie? Jealous that your old Mum and Dad can party all night long and still go some more?" Oscar smiled.

'Jealous,' he'd said.

Jealous.

More than the ache in my back, more than the weakness in my legs, when I heard that word, I felt that same dull pounding in my chest. I didn't know what it was until that moment. Stood with my head resting on Oscar — remembering Dad's firm grip, remembering Mum's beautiful blonde hair as she'd stood beside my Ruby on the most special day of our lives, while I'd had to cover my gray in a hat — my chest pounded, and then it eased.

That's what it was.

'Jealous,' he'd said. Jealous of not having been born in Earth's gravity. Jealous that I only had sixty years, while they would have thirty times more.

"Yeah, that must be it, Dad." Charlie laughed.

V

"Push! You can do it. Keep breathing."

Voices drifted through the other wall inside the dome. My heart raced. My Ruby would be gripping Chris in one arm, and Mum in the other. I yearned to be there for my little girl, just as I'd wanted to be there the first and second time she'd given birth. But I wasn't much use in that room.

She'd only have been worried about me. It was much better that I watched the children.

Her screams echoed through the dome. Tears were being shed and I winced at the sound of them. They tugged me towards her, pulling at my heart. When Ruby was born, Oscar had cut her cord, but the string that binds a mother to their little girl can never be broken. Her pain jarred through my bones. I'd have done anything to take it away.

"That's it. Keep going. One big push."

How much longer was it going to take? Why wasn't it over yet? Then I saw that the little one was waving at me from where he played at my feet.

"Pardon me, dear," I said. "My mind was elsewhere. What is it you want?"

"I'm scared, Nan," Tim said. His younger sister was playing at the far end of the room with the boy she would wed one day, quite content. Oscar kept a watchful eye on them, when he was awake. He was dozing now.

"Scared, Tim?" I said. "What is there to be scared of?"

"Scared of Mummy's screams."

I took his hands in my wrinkled palms. "I know what you mean. But it sounds worse than it is. I remember back when you were born, and it was no different then. And you and your Mum both turned out alright, didn't you?"

He nodded.

"Why don't you play with your toys and try to forget about it?" I said. I wanted to get down on my knees and pick up his stuffed animals to enact some kind of drama as we pretended we were somewhere else. But my knees couldn't take it these days. Sitting down was bad enough.

He started to pick up a stuffed animal, when another scream of Ruby's penetrated the dome. He dropped it. "Will you tell me a story, Nan?" he asked, once the outburst had faded.

"Of course I will." I patted on the seat next to me, where he promptly came and nestled himself. "Back when I was your age, your Great-Nanna June used to tell me stories. Let's see. There was this one story that I always liked hearing. It was about a horse who rode up to the forest." I paused, expecting him to ask me what a horse was, or a forest. But he said nothing. "Do you know what a horse is?"

"Of course I do," he said.

"You're a clever boy. How is it you know so much about horses?"

"Great-Nanna June told me this story before."

I just nodded.

Great-Nanna June. Mum had beaten me to it. Again.

I tried not to resent her, but I couldn't help it.

"Great-Nanna June plays with my toys sometimes," Tim said.

No problems with her knees.

My chest tightened, closing off the air. Breathe, Penelope. Just get a hold of it.

I should be glad about this. After all, Mum would always be there to look after Ruby and Tim, even when I couldn't anymore. She'd be holding the hand of the little girl playing in the corner years from now when she'd be giving birth, long after I was gone. I owed her for that. She was my Mum. I owed her for everything.

"One last push," and a final scream, and then the sound of new life echoed.

"Did you hear that Tim?" I said.

"What is it?"

"That's your baby brother. He's arrived safe."

Tim smiled. Ruby was okay. My darling girl. Another thing I owed to Mum. Another reason to resent her. Another pounding in my chest that I would try my best to suppress.

"What happens after the horse rides up to the forest?" Tim asked.

"That's a very good question, young man."

VI

The view looked lovely. It was vast. Open. I could see far away. The sun was red. I liked red. I wanted to go and see it closer.

Who was that, holding onto me? Was that you, Oscar?

I looked around and saw lots of people standing together. Everyone looked very nice. Very smart. I was smart too. I wore my ruby ring which fit over my gloves.

Ruby. That was who it was. She was the one holding onto my arm. She looked pretty. I craned my neck for Oscar, but I didn't see him anywhere.

"Where's your Dad?" I asked Ruby.

"What is it, dear?" she said.

"Your Dad. Where is he?" She just shook her head. She looked confused. Oh, Ruby. Didn't I raise you to be more polite than this?

"Do you mean Oscar?" she whispered.

"Yes."

"That's why we're here, dear," she told me.

I didn't know what she meant. Were we looking for Oscar? Had he gotten lost playing hide and seek? The little rascal. He always got up to some mischief or another. Where could he be?

At my other arm, an old lady gripped hold. I didn't recognise her.

"Do you know where Oscar is hiding?" I asked her.

The old lady's eyes filled up with tears.

"No need to cry," I said, tapping her arm. "The little scamp. Just wait until I find him. I'll give him a piece of my mind."

"It's okay, Mum," the old lady said.

Who was she talking to? It looked like she was talking to me, but that couldn't be right.

I turned back to the young girl at my other arm. "Ruby, where's Oscar?" I asked.

"I'm not Ruby," she said.

"*I'm* Ruby," the old lady insisted.

"You can't be my Ruby. You're too old. Ruby's not old. She's young and has lovely yellow hair, the color of sand. Where's Oscar? He'll clear all this up," I asked loudly.

"Calm down, Mum," the old lady said.

"I am calm," I told her. "Where's my Oscar?"

"It's been two years today, Mum." Tears filled the old lady's eyes. I felt sorry for her.

"Two years? What are you talking about, dear?"

Everyone wore black. We were on the edge of a cliff. I looked around. The view was lovely. I recognised it now. It hadn't changed a bit. Not since me and Oscar shared a little kiss and carved our names in the rock.

People stood around a pile of stones, each adding one more. I had a pebble in my hand. I was the last person to put one on.

The two ladies at my arms helped me walk up to the pile.

Underneath the pile, words had been engraved.

OSCAR

PENNY

RUBY CHRIS

CHARLIE ISABEL

LORI CALEB

The words were faded. I could hardly read Oscar's name, or my own. Who were all these other names? Chris, Isabel, and Caleb? Graffiti. They'd ruined our carving. I didn't like this pile of stones being near our carving. It wasn't right. Oscar wouldn't like it either.

I bent down, and put my stone on the ground. I started taking the rocks off the pile, one by one. They were heavy to lift, but I wanted them gone.

Someone at my arm was pulling me away.

"Stop it, Penelope. You leave those stones alone. Understand?"

A young man appeared at her side. "Leave it, June. If she wants to cause a scene, let her," he said.

The old lady on my other arm wasn't helping any.

Two years she'd said. Two years since what?

Just wait until I found Oscar. He'd clear all this up.

At least the view was nice. The sun made everything look pretty.

I walked back to the shelter quietly. People around me seemed somber. And on such a nice day as well. Something sad must have happened for everyone to behave so drearily when the sun was so pretty. Maybe Oscar was back at the shelter waiting for us?

But when I got back, he was nowhere to be found.

I wandered all around my dome looking for him.

"Oscar? Where are you Oscar?" I called out. But he was nowhere.

The wall turned and the dome went dark. I made my way to bed and tried to sleep, but I couldn't. I didn't like those stones being there, piled up like that. They had to go.

I stepped out of bed and put on my coat, crept through the dome, and left the shelter. Outside, the sun was just as nice as ever. Everyone was missing the glorious day by sleeping. I took a whiff of my inhaler. Mustn't forget that. That was one of the rules.

My progress over the rocks was slow. The pools looked nice. I wondered if I'd spot an animal today. Mummy said there might be an animal somewhere. I just had to keep a lookout for it. I wondered if Oscar had spotted one by now.

"Don't dawdle, Oscar," I told him, turning around. He was always slowing us down, playing in rock pools. Where did he go? Was he hiding in the mist?

Hide and seek. I wouldn't let him beat me again.

"You can't hide forever, you little rascal," I shouted.

I kept a keen eye out for him. The mist was thick today.

Where was I? I didn't recognise this place. It grew cold. In front of me, I could see a big shadow in the distance looming. It was dark there.

Maybe there were animals in the dark? Didn't Daddy say something about that?

No. I couldn't go there. Mummy taught me the rules. Never go where it's dark. That was the first rule I ever learnt.

I turned around, but I was lost.

I kept walking. My legs tired. I needed to rest. To sit down. I started coughing. I couldn't breathe.

When was Oscar going to get back with my inhaler?

I lay on the ground.

There was that voice again. "Penelope? Where are you, Penny?"

I coughed some more. The air was cold here. It hurt my chest.

Through the mist, someone approached.

Oscar?

No. Mummy.

She came up to me and lifted me up, but I seemed heavy to her.

"I'm sorry, Mummy. I forgot my inhaler."

"It's right here, dear," she said, and picked it out of my pocket, putting it to my mouth. The air tasted nice. I didn't want to cough anymore. But I was still cold. My nightgown was usually good at keeping me warm. But not outside.

"Oscar's hiding somewhere. Will you help me find him, Mummy?"

She started to cry. She looked so pretty, even when she cried. Her hair was lovely.

"Don't cry, Mummy. Why don't you tell me a story? I always like your stories."

She wiped her eyes. "We need to get you inside, Penny. The chill will do you no good."

"Just one story, Mummy. Please."

She looked back at me and smiled a little. "Okay. Just one. The horse rode up to the forest," she said.

"What happens next?"

Her smile spread into her eyes. I liked Mummy's smile. She gripped my hand. My hand was so weak and wrinkly. How did it ever get that way?

"Well," she said, "the horse saw all the beautiful trees and the flowers. He sat down, tired after his journey, and in the shade of the sunshine, he closed his eyes and started to fall asleep. He dreamt of a forest with big trees and gentle flowers. It looked like a marvelous, magical place, so in his dream, he set out to find it. After a long journey, he glimpsed the first tree in the distance, and neighed with delight. And the horse rode up to the forest."

Mummy stopped.

"And what happened next?" I asked, and she told it to me all over again.

I always liked that story. I must remember to tell it to Oscar when we're married.

I felt sleepy, and then I noticed that we were outside. A young lady held onto me. She looked a bit like my Ruby, just as pretty as the day she was married.

"What are we doing all the way out here?" I asked.

"Let's get you inside."

"It's so nice out here, Ruby. Just one more minute."

"It's okay, darling. Mummy's got you," she said.

I looked up at the sun in the sky. It was so red. I liked red the best. Red was my first color.

Why was I so tired? I closed my eyes, expecting everything to go red, but it didn't. It just turned a horrid, empty, endless black.

CASSANDRA

I

TRANSCRIPT OF CLINIC SESSION 431
PATIENT: Cassandra (Biology — Orbicon Employee)
CONFIDENTIAL

JUNE: Do you regret coming here?

CASS: I don't know.

JUNE: Come on, Cass. You can talk to me.

CASS: It isn't an easy question, June. So much has happened. Where do you expect me to even start with a question like that?

JUNE: How about the launch?

CASS: The launch? You're serious?

JUNE: Do you remember when we launched?

CASS: Of course.

JUNE: How did you feel back then?

CASS: Truthfully? Angry. I was so angry. Leaving Earth with only six months to live. Who wouldn't be mad about it? Everything felt so raw. Well, you know what it was like.

When Dr. Rolands had stood behind that podium and announced her theory would kill us after six months, I couldn't help myself. I shouted out. The director of

Orbicon gives us our mission and there I am, hollering at her like a cowboy who put his spurs on backwards. I was livid. Over those next few weeks, I'd go home at night, after another long day of training, and grit my teeth, scream noises into my pillow, chuntering at myself. It wasn't fair. Why was I even going? Y'know?

JUNE: Go on.

CASS: You sure you want to hear this, June?

JUNE: I want you to talk to me. If talking will help you to answer the question, then let's talk.

CASS: We might be a while.

JUNE: Do you think I've got anywhere else to be right now? We've got time. So . . . do you regret coming here?

CASS: Right up until the launch, I was a mess. Angry, y'know? But when we arrived, having traveled on the doctor's 'gravitational wave propulsion' to the furthest reaches of Trappist-1E — I can't believe we're still calling it that, by the way — I was determined not to die bitter about it.

The rest of you seemed pretty resigned to our plight. It was only fair I try and do the same. Max's motivational speeches were good for that. And you always calmed me down, June. A few weeks after we'd built the shelter, I came to see you in your clinic. I'll never forget the look on your face when I stood there screaming for a full five minutes. Talk about a rabbit in headlights. Y'know, it's been such a long time since I heard that expression, but that's exactly the look you gave.

You just sat there, calm as you like, and said 'Can you put your feelings into words?'

I said, 'Does 'Aaargh' not count as a word?'

You know what you said? 'I'd prefer to have more than one syllable to go on.' Talk about playing it cool. Shy, but sturdy, that's you, Junie.

Anyway.

My studies of the mist, which had condensed to form pools of water on the surface, was what kept me going during those days. Where there's water, there's life — first rule of biology — so I was always hopeful I'd find some spore or bacteria or plant growing. I didn't get my hopes up too much though, not enough to expect I'd ever come across an animal in the pools. But there might be some fauna or flora. Even the thought of plain old moss would be something. Besides, I've always liked walking. You said it would help me to channel my feelings about the mission if I walked. I'd be able to stomp out my anger in a heavy spacesuit until my boots were almost worn away to nothing. You said, 'Take it out on the planet.' Well, I did.

JUNE: I'm glad that advice helped.

CASS: I'm not sure it helped the planet much. I must've worn at least half of it away by now!

So, I took my daily trek alone, which was a good thing for everyone. I can't imagine having to explain myself to one of you, why I stood slamming one leg and then the other into the ground over and over again, like a two-year-old throwing a fit. Bits of rock would crumble away if I caught the ground just right. When I went back to the shelter, I'd take the crumbling parts with me, and analyze the minerals. Hooray for tantrums, I guess.

It was Harold — no. It was Kirk who first realized the truth of our situation.

By that time, I'd left my study of the rock pools and turned my hand towards cultivating soil. I thought a garden might be nice, not that we could grow much, but I missed the taste of proper food. All our meals came out of a microwave and plastic packet. What I wouldn't have given for a baked potato. Sonja was the same. Although it was much worse for her. She was the foodie. But she never complained about it. In that way, we were quite different.

I'd ask her, 'Aren't you tired of the same old thing over and again?' She'd just sigh.

'The only time I'm tired,' she said, 'is after a dozen laps of this place.' She ran every day. I didn't have the patience for it. Besides, I liked my curves the way they were. And it wasn't like I needed any more exercise, with my daily stomp.

JUNE: It's best not to compare yourself to Sonja when it comes to exercise. Trust me.

CASS: Why, June, do I detect a hint of jealousy in there? You've got nothing to be jealous of. You're gorgeous just the way you are.

JUNE: Don't think flattery will get you out of this.

CASS: And you're smart, too.

JUNE: I remember Sonja being so happy when you fixed the inhalers so we could get outside without having to wear a spacesuit.

CASS: When I told her, she practically squeezed the air out of me, she hugged me so tight. Sonja's always been like that with everyone, though. Such a sweet girl.

Anyway. What was I telling you that for?

JUNE: You were saying that Kirk was the one who figured it out.

CASS: Oh yeah. I remember him sitting us all down and telling us that Dr. Rolands had only been half right. That we'd have at least thirty years here.

There was always something about Kirk which I couldn't figure out. He was hardly sociable. He kept himself to himself, and he was scrawny. His scruffy beard looked like it'd make for a fascinating biological analysis all by itself. But I couldn't help liking him. Maybe it was how miserable he was. Maybe his melancholy was just part of his charm. He wasn't anything like the rest of us, or at least, he didn't talk like the rest of us. Even when he told us that we'd be getting thirty years of life, he didn't sound excited about the prospect.

I was glad that night when everyone spread out through the shelter, leaving the two of us on our own. I kept him dancing for as long as I could. I thought maybe he'd notice me if I busted a few moves in front of his face. But he was more interested in talking. Trust Kirk. There I was, throwing myself at him, giving him my best eyes, and all he wanted to talk about was some math problem.

JUNE: Classic Kirk.

CASS: Uh huh. It wasn't until the next day that he explained it all to us. He waltzed in with a clipboard and a grim look. You remember? 'So, if my calculations are correct,' he said, 'there's a likelihood that our lifespan here could extend beyond my initial thirty year estimation.' I was tired that morning, but I did my best to look interested in what he was saying. In truth, I was wondering which part of his beard I'd take a swab from if I got the chance.

Then everyone else gasped.

'Say that again, Kirk,' I asked.

He sighed with the patience of a toddler. 'A thirty year lifespan could mean 1,800 years of life here.' Normally, I liked the melancholy in his monotone voice, but this was too moody even for me.

So I balked, didn't I? 'Are you being serious?' I said.

'Sadly, yes.' He hung his head.

'What do you mean, sadly? Isn't that great news?' Was I the only one not getting it? Everyone else just stood there with their jaws flopped open, trying to take it in.

'We won't know for certain until we've lived many more years. Give it ten years. If we haven't aged in that time, then we'll know I'm right.' He couldn't help looking cocky. That was just him, wasn't it?

I laughed at the thought of it. I'd been so angry at having come here, and now, he was telling me that I'd be living sixty times longer than I would've done if I'd stayed on Earth.

You looked so stunned, June. I remember whispering to you, 'I think the word you're looking for is 'aargh'!'

JUNE: I remember.

CASS: Kirk was so . . . he was . . .

JUNE: It's okay. We've made some progress today. Why don't we leave it for now, and pick this up next time?

CASS: Are you psychic as well, June?

JUNE: Come on. Let's get you a drink.

CASS: Yep. Definitely psychic.

II

TRANSCRIPT OF CLINIC SESSION 432
PATIENT: Cassandra (Biology — Orbicon Employee)
CONFIDENTIAL

CASS: Has it been a month since our last session already?

JUNE: Time flies at our age, doesn't it?

CASS: So where did we get to?

JUNE: You remember the question we're working on?

CASS: I think so. Do I regret coming here?

JUNE: That's right. The last thing I noted down was Kirk, and him saying 'give it ten years.'

CASS: Sounds accurate.

JUNE: Do you feel ready to pick back up where we left off?

CASS: No time like the present, right?

JUNE: Okay. If you want to stop at any point, just say so. We're making good progress.

CASS: Yes, please. Can we stop right now?

> . . .
>
> I'll take that as a no.
> Okay.
> So, I guess, ten years went by. None of us felt any older. Was it really ten years? They passed so fast, in the blink of an eye. My garden was growing all sorts of good things by now. I'd been able to rescue some of the raw vegetables from the microwaved packets to plant, and we ended up with a nice variety of things. The greenhouse smelt of leaves that grew through the soil. I loved it — that

earthy smell. It took me right back to my parents' house and their allotment on Earth.

I harvested more than enough for the six of us, and I'd set up another dome full of soil, which I'd built myself, just in case anything happened to the first one. It took me years to finish, and I was always in my spacesuit, which hid my figure. I blame that for a great many things, not least of all for what Kirk had told me.

JUNE: Those spacesuits always were the worst.

CASS: Name me one sane person who likes wearing them.

JUNE: So, what did Kirk tell you?

CASS: It was long after you and Harold got married. Max and Sonja were the next to get hitched. That left me and Kirk, and I was always hopeful he'd show an interest, but he spent most of his days sulking in his room. Whenever I saw him, I was always hidden by my hulking great suit. It was hardly appealing. My face was constantly covered in soil, and my hair was fastened in a ponytail, which gave me a squarer jaw. I could hardly blame him for taking me aside and telling me what he did.

'Look, Cass,' he said. 'We get on great, and we're good friends, but I just don't feel that it'd be right — the two of us. We don't add up in that way. With the others getting married, I don't want you to have any false expectations. I wouldn't want to hurt you.' He'd been morose since Sonja and Max had tied the knot.

I told him I understood. Thanked him for his honesty. I mean, of course I understood, but I didn't like it much. I wasn't an enticing enough prospect for him. If only I'd finished the inhalers sooner, then I could've worked on the dome in my tightest clothes, and we might've had a different kind of conversation.

So I guess I was grateful when you and Harold came in one day for breakfast in the main hub to tell us your news.

'We're having a baby.' It was you who said it, June. It took us all by surprise.

We were all like, 'Congratulations,' 'I'm so thrilled for you,' 'I can't believe it.' And then Kirk just stood there and said, 'What!'

Harold didn't like his attitude. 'You heard what June said. We're having a baby.'

Kirk was furious. 'Do you know the implications of what you're doing? It's reckless. That's what it is. You're living on Earth's clock. Your baby will be living on Trappist-1E time. It's been ten years. We know how long you'll all last. But there's no reason to expect your child will live that long. Sixty years here, and we age one year. Sixty years for them, and they might be dead. Do you know how stupid it would be to have children?'

Kirk had such a way with words, didn't he? But he was only looking out for you. He cared, in his own way.

You stared at him, June, with those resolute eyes you sometimes make. 'We've thought about the implications, Kirk,' you said. 'And we're having this baby.' You were so stalwart.

JUNE: What other way was there to be? You're a mother, Cass. You understand.

CASS: Kirk didn't. He stormed off to his room, and the rest of us congratulated you. I followed him and knocked on his door.

'Go away,' he said.

'It's Cass,' I said. 'Can I come in?' There was a pause.

'Fine,' he said, and I opened the door and perched on his desk as he lay across the bed with his back to me.

I told him, 'I know you think it's a bad idea, Kirk. You don't have to explain it to me. But I wanted to see if you were alright.'

'I'm fine,' he mumbled. 'It's them you should be worried about.'

I so wanted to cheer him up. 'Come on, mister doom and gloom, aren't you the least bit intrigued as to what June will look like when she's fat?' I said, and he turned over, stifling a grin.

'It's not that I'm unhappy for them,' he said. 'It's just that . . . never mind.'

I pressed him. 'It's just what?'

'I don't want to talk about it.'

'That's fine. We don't have to talk.' We stayed in silence for a little while. 'What did you mean when you said 'we know how long *you'll* all live'?' I asked. 'Don't you expect to live out your days like the rest of us?'

He sat up on the bed and sighed. 'Listen, Cass. I only had a handful of months left to live on Earth. You know that already. So if I'm aging on Earth time, then I don't have hundreds of years like the rest of you. I get my thirty years here, and maybe an extra ten, fifteen years at the most. Which means that I'll be long gone soon enough. I know what it's like to sacrifice things. So you can't blame me for feeling angry at Harold and June. They've been stupid, and I don't want to see them hurt.'

JUNE: So that was why he'd turned you down.

CASS: It had nothing to do with my body, and everything to do with his.

I remembered what he'd said before, about not wanting to see me hurt, and it all made sense. The penny had finally dropped between us.

I left the room before I burst into tears, or started shouting. Who did he think he was, trying to dictate everybody else's lives just because he wasn't going to last as long as the rest of us? It made me mad. So I got to work. I'd have plenty to do if babies were coming. I was a biologist, and there'd be extra mouths to feed.

I knocked on Max and Sonja's door. Sonja opened, and let me in. I confided in her what Kirk had said. She knew I liked him, so she understood why I was upset.

'Maybe Kirk's right,' she said.

'What do you mean?'

'Well, maybe you'd do better waiting for Harold and June's baby before you settled down. It could be a boy?'

I laughed. She knew what to say to make me laugh.

'Or better still,' I said, 'I could wait until you and Max have one and take my pick.'

She laughed too.

I think it was in that moment that I realized the implications of what was about to happen.

'Sonja,' I said. 'Are we starting a colony here?'

She thought about it. 'I guess so.'

Suddenly, everything was different. I had to think, so I said goodnight, and left for my greenhouse. I always thought better surrounded by nature, although it was hardly natural to be harvesting plants on a planet comprised entirely of rock.

Colonization held long-term implications. I calculated it. If you and Harold had children, and Max and Sonja had children, and then for argument's sake, let's assume that those children married and had children of their own, in three generations, we'd hit the ceiling for the potential growth of the colony. No more children. That's what it boiled down to. But if the colony was to grow naturally and sustain that growth, then more DNA was needed in the mix.

JUNE: I can't believe that's what you were thinking about the night we told you we were pregnant.

CASS: What else was there to do? According to the legend back on Earth, Noah had three sons that came out of the ark — Shem, Ham and Japheth — and those three men were enough to fill the Earth. There were three men here. Max, Harold, and Kirk. That was the bare minimum we'd need if we were to fill Trappist-1E. I stayed up all night working it out. We'd have to control which children were permitted to procreate together, but if we all had enough kids, then after about three generations, it would be fine for them to start marrying who they wanted. There'd be enough biological diversity to make it sustainable. Which meant one thing.

I printed a fridge that could be run on solar energy. I'd need something cool to store specimens. Then I printed a plastic cup. I went back to my room and spent some time curling my hair just right, and choosing my most attractive outfit, thinking it would make all the difference.

Then, with cup in hand, I marched to Kirk's room and banged furiously on the door.

'Go away,' he said, but I kept banging, until eventually he was forced to open up.

I barged past him into the room and stood there with a hand on my hip, and he turned around, gawping.

'I know what you meant before,' I said. 'I know you think that by us just being friends, then you're protecting me from heartache when you eventually pop it, but that's not your call to make. Not on your own anyway. And it's only meant we've wasted good time.'

He was going to interrupt me, but I threw my finger up in the air and he kept schtum.

'Math, math, math. That's all it ever is with you. Numbers and figures. Well I've run the numbers. If Harold and June are having kids, then Max and Sonja will be next. We need three biological pairs to produce enough diversity so that there's no cross-genetic contamination in order to foster a colony. Which means that you need to get me pregnant.'

He stepped forward, about to object, but I stepped forward too, and my eyes flashed a warning to tell him he should back down while it was still good for him. He shriveled beneath their fury.

'There's no point trying to argue, Kirk. We're way beyond that. There are only two ways that this can happen. The first is that you can fill this cup. I'm a biologist. I can do the rest.' I slammed the cup on his desk behind me, and took my palm away from where I'd clenched it.

'What's the second way?' he asked, sheepish.

'The second way,' I said in almost a whisper as I flicked my hair back and leant against the desk, 'is much more fun.' I bit my lip, waiting to see what he'd do.

He stood for a moment, staring me down, calculating his options. Then he walked towards me and leant over where I stood, picking up the cup. He stepped back, walked over to the bin he kept by his bed, and tossed it away.

Then he looked at me and smiled. He started walking towards me with serious intent.

'Not so fast,' I told him. 'You'll have to make me an honest woman before we colonize this planet.'

He stopped in his tracks and laughed at me. 'You want to get married? You'd have to be the last girl in the world,' he said through a grin.

'Good job I am then, isn't it?' I kissed his cheek and left the room. He stood in the doorway.

'Tomorrow?' he said.

'I'm free now,' I told him.

Five minutes later, we were hitched.

I'll admit that my first wedding could've been a bit more romantic. But just because it wasn't filled with romance, didn't make it any less memorable. In fact, of all my weddings, I'd have to say that it was the most enjoyable of the lot.

JUNE: I remember your first one. You woke us all up at some ridiculous hour so Max could stumble over a few lines and you could repeat your vows.

CASS: They were good times, right?

JUNE: Absolutely.

CASS: I miss him so much, June.

JUNE: I know. Next time, you can tell me about Beverly.

CASS: Alright. But I'm gonna need something stronger than water.

JUNE: Deal.

III

TRANSCRIPT OF CLINIC SESSION 433
PATIENT: Cassandra (Biology — Orbicon Employee)
CONFIDENTIAL

JUNE: What do you remember about Beverly?

CASS: Everything.

JUNE: Where do you want to start?

CASS: Beverly was our first. She had auburn hair the same color as the sunlight, and Kirk's eyes. We'd worked it out that she'd be marrying your boy, Luke. Your little Penelope would marry Oscar, Sonja's boy. Then our second would marry Sonja's second, and then it would be a case of genetic matching for who had a third. With the specimens I'd taken from Harold, Max, and my willing Kirk, I could analyze and test for which pairs would match best.

But that hardly matters. What mattered was Beverly. She was lovely. Both Kirk and I agreed on that.

JUNE: What was it like, becoming a mother on Trappist-1E?

CASS: Are you kidding me? It changed everything. Not just for me. For all of us. The whole atmosphere of the planet was somehow different. The sun was that little bit brighter. The air, a little warmer. And the greenhouse, a lot bigger.

I always worried about the food. I still do now. Was there going to be enough? If we ran out, would we be able to grow more in time? It was all I thought about while I sat cradling Bev. That, and how gorgeous she was. So tiny.

'At least when I'm gone, you'll have something to remember me by,' Kirk muttered while she slept in my arms.

'Do you ever not mope?' I asked.

He laughed. 'You were the one who insisted on marrying me.'

'Yeah. Remind me why.'

'You just couldn't resist the beard,' he said. He could be quite funny when he wasn't miserable. At least Bev inherited his humor before she inherited his whine. Who knew someone so dour could make the happiest little babies?

They were happy times, though. It seemed like we were raising Luke as much as we were raising Bev. He spent all his time in our dome playing with her. Kirk never liked Luke, even when he was little. I guess that's just a Dad thing. When he got older, Kirk was always wary of him. No offense, June.

JUNE: None taken.

CASS: Do you ever think about Luke?

JUNE: We're here to talk about you. Not me.

CASS: I know, but . . . do you ever think about him?

JUNE: What parent ever stops thinking about their children?

CASS: Where were we?

JUNE: You said Kirk was wary of him.

CASS: Oh yeah. He was always mumbling to himself back then. 'I wish we could do something about that boy.' Stuff like that.

'It's all worked out. You can't go changing things now,' I'd say.

'I don't like him.'

'You don't like anyone.'

He smiled, as if he was proud of it somehow. 'Why does Beverly even have to get married anyway?' he asked.

'It's what she wants,' I said.

He shook his head. 'It's not what I want.'

'What is it you want, Kirk?'

I don't think he ever answered that question in all those years.

JUNE: Do you think he even knew?

CASS: Does anyone?

JUNE: Beverly was such a beautiful bride.

CASS: She married when she turned twenty-years-old. They all got married when they hit twenty.

Kirk had worked out the specifics of her dome, and Max built it for us. He didn't have to, but he wanted to. He was the captain, after all, and the engineer.

The wedding was short. All of them were. Bev had chosen me and Penelope as her bridesmaids. Penny was a sweet girl. She and Oscar already had a little one of their own, only a few months old. Ruby. She was the spitting image of you, June, even at that tender age.

Luke was nothing like you, though. He was Harold's boy. Always some scientific principle at work in his brain. He even stood like Harold, that same meditative lean arching his back, and his hand glued to his chin, which made him look intelligent, at least.

Being a bridesmaid used to be exciting. You got a chance to print out a nice new dress. And you didn't have to do anything but turn up and look good. Or should I say, look young. I've lost count of how many times I've been a bridesmaid. But the last time was a long time ago. So long ago. Time is so — you know what? Let's not go there, shall we.

JUNE: Good idea.

CASS: So, Bev got married, as did our second and third before Kirk became ill. It was one of the things I appreciate most, that Kirk lasted long enough to see our kids marry.

He'd suffered for weeks before his condition worsened. We tried all we could to make him comfortable. That last night we were together, I'll never forget it.

I sat perched on the bed stroking his hair. Bev was in labor in her dome, through the plaza that connected us to the main hub. She must've left her door open, because we could hear everything that was going on.

'You should be with her,' Kirk told me.

'I'm right where I need to be.' I stared into his eyes. He looked upset.

'I told you, didn't I? Do you remember? That I didn't want to hurt you.'

'You haven't hurt me yet, have you?'

'Cass, I'm—'

'Ssshh,' I said. 'Get some rest. You need to keep your strength up.'

He looked so weak. Then the screaming stopped from the room beyond. We both stared at each other. We stayed that way for about an hour, and then Sonja appeared in the doorway, cradling a tiny baby in her arms.

'Bev wanted me to introduce you,' she said.

I helped Kirk to sit up in bed. Sonja passed me the newborn.

'Boy?' I asked.

Sonja nodded.

'What's his name?' Kirk asked.

'Bev isn't sure yet.'

Kirk thought about it. 'Tell her I think he looks like a Christopher,' he said.

'I will,' Sonja promised, hovering in the door.

'Although I doubt she'll use it,' he mumbled to me.

I laughed. He never changed. 'Do you feel up to holding him?'

He nodded, and took the baby in his arms for a minute or so before passing him back. The boy had been sleeping until Kirk had taken him. Maybe he was tickled by the beard and it caused him to stir. But he looked up at Kirk with the most vivid expression. Then he drifted back off to sleep in my arms.

I passed him to Sonja and told her to thank Bev for us. She disappeared.

'He's got my eyes,' Kirk said with pride. And he was right.

'Christopher? Seriously?' was all I could think to say to him.

'Would you have preferred something more banal, like Wesley Cecil Cuthbert Fitzpatrick?'

He closed his eyes and I kissed his forehead. He would never . . .

JUNE: It's okay, Cass. Just breathe.

CASS: I'm sorry . . .

JUNE: You okay to continue?

CASS: Where did I get to?

JUNE: You said, 'He would never . . .?

CASS: . . . He would never open his eyes again.

IV

TRANSCRIPT OF CLINIC SESSION 434
PATIENT: Cassandra (Biology — Orbicon Employee)
CONFIDENTIAL

JUNE: I'm sorry I cut our last session short.

CASS: It wasn't your fault that I couldn't stop crying, was it?

JUNE: Still, I'm sorry.

CASS: June, do we have to keep doing this?

JUNE: I think it's important.

CASS: Why? Why are you making me relive all of this?

JUNE: Regret is a dangerous thing, Cass. Particularly if it's allowed to spread throughout the colony.

CASS: Are you saying that I'm bad for the colony?

JUNE: Oh, Cass. It's nice to see some of that old fire still burning away in there. People are worried. And who wouldn't be?

CASS: I don't know what they've got to be worried about. People are idiots. You know that, don't you?

JUNE: Let's just get to the bottom of this question, shall we? Over whether you regret coming here.

CASS: What do you want me to talk about next?

JUNE: Why don't you tell me about Chris?

CASS: Chris. You mean Bev's first little boy? Born the night Kirk . . .

No, I won't cry again. I'm not falling for your tricks, June.

JUNE: What do you remember about him?

CASS: Chris was . . . he always reminded me of Kirk. So much that I could scarcely stand to hold him for that first year. It wasn't much of a help to Bev, but I couldn't stand it. Losing Kirk paralyzed me. I mean, I always knew I'd miss him when he was gone. I'd known that before I'd marched into his room and told him to marry me. But I wasn't expecting it to feel like it did, how empty things would become without Kirk. I still miss him now.

JUNE: I think we all do. He was the first person we lost on Trappist-1E. It's no wonder you found it so hard to accept.

CASS: The rest of you were a comfort. We were a team. A unit.

JUNE: What did Kirk used to call us? It wasn't the lucky five.

CASS: The fortunate five. I think he was being sarcastic. Which doesn't sound like him, does it? But he was right. We were together. The five of us. You all did what you could. It's just . . . the nights were—

. . .

The nights were the hardest time, and I'd sit outside, watching the sun while everyone else slept. What would I have done without the kids?

There were our three. Beverly was first. Then came Felicity. And Phillip was our little boy. Phillip had just turned twenty when Bev gave birth to Chris. Phillip was newly married, but he and Chris were inseparable. We had to force them apart so Chris could play with Ruby. Do you remember? All those tantrums. You used to blame it on the thick streak of red in their hair. Remember?

Felicity took after Kirk, though. I remember one time finding her laid out on her bed with her face on her pillow

— she was maybe about eight — and when I asked her what the matter was, she just said, 'Life isn't all it's cracked up to be sometimes, is it, Mum?' Kirk was so proud of her when she said that.

'She gets it. Eight years old and she's figured it out,' he'd boasted to everyone.

I missed telling Kirk those little stories. We used to laugh over those anecdotes right up until the end. The more time I spent with the kids, and particularly with the grandchildren, the more I missed telling Kirk about them. That's when you suggested that I find someone else to talk to, to share them with. So when I used to sit outside through the nights, I used to tell them to the sun. It just hung there, listening. A sad substitute for a man, but it made me feel a little better, and it was hardly going anywhere.

JUNE: You used to talk to the sun?

CASS: Still do.

JUNE: I never knew that. Why didn't you come and talk to me?

CASS: I'm talking now, aren't I? Besides, how could you have understood? Nobody could. I was the only one to lose a person. Someone that close, anyway. It'd be years before Penny.

. . .

Sorry, June. I didn't mean to—

JUNE: It's alright, Cass. So tell me, how did it make you feel — talking to the sun?

CASS: Like I was going crazy! I mean, who talks to the sun except crazy people? Right? And then one day, Sonja told me Max still talked to Orbicon through the communication equipment he kept in his dome.

Sonja told me, 'He'll never get an answer, but he feels better doing it, so I won't dissuade him.'

That made me feel normal, at least. Well, as normal as you can on a lump of rock thirty-nine lightyears from what used to be home.

JUNE: Where do you think of when you hear the word 'home'?

CASS: That's a big question, June. And what has it got to do with regret?

JUNE: Maybe nothing. Maybe everything.

CASS: We'll never finish if we start down that rabbit hole. Come on. Where did I get to?

JUNE: Felicity.

CASS: Alright. So Felicity's dome was much plainer than Bev's. It was angular inside. She'd wanted as many mathematical oddities in its design as possible, so there was always some surface or wall that seemed out of place somehow, like an interior optical illusion. But it might have been the awkwardness of it all that made her feel like it was home.

It was in Felicity's dome where I sat with her and Bev talking about Chris and Ruby's wedding, only a week away. It had come round so fast.

Felicity complained that Ruby wanted it outside. 'Outside! Can you believe it!'

I remember them talking about how long it had been since Penny's wedding, and Bev said it felt like a lifetime ago.

'Watch it, you two,' I scolded them. 'Give it a few years and people will be saying the same thing about Chris and Ruby's wedding.'

'Oh, don't say that, Mum. You'll make us feel old,' Bev said.

'We *are* old, dear,' Felicity reminded her. Ever the realist.

I hated seeing them wrinkle, especially when my skin was still so fresh. Looking at the three of us, I could've been their daughter. Freckles were the closest thing to a tarnish on my face. But every time they smiled, the cracks and lines grew longer and thicker on them. And it wasn't like looking at the grandchildren was any easier. Chris resembled Kirk more than ever, especially around the eyes. But that was a good thing, no matter how hard I found it.

'What are we going to do about the food?' Bev asked. She was definitely my daughter.

I told them not to worry. I'd been working a lot in the greenhouse. Even offered to show them what I'd grown at first light.

Felicity was looking after the tykes that day. So, Bev said she'd come with me and sort out the recipes from our new supplies. Felicity could always help with the flowers.

You should've seen their faces when I mentioned flowers.

'Flowers? What do you mean?' Felicity asked.

'I've developed green thumbs these past few weeks,' I said.

'You ought to get June to take a look at that. Perhaps she can give you some medicine. It's not contagious is it?'

I laughed. 'No, it's an expression from Earth. It means that I've been busy in the garden. I've been growing flowers from the potato plants. I think we can make them into a bouquet for Ruby. She'd like that, wouldn't she?'

'You never got flowers for me when I was married!' Felicity burst, outraged.

'You're right. I'm sorry, darling. I should've spent more time growing you flowers, and less time building you this ridiculous dome. You know what, let's turn the clock back. You'll have a lovely bunch of posies on your wedding day, but no bathroom or kitchen. I'm sure you'd prefer that.'

'Very droll, Mum,' she said.

I had my moments.

'Well it's not like Chris is bringing anything else to the party, is it?' I said, looking at Bev with disapproval.

'Don't blame me. It's these kids today. That's the way they want it. I'm sure Ruby will be very happy with flowers, Mum. I'll be ready to tour the greenhouse whenever you want to call around.'

It was mid-morning the next day that we'd made a start, and by half-light, we'd come up with a few good dishes. A week would be plenty of time to do the cooking, and Felicity helped me with the flowers, grudgingly.

JUNE: I don't think any of us will forget that wedding.

CASS: Chris looked so dapper on the big day. He'd printed out a suit that fitted him nicely, and if I squinted really hard, it was almost like looking at Kirk. I'd been to other weddings on my own, but this one was the hardest yet.

After they'd said their vows and strolled through the compound into their new dome, we ate — the food

could've been nicer, but at least there was plenty of it —
then we danced. Kirk had never been much of a dancer,
but at least he would've been someone to sit with in the
corner, mocking the whole affair. Everyone took it in turns
to do the sympathy waltz with me. First Max, then Oscar,
even Chris. But at least the flowers looked nice.

That night, I sat outside and talked to the sun. Don't
judge me, June! 'It was a lovely night,' I said. 'Penny and
Oscar were so grateful. Ruby seems like a nice girl, and
Chris is happy. They're all happy. Well, at least they tell
me so. Beverly could only manage a few dances though.
Mother of the groom. Our Bev. I can hardly believe it. But
she's looking her age now. I hate to say it, but watching
her tonight, she's slowing down, like she's been around
the sun a few too many times. I can't stand the thought of
losing her. But I know it's only a matter of time. What am
I going to do then?'

It was the first time I'd said it out loud. And I realized,
I didn't have an answer to that question. All I knew is that
I felt alone, a feeling that would intensify as one by one, I
watched them fade.

First it was Beverly. Then Felicity. I had only Phillip
left. I cried on his shoulder so many times, but even he'd
be gone soon. My last connection with Kirk. It was like
losing him all over again. For every new baby Chris and
Ruby had, I was forced to say goodbye to one of my own.

You and Sonja were the only ones who understood.
You'd lost Penny. You knew what it was like to feel that
hole that opens up inside of you which can never be filled.
That deep, condemning pit. I was so angry all over again.
It was all so raw. That feeling of screaming at the walls

before we'd left Earth – it was a picnic compared to losing our children.

JUNE: It doesn't get any easier. Ever.

CASS: By this time, you'd given birth to nine, and Sonja had seven. You kept going, popping them out, and you could keep on going for years yet. Even when you lost your kids, you never ran out of children. Not like me.

When Phillip finally breathed his last, I had no more shoulders to cry on. Kirk was gone, and there'd be no more cherished childish anecdotes to share. Rage festered in me all the time. I came to you then, didn't I? But you didn't know what to suggest, and all our conversations ended up the same. I didn't have an answer, and neither did you.

JUNE: I remember you were so lost.

CASS: Lost. Exactly. I stayed that way for a whole year. But then David happened.

V

TRANSCRIPT OF CLINIC SESSION 434 (cont'd)
PATIENT: Cassandra (Biology — Orbicon Employee)
CONFIDENTIAL

CASS: David was your fifth, right?

JUNE: He was only two when Chris and Ruby married.

CASS: It feels weird to think about him as a baby. After everything. It's just weird talking about him at all.

JUNE: That's not totally true is it.

CASS: What?

JUNE: You'd be happy to talk to me about him if I weren't his mother. But it's okay. I want you to feel comfortable talking to me about David.

CASS: You sure you want to know?

JUNE: Of course.

CASS: Don't say I didn't warn you.

JUNE: It's important you talk about him. You didn't spend a lot of time with David until he was about twenty, right?"

CASS: By the time he reached twenty, there was enough biological diversity in the colony that we weren't forcing the children on one another. He was one of that first generation who had a choice. And he'd chosen abstinence.

I could understand why. He took after Harold. Lank, like you, June, but his face was a double of Harold. And boy, could he waffle. There was always some field of study to embark on. First it was telescopes, as far into the sky as could be seen. Then it was the Trappist-1 solar system, and the rate of orbit. Then the other planets. Until, in his thirtieth year, his interests reached Trappist-1E, and he started analyzing my soil.

JUNE: We were so pleased when he'd got his head on the planet after spending so long obsessing over the stars.

CASS: I was just happy someone else was showing an interest. It had been me and the soil for so long. Just the two of us. And then David showed up.

'How did you manage it Cassandra?' he asked over and again, knocking on my door and plying me with questions. The perfect distraction. 'I just don't understand it,' he'd say. 'How can you cultivate a dead rock to produce life?' When he was baffled, he looked even more like Harold. It was uncanny.

'There's life in everything, David,' I'd tell him. 'I guess that's the difference between a physicist and a biologist. A physicist looks at what things are, and a biologist sees what things could become. You've got to find the life in something, and then draw it to the surface.'

'It's a marvel,' he would say, with his hand on his chin.

JUNE: He used to do that a lot, didn't he?

CASS: All the time. His hand was on his chin so much, it could've doubled as a beard.

We used to tour the greenhouses together. By now, there were four of them producing food for the whole colony. I explained to him how the ecology of Trappist-1E could be manipulated to maximize growth.

'It's constant heat from the sun. Constant water from the mist. Ideal for growing anything you want.' Each visit to the greenhouse lasted longer than the previous one.

And then, one day, he knocked on my door, and I invited him in, still half-asleep. Mornings were still mornings, no matter what planet you're on.

'I've hit on an idea,' he said, with passion in his eyes. 'What if we annexed a greenhouse onto each domiciliary dome? Every family could grow things in addition to the food produced from the greenhouses. Then, if it's successful, we could reduce production enough to clear one of the larger garden domes. We could use it for experiments, biological testing, growth studies, genetic engineering. What do you think?'

He was far too enthusiastic for such an early hour in the day, but I could see the sense of his idea. 'Sounds good, David. Why are you talking to me about it? Why not go straight to Max?'

'I was hoping you'd come with me to see him. I know you've been here from the start with him, and I hoped you might help me with the project.' He seemed shy. More than usual.

'I'd love to help out,' I said. 'Now how about some coffee and then we'll go see Max?' Coffee was one of the first beans I'd grown from our stash. I don't know what I'd have done without it all these years. Odd that, even after all this time, I haven't ever tired of the taste.

Anyway, Max was up for the idea, and he said we could print out whatever we needed.

David spent every day in the greenhouses with me, designing the pods that we'd attach to each dwelling. I think it was a bit too humid for him, but I always preferred being surrounded by soil. The pods were up in no time, and within three months, we'd cleared the smallest of the garden domes to start our experiments.

JUNE: I always thought clearing the dome was your idea, Cass.

CASS: Nope. It was all him.

He was the one who suggested that we take a survey of biological traces in the rock pools, too. I told him that I'd done that years ago, and he asked how far I'd got with it.

'As far as the edge of the plateau,' I told him.

'You mean you never scaled the cliff top and examined that large pool at its base?' he asked.

'No. Never.'

'Never say never,' he said through a smile, and twenty minutes later, he returned with some clips, hooks, and ropes.

'What are they for?' I asked.

'Pack an extra inhaler. We're going climbing.'

I had no idea he was so strong until I saw him abseil. His scrawny arms lowered his body over the edge with such poise and control. He held himself on the rocks firm, and . . . well, anyway, he fastened the pulleys into the cliff face so we could climb back up. By the time he reached the bottom, he hadn't even broken a sweat.

He clambered back up to join me on the top, and asked me if I was ready. I wasn't. My heart was pounding.

'Are you sure this is safe?' I asked him.

'Don't you trust me, Cassandra?' he said.

'Of course I do, but—'

'Then it's safe.' He smiled, but I was still terrified. 'Are you ready?" he asked again.

I nodded my head, and he started lowering me backwards over the edge of the precipice.

'Lean back into it,' he said. 'You won't fall. I've got you.'

Once my weight was over the drop, my heart erupted inside my chest, pounding so hard and fast.

'When you're ready, you go as quickly as you want. Remember it's your hands that slow you down.'

I drew a deep breath, closed my eyes, and then I let myself drop, screaming as I plunged through the air with the rope between my fingers. I screamed all the way down, but when I got to the bottom, I was so relieved, and adrenaline rushed through me so hard, I couldn't stop myself from smiling.

David appeared next to me in moments. 'That wasn't so bad, was it?' he asked.

'Can we go again?' I said.

'All in good time. Let's take a look at this body of water, and see what we learn.'

At the foot of the cliff, a huge lake stretched out. It could've been a small ocean. After we did some studies and took samples, David suggested we dive in, to take a closer look.

I didn't want to disrupt the water. It might taint it somehow. But he insisted, and in the end, I conceded. Stripping down my outer layers, I gingerly lowered myself into the pool, the sun tingling my skin. The water was warmer than I'd expected. I felt weightless for the first time since being in space. My hand was always on the rocks, and I stayed close to the edge, never straying too far from my inhaler.

David, on the other hand, was swimming across the water as if he were a fish. Not that he'd ever seen a fish, of course.

'Over here, Cassandra,' he shouted.

'What is it?' I asked.

'I don't know, but whatever it is, it's green.' Green! I mean, can you imagine the possibilities flooding through my head?

I swam to where he treaded water. When I reached him, he pointed beneath his legs. A large patch of dark green grew on the lakebed.

'What do you think?' he asked.

'I don't know. It could be anything. Oh, David, do you know what it means? It's the first traces of a biological imprint on another world.' I forgot we were in the water, and I threw my arms around him. Our bodies touched beneath the ripples of the pool. His legs kicked, and so did mine, but our torsos were stuck together. It felt strange, having his body so close, but I couldn't tear myself away until we'd started sinking.

'We need a sample,' I said, as we parted.

He thought about it for a moment, and then took a deep breath and disappeared beneath the surface of the water. I watched him swim to the bottom, where he stayed for a moment or so, before he returned to the surface with a rock in his hand, covered in the mossy, green growth.

He shook the water from his head. His spray splattered me, but I didn't mind. I was too fascinated by his finding.

'One sample,' he said. 'As requested.'

'Quick, let's get it back to the greenhouse to study it.' My wet undergear clung to my skin as I raised myself out of the water, but dried off in minutes. The sun was so warm. Once we'd dressed and packed our things, David tied the rock samples to his back. We scaled the cliff and returned to the shelter.

It was such a lovely jaunt. I hadn't had fun like that in a long time, but for the next three days, I refused to accompany him back to the water. I was determined to study the strange moss for clues as to how it had developed and what it signified, whether it was alive or not.

On the third day, with my head fixed to the microscope, I heard the door open. David entered, hands behind his back. 'David, come in,' I said. 'I'm just doing an analysis of your finding.'

He smiled. 'You mean *our* finding?'

'No it was you who found it, fair and square.'

He joined me at the microscope, and I moved my head back to give him a peek at the sample. 'Fascinating,' he said. We watched the cells move and scurry across the glass palate.

'What is it you've got there?' I asked. His hands hadn't moved from behind his back, as if he was hiding something.

He stepped away from the microscope and faced me with an anxious look.

'David, what's wrong?" I said.

'I've not been totally honest with you.'

I folded my arms. 'What do you mean?'

He coughed. "You remember when I suggested that we design an annex so that each dome could be given soil to grow its own food?'

'Yes, of course I do.'

'Well, the reason I wanted access to some soil had nothing to do with food. It was because I wanted to surprise you, and grow you these.' He produced a bouquet of flowers from behind his back. They were the same flowers I'd grown for Ruby's wedding all those years ago.

I took them and smelled them. Their aroma was divine.

He stood smiling. 'Do you like them?' he asked.

'David, I love them. But why would you go to such trouble for me?'

He ran his hand through his hair. 'Isn't it obvious, Cassandra?' he replied. A look of hopefulness filled his eyes. 'You're a marvel.'

I didn't care that he was scrawny, goofy, and looked like his Dad. I didn't care that he was in his thirties, pensive, and fancied himself an intellectual. It had been so long since a man had looked at me that way. I threw the flowers on the desk, pulled him close, and kissed him.

VI

TRANSCRIPT OF CLINIC SESSION 434 (cont'd)
PATIENT: Cassandra (Biology — Orbicon Employee)
CONFIDENTIAL

CASS: He was such a good kisser. He—

JUNE: Alright. I get the picture.

CASS: Sorry, June. But you said you wanted to know. Do you want me to tell you what happened next? We—

JUNE: Why don't we skip ahead a little, huh?

CASS: Alright. You sure you don't want the details?

JUNE: I remember the conversation when you came and told us about the two of you.

CASS? Alright, June. I can take a hint. We can move on if you really want us to.

JUNE: Was telling us about it as awkward for you as it was for Harold?

CASS: Oh man! Harold's face! Do you remember?

JUNE: He looked so baffled by it.

CASS: For all his brains, he couldn't get his head around it. Thank goodness you caught on quicker, June. Otherwise we'd have been there all night listening to him saying, 'What do you mean, you and David?' You remember what you said to me?

JUNE: No.

CASS: 'I couldn't ask for a better daughter-in-law.' That's what you told me.

JUNE: It was true.

CASS: You've always been my favorite mother-in-law, June. Always will be.

. . .

I understood why Harold was so confused. It was odd, even I'll admit that. But that didn't make it wrong. After it had sunk in, you turned to me and asked me if I was ready for it. You said, 'You know where it's going, don't you?' I told you I was ready. But I'm not sure I meant it. I think you understood, even back then, but you just hugged me, while Harold was still trying to puzzle it out.

When Max and Sonja found out about David, they wouldn't stop laughing. 'Didn't I tell you that you'd end up with one of Harold and June's?' Sonja told me.

Max said he was happy for me. 'Just tell me one thing, Cass. Have you always had the hots for Harold? They look so alike. You can tell me. I won't blab.' I punched his arm so hard, I think he regretted it. But, to be honest, I didn't mind the teasing. I would've done the same to him.

JUNE: Am I misremembering it, or did the wedding come round really fast?

CASS: We got married the next month. I'd wanted to marry David right away, but he craved the romance of it all. You remember the wedding, don't you?

JUNE: Of course.

CASS: It was so big. David saw to that. The first dome we'd built had become the central plaza by now, connecting the other domes. David insisted the atrium be converted into party central, with flowers twined all the way through, up the walls, over doorways, you name it. David would come to live with me in my dome, so the ceremony was a little unusual. No dome bestowal required. Just a simple, old-fashioned 'you may now kiss the bride' kinda thing. Y'know?

I adjusted my usual bridesmaid's dress to reveal a little more shoulder, and I got ready in my room. Sonja helped me with my hair. She was always so good at it, and charitable with her skills. She curled it into ringlets and mixed me out a lipstick the same shade as my hair. You joined us after a while, June, and told us that everyone was waiting.

JUNE: You seemed nervous.

CASS: Did I? I just remember feeling like I wanted it done.

I walked down the aisle with you at one side, and Sonja at my other. David was waiting for me at the far end, between two pillars. I always hated walking down the aisle.

JUNE: His vows were so long.

CASS: Tell me about it! Much longer than I'd expected. And mine were so flimsy, but nobody minded, least of all David.

We ate in the atrium, and danced into the night. I danced with so many, I lost track. Every now and again, I'd be dancing with one of Christopher's kids and I'd see those same eyes of Kirk's staring back at me. A twinge of guilt pricked at my heart, but the feeling passed. And when the music finished, I took David by the hand and led him into my dome, and I forgot all about my guilt.

JUNE: You were happy that day.

CASS: The next morning, he held me in his arms, and we watched the room turn to reveal the sun. It looked new somehow.

I whispered to him, 'David?'

'Yes, Cassandra,' he replied.

'Just checking you're still here,' I said.

'I'm here, darling.' I loved hearing those words.

Nine months later, we had our first baby. James. Our second and third came almost immediately afterwards. Everybody thought we were rushing things, but we had plenty of help with the kids, and David wasn't getting any younger. Our second was Carla. David wanted that name, and I'd always liked it. Our third was Louisa.

James grew fast. It was strange how different he looked to Phillip. And he cried all the time. The total opposite to my first three.

Carla was always tiny. A cute thing. She was quiet, born inquisitive. I could put something as simple as a piece of tissue in front of her and she'd spend hours trying to work it out.

Louisa was more like David, and the only one who got my red hair. He was such a great Dad.

JUNE: He was so proud of those kids. He couldn't get enough of them.

CASS: It's why he wanted to look after the children while I studied our specimen — the moss from the water at the foot of the cliff. When I was needed back at home, he'd carry on my work, so we made some good headway in understanding the biological potential of the planet.

It was exhilarating, having something to study, and I started growing the moss in the greenhouse, until it spread enough to cover a good part of the soil. But despite my studies, I was careful not to waste a moment of time with the kids. I made use of every minute, and every day became a new adventure.

JUNE: Happy times.

CASS: I just wish they could've lasted longer.

We never went back to the pool at the bottom of that precipice again. We were too busy on the plateau. And David grew increasingly tired with each day, so that by the time we were able to leave the children, he never would've made the climb.

Still, we talked of it often. I joked that he'd only got me down there to get a peek at me in the flesh, and he didn't deny it. Ah, David. He was a charmer.

Then, before I could blink, Louisa was having her hair done and her dress fitted, and the atrium was decorated for her wedding.

She looked beautiful. David was using a stick to walk at this point and his hair was silver. Some things get better with age, and some things don't, but David was one of those things which kept improving. A real silver fox. He even made the walking-stick seem sexy.

JUNE: Cass. Please.

CASS: Oh, right. Sorry, June. But you can't deny he turned into a looker in his later years. Maybe there's hope for Harold yet!

. . .

Anyway.

Despite the pain, he still managed most of Louisa's wedding day. He wasn't going to let a little thing like pain stop him from seeing his daughter get married. I would've danced all night alongside Louisa, but I had to get him back in bed and rested before the music had even begun. I could hear it from the dome, and David insisted I go and dance. So I told him that I'd dance if he wanted me to, and I stood up and threw my limbs around wildly while he lay in bed laughing and watching.

Carla was a great help in my studies, and in taking care of David, the longer he was in bed. By the time James had finally gotten round to marrying, David was in a wheelchair, and he only made the ceremony. That time, I did leave him so I could dance, but only for a little while.

I had to watch him fade, the same way I'd watched Kirk fade, until he breathed his last. You don't know what that's like, June. I mean, imagine if Harold was going through it. I know David was your son, but he was my husband, the father of our children. And he was gone. Another one gone.

There's no way to explain the hole that swallows you. The emptiness. Like something's always missing. He'd made me forget that sorrow after losing Kirk, and when it returned, it broke me to pieces. I ran outside and screamed at the sun until I was red in the face. There were no words. Just one, long, agonizing scream, until I ran out of breath and needed to get back inside to inhale.

JUNE: I'm so sorry, Cass.

CASS: Don't be. I loved him. Is that something to be sorry for?

JUNE: Losing him was heartbreaking for all of us.

CASS: Hearts break, June. It's what they do.

JUNE: Are you okay?

CASS: I want to scream, June.

JUNE: Come here.

. . .

CASS: This doesn't seem very professional. Do therapists normally hug their patients this long?

JUNE: I won't tell anyone if you don't.

CASS: What would the boys say if they saw us now?

JUNE: They'd probably want in on it.

. . .

Do you feel up to continuing?

CASS: Haven't you got what you need yet?

JUNE: We've barely scratched the surface. I'll have to go over my notes. What about if we take a break, stretch our legs, and meet back in, say, an hour?

VII

TRANSCRIPT OF CLINIC SESSION 435
PATIENT: Cassandra (Biology — Orbicon Employee)
CONFIDENTIAL

JUNE: Feel better after your walk?

CASS: Don't play coy with me, June. You've been busy. Haven't you?

JUNE: What do you mean, Cass?

CASS: I saw Mark come in here while I was supposed to be walking the complex, and Max too. What did you say to them? What exactly is going on here?

JUNE: I don't know what you—

CASS: Save it, June. How long have we known each other? Let's not do this. You're smart enough to know not to push me. Right?

JUNE: We're just worried about you, Cass. That's all.

CASS: Worried? Pfft. What for?

JUNE: How long have you been living in that makeshift dome by the lake? You haven't been near the main complex in years. You said yes to Mark and then you just disappeared. And now you're back, like nothing happened. What's he supposed to think?

CASS: If Mark's worried, he should be talking to me about it. Not you. Besides, even if that's true, what gives you the right to go rooting around in my past? What does Max think you'll find? An excuse to lock me up? I went to the lake, not his precious, forbidden dark zone!

JUNE: Cassandra. There are only a handful of reasons why you'd disappear to that shack. And even fewer why you'd return. I want you to understand what you're getting yourself into.

CASS: Because you think I'm making a mistake? Saying yes to Mark.

JUNE: I don't want you doing something you'll regret. One lifetime of regret is enough for anyone.

CASS: I'm sorry, June. I just, I feel so alone.

JUNE: You're not alone, Cass. I'm trying to help. Now, are you happy to continue?

CASS: . . . Fine.

JUNE: Was it before or after David's funeral when you took Carla to the lake?

CASS: Before. I wanted to see it again before I laid him to rest.

JUNE: You printed out a shelter and some air-tanks so you and Carla could refill your inhalers for a few days. And then you came to see me.

CASS: When I came to tell you what we were planning, you just hugged me and sobbed. I was still too angry, too bitter to cry about it, but I held you all the same.

JUNE: It was hard to say which of us was a bigger mess.

CASS: That's right. You with your tears, or me with my bitterness. I don't suppose it mattered.

JUNE: You spent days down there. Was that when it first got established, do you think? This pattern of you going to the lake?

CASS: I hooked up the rigging with the ropes just like David showed me, and then I scaled the rock face, making sure it'd hold before Carla tried it. There was no thrill this time. Nothing. Just the mechanics of threading the rope through my hands, and a gust of wind on my face. Carla squealed when it was her turn.

JUNE: Sounds like Carla.

CASS: Yep. At the bottom of the ravine, we studied the water. It was clear for the most part, but a peculiar murky scum had collected at the edges. Carla asked me why her Dad hadn't taken a sample of the foamy stuff last time, and I told her that it wasn't there last time. The water was completely clear before. I put up the makeshift shelter while Carla scooped up samples of the scum into test tubes. She wanted us to test it. She was so excited about the sticky goop.

JUNE: Harold and I always used to laugh about how much she took after you. If there was ever a competition on excitement over sticky goop, she'd have given you a run for your money, Cass.

CASS: We stayed down there until the inhalers were almost dry and the tanks we'd brought were empty. Then we collected our samples and packed up ready to go. She started climbing, but I held back.

I walked to the water's edge. The sun's red rays reflected across the surface, bathing it in a lovely crimson. I looked across at where David and I once swam and tried to imagine him diving down all over again. I could almost see it, the memory was so fresh. So I whispered my goodbye to him across the water, and then I started climbing.

JUNE: And then it was the funeral.

CASS: Let's skip the funeral, shall we?

JUNE: By all means.

CASS: Okay. So, afterwards, I spent days alone analyzing the thick murk we'd taken from the water. It had cells in it. Not cells like the ones I'd discovered on the moss, but cells that were more similar to an animal. If they'd formed in the pool by themselves, I'd have been astonished, but I realized what they were the instant I saw them up close. I'd spent so long studying specimens of one sort or another, I recognised some of the markers as my own DNA, and some as David's. When we'd taken a swim, we'd contaminated the water, and this was the result.

JUNE: And that's when you smashed up the lab, right?

CASS: I threw my arms across the desk and trashed the microscope. And then I went to work on the rest of it. I cursed David for making us go in the water. But then I remembered him, and his hopeful eyes, and I couldn't be angry at him. After a while, I decided it was nice to think that a part of him — a part of us — would always be in that pool. It would always be our spot.

JUNE: Max forced you to come and see me after the damage. Said you posed a security risk. Is that when our sessions like this became more regular?

CASS: Probably.

JUNE: And in return for coming, you asked Max if you could build a dome at the bottom of the cliff?

CASS: It was so I could study the lake more easily.

JUNE: Are you sure that's why?

CASS: What are you trying to say?

JUNE: It didn't have anything to do with David? With that hole you needed filling?

CASS: Max said it would be fine, but there was no rush. I don't think he wanted me to be out of eyeshot too soon. Maybe I hadn't let go of David yet. I don't know.

JUNE: Maybe you still haven't?

CASS: It was so long ago.

JUNE: But it still feels raw, right?

CASS: Carla and I worked on the plans for the dome, but we couldn't make everything fit into such a small space. We left it after a while, and kept growing the moss up top, to see what effect it would have. We'd go back and forth down the cliff quite often, visiting the pool, and measuring the effect of our cells and how they developed in the water.

Eventually, we weren't able to take as many trips. Carla was getting old. James' little ones needed supervision, as did Louisa's, and before long, I was landed with more grandkids, trying to find ways of comforting them while they watched their parents grow frail, knowing the same thing would happen to them. James went first, then Louisa. Carla never married, so I had to grieve alone for her. I was never sure if she'd made a mistake or not, deciding not to marry — whether I was grateful, or disappointed by it.

JUNE: And then you started seeing Bill?

CASS: A few months later, I went back to my plans for the shelter. Max's boy, Bill, was an architect. I thought he might be able to help. So I invited him round for some food one evening. He was twenty-two. Strong. Handsome. We talked about the plans, and visited the site. Over those next few weeks, building the dome, we worked together. Close at first, and then closer.

By the time the dome was built, it was both of us moving into it together.

The wedding was at the main hub. Sonja looked beautiful. I had Max walk me down the aisle that time. The dress was much the same as before, but I put sleeves on it, and I wore my hair differently.

JUNE: What was it like, being away from us after all that time? You were the first to move away from the main atrium. I thought you were so brave, Cass.

CASS: I loved the dome Bill made us by the waterside. It was beautiful there. Peaceful. Tranquil. Bill told me that my hair was like sunlight, and my freckles were like the stars. He was always saying things like that to get me to pay more attention to him, and he was tenacious — so strong, so muscular — a good distraction. Most days would pass where I'd get no work done at all. I'd just lay there in his thick arms with my head on his chest, my auburn hair running down his torso. Some days I'd accidentally call him David, or Kirk, but he never seemed to mind.

Every morning I'd wake up and squeeze him, and say the same thing. I'd say, 'Just checking you're still here.'

'I'm here, baby,' he used to reply.

I loved our little dome away from home, but when the kids started coming, we were forced to move back into my old dome inside the complex. There just wasn't enough space down by the lake.

Every morning, he'd say, 'I'm here, baby.' Until he wasn't.

Oh, June.

JUNE: It's okay. Take your time.

. . .

You had five more husbands after Bill. Right?

CASS: And I've lost every single one. It's okay for you and Sonja. You married Earthmen. But me? I'm on a carousel. An endless cycle. How many times can a person lose the ones they love before they start to lose themselves?

JUNE: Do you really want to go through all that with Mark again?

CASS: Would you rather I stopped living altogether? What else am I supposed to do? Besides, it's not like I haven't had my share of happiness.

JUNE: I don't want to lose you, Cass. Not to regret. Not to this cycle you're on. It's been eight hundred years we've spun around this sun, and I couldn't face it if we lost you. I'm not saying you shouldn't marry Mark. He's a nice guy. I just don't want it to break you when his time comes.

CASS: Pass me the bottle.

. . .

Y'know, June, I've given birth to over twenty children. I've fallen in love so many times, too many times, and watched my sweetheart fade in front of me. I've watched the colony grow until it's now filled with people. It's a hive, and in each corner there's a reminder of both happiness and loss. I see my husbands in the eyes of others, or the stride of some, in a stance or a twitch or a laugh. It takes me back every time. Is it wrong to keep missing them, after all this time?

JUNE: Of course not.

CASS: But it feels it. It feels wrong. Some days, I can't miss them. I'm just numb to it. And at other times, it's like if I close my eyes, they're still here, holding me. And when I open my eyes, they're gone all over again.

I've stopped being mad about things. I used to be so angry. But nothing seems raw anymore. Not until you make me remember the early days. The way I used to be. That never goes, the memories. That's what pain is. It's a memory. And every time you poke at it, the fire stokes and it keeps burning. It keeps me burning, June. If I didn't have it, what would I be? A shell of a person. That's what I'm becoming. That's what I'm frightened of. I've got used to the way things are, as if living eight hundred years is normal. Or maybe it's just taken me this long to accept things the way they really are. You know how old I really am right now?

. . .

Eight hundred years on this world makes me thirty-nine in Earth-years, and I'm only just starting to get a few strands of gray. The first wrinkle that came, I was so relieved I remember laughing. My husband — I think it was Harvey, or it could have been Ralph, it's hard to keep track of the later ones — didn't get what I was so happy about, and I didn't bother to explain it.

JUNE: How could they understand? We've been young for so long.

CASS: Too long. You say one lifetime of regret is enough for anyone. I've lived a dozen lifetimes. I've got heartache in my bones, but I've also got more joy than a person has any right to experience. So many anecdotes, that if Kirk were still here, I could keep him talking for a hundred years. I regret a great many things, June. But do I regret coming here?

Honestly. I don't know. But I don't think that matters. I mean, I've still got a thousand years to figure it out. Right?

JUNE: Pour me a glass, will you?

. . .

Here's to you and Mark.

CASS: Don't worry, June. No matter what happens, I'm not going anywhere.

MAX

"This is Captain Max Shelby of the Icarus One, broadcasting on all frequencies. Houston, do you copy? . . . . I don't know why I still do that. It's not like you ever answer. Anyway. Mission update. I'll have to be brief.

"Today marks the thousandth year since our arrival, Trappist Time. It'll be over sixteen years, Earth Time. There's this big party they're holding to celebrate, although I don't know what we're celebrating.

"We were supposed to have six months to complete our mission. I had every excuse to fail. What were the chances of us finding a habitable exoplanet in a pocket of space within six months, when the best minds on Earth had been searching for thirty years? But I always believed we'd succeed. Always.

"It's been a thousand years since we landed. I've had the same mission for a thousand years. What excuse is there for failure . . . .?

"I'm meeting Bjorn later to train him how to broadcast, so you won't just be receiving reports from me. He's a good kid. They all are. I've gotta start thinking about the future. About how to continue the mission after I'm . . . ."

"That's Sonja calling me. Party time, I guess. Max Shelby signing off, over."

I flicked the switch as the door whooshed open, and her shadow rippled across the transmitter array.

"Ready, babe?" she asked.

My shoulders slumped. "Sonja, I don't want to go."

"What's wrong, hun?"

I spun in my chair to face the transmitter. "Why are we doing this?"

"Oh, come on. It'll be good for the colony."

"No. I mean. *This*. In the time we've been here, we could've done so much more. It's been sixteen years. Where's the backup crew? Why haven't they sent a relief team?"

"You still remember Earth?"

"I think about it every day."

"Then you'll remember how bad it was. The way things were going, who knows if there's anybody still left on Earth to save?"

"What are you saying, Sonja?"

She rested her hand on my shoulder. "I'm saying, look around. Look at everything we *have* achieved. This is the future. It always was."

I shook my head. How many times had we gone over this? I stared up at her, my mouth poised to argue, but the spark in her eyes soothed the storm. Her fingers played with my ear, and I shrugged off her tickle.

"Come on, old man." She yanked me upright. "Let's go have some fun."

The atrium was alive with noise. A carnival of confetti flitted around the dome. Punch replaced water in the fountain. Bodies swayed to June's disco tunes beneath banners that read 'Happy Landing Day.'

"Max!" Cassandra wailed, pushing through the fray. "You came!"

"What did I tell you, Cass?" Sonja squeezed my hand.

"There's life in the old dog yet!" Cassandra necked her glass of punch.

"I can't stay long," I said. "I'm supposed to meet Bjorn soon, so I can train him to use the comm."

"You're not still broadcasting on that thing, are you?" Cassandra scowled.

"Our mission's not finished."

"Pfft. Don't talk nonsense, Max. Do you really think anyone's listening to those stupid messages?"

"I have to believe that they are. For the sake of the mission." *Just drop it, Cassandra.*

Her hand found its way to her hip. "The mission's changed. Forget about Earth, Max. They forgot about us."

I stiffened. "No."

"We failed."

"I won't accept that."

"Oh, face facts. Harold's been mapping nebulas for how long and come up dry? How much longer is it going to be before you learn to accept it? We failed Earth. Are you going to fail the colony too? When are you going to let us explore this planet instead of keeping us prisoner inside your perfectly engineered little cage? That mist on the horizon and the darkness beyond it – we don't even know what's out there, and you've got us cooped up here toasting to what? A happy landing? When are you going to accept that things have changed?"

We stood glaring at each other while around us, bass thumped and our children's laughter trickled in waves. Sonja sighed. I tugged myself free from her, and met Cassandra's bull-headedness with ice in my eyes. "The situation may have changed," I said, "but our mission is still the same. We stay together. We survive. We consolidate our resources. You saw what happened to Earth. I won't let it happen to us. Understand?"

She laughed. "Aye, sir."

My cheeks flashed hot. "It isn't over until I say it's over. Is that clear?"

She bowed in a mock-curtsy. "Whatever you say, Captain."

I turned to Sonja. "If you find Bjorn, tell him I'll be at the comm station."

"Don't go, hun," Sonja pleaded. "Stay a little longer. Enjoy yourself for once."

I smiled at her, and disappeared into the crowd, pushing my way back to our dome.

The door shut out the hubbub of the carnival. I rushed to the array and hit the switch.

"This is Captain Max Shelby of the Icarus One, broadcasting on all frequencies. Houston, do you copy? . . . . Can you hear me? . . . . Is there anyone there? . . . . Henry! Henry Rolands! I know you're listening. I know you can hear me. Why don't you answer?

"You gave me this mission, Henry. Remember? You sat me down and told me this mission was never about Trappist. It was always about Earth. To broadcast coordinates of a habitable planet. 12 billion people depended on our success. Depended on me. 12 billion voices clamoring in my head every single day for a thousand years, screaming the call to succeed.

"You sent us here to do the impossible. And you knew it, didn't you? That it was impossible. What were we? A PR stunt? A last ditch Hail Mary? 'Failure is not an option,' you said. Those were your last words to me. But you knew there was no way to succeed.

"Why send us? To give the masses some hope before they all got snuffed out by some tidal wave or something? Sonja's probably right. In sixteen years, you could've wiped yourself out a dozen times. Answer me! Why don't you answer?

"Cassandra says we failed. But it wasn't her that failed. It was me. I was the captain. I was responsible. You gave me the mission, and it was mine. And I . . . I fai . . . No. Failure is not an option. I won't fail.

"Harold has his students and he's teaching them to operate the telescopes. Well, I'll do the same. I'll teach these kids to fulfill the mission. Make sure they don't forget why we're here. If I can't save you, maybe they can.

"Are you listening? You hear me? I don't care if it's impossible. You won't beat me, Henry. You won't beat me."

"Max . . . ., Max . . . . ?"

I snatched the microphone. "Houston! Houston is that you, over?"

The door whooshed open behind me.

"Max, there you are. Didn't you hear me calling you?"

I slumped, and dropped the mic on the desk. "I heard you, Bjorn. I just . . . thought you were someone else."

"Sonja said you were waiting for me. What did you want to show me?"

"Take a seat."

He pulled up a chair.

I spun in mine and faced him, man to man.

"Bjorn. What I'm about to tell you is classified. Do you understand?"

"Classified?"

"I'm giving you a mission, Bjorn. I'm putting you in charge."

"In charge of what, Max?"

"Of the future of Earth. There are 12 billion people on Earth. 12 billion lives. And I'm giving you the mission to save them."

His jaw dropped. He shook his head, but I grabbed his shoulder and forced his eyes to lock with mine.

"Bjorn. Listen to me carefully. This is your mission. Your duty to the people who brought us here. It's a sacred trust. You'll be sitting where I am one day, passing this on to the next generation until it's completed. So you have to understand how important this is."

"But . . . you'll still be here, won't you?"

"Maybe. Maybe not. I can't keep doing this forever."

"Alright, Max. But . . . 12 billion people?"

"That's right. They're counting on you. And Bjorn . . . failure is not an option."

GERARD

I

408 AE[*]

Many were packed into the great hall. Joseph had called a gathering of the council. I sat beside him as he called for order.

"My brothers," he boomed over the mutter of the assembly, raising his hands to quiet the uproar of the people. "Hear me, brothers. You have been called. Now, pray silence, I beg of you."

The din continued, relentless and considerable. Discontent among the citizens was no secret. Rather, it spread wide as moss, touching every quarter of the city, and growing more fervent with each rotation. No wonder such loud echoes of rancor filled the great hall.

"My brothers and sisters," Joseph cried with a voice strong as an army. "Please, let us be reasonable. We are not here to bicker, but to think and act. What are we to do about this spreading plague?"

He was right to speak of it as a plague — the moss creeping through the city's walls. It had begun in the Dome of Cassia. A dark green scourge that first spread through the soil, polluting its fertility, so that nothing could be grown in the House of Green. Now it multiplied

[*]AE: After Elders, Trappist Time

across every surface, clogging motors and filling domes that were already falling into disrepair. Once it took hold, it would not be removed, and it ate through the metal with an appetite voracious and unquenchable. Only hours ago, scouts discovered it threatening another House of Green, the Dome of Cassia, without which, it would be impossible to feed many in the overcrowded city.

"What are we to do, indeed," Thomas roared from the crowd. At the sound of his voice, many stopped to listen to his words.

Thomas was a popular man. He was of a pure line — heir to one of the last sons — and he had wed the most beautiful of all the living. Dinah. It was said by many that Dinah was as lovely as the Lady Sonja herself. They were wrong. She was far lovelier than that. Little wonder that Thomas spoke, he commanded the ear of the people. Even more so, perhaps, than Joseph.

"I put it to you, Joseph, that the Scourge of Cassia is but a sign. The Elders are displeased with us, and so they punish us with this tormenting weed."

The stamping of feet heralded Thomas' words as well-received. Joseph sat above the crowd, watching carefully, holding court, while the people urged Thomas forwards until he stood before the Seat of Maximus, staring Joseph in the eye.

"If what you say is true, Thomas, then we must discover the reason for the Elders' displeasure, and in haste, for the scourge has spread enough already. Soon it will bring the end of Cassia's largest dome, from which our stomachs reap the bounty."

Joseph was as much a believer in the Elders as anyone else, but I could not be so sure about Thomas. He claimed to be devout, but I never sensed conviction in him. And his ambitions were hardly congruent with those of a true follower of the Laws of Juniper. Even now, he sought to break them.

"I know well why we have incurred the Elder's displeasure," Thomas called out, so that all might hear. "Is it not from Cassia that this scourge was made? Was not Cassia the one who first ventured out across the sward into the unknown, seeking to discover what was hidden, and would still be hid heretofore had it not been for her fabled curiosity? Was it not Cassia who gave us the power to breathe amidst this air, with the sacred chalice of inhalation, so that we might roam new territories in her same spirit? To explore. Where is that spirit now, I ask you? What great new discovery is it that we are seeking to uncover? We have lived among these ruins of former times for long enough, in the shadows of our forebears' accomplishments. But now, we must stand in our own right. We must expand. We must discover. We must reach into the world around us with the spirit of Cassia as our guide."

There was a great stamping of feet at his speech. But Joseph had expected this. It was widely known what Thomas sought, and Joseph was not fool enough to ignore it, nor to be ill-prepared.

"You forget, Thomas, that it was Cassia who brought the weed to us in the first place so as to warn us of the dangers in the world. Would you take her warning lightly? We have existed for many generations in peace, without trouble or torment. So why now would Cassia be angered by our way of life, when we seek only to follow the Laws of Juniper?"

Joseph may not have been as popular as Thomas among the people, but he spoke with the Voice of Maximus. None could dispute it, and there was as much stamping of the feet at Joseph's words as there had been at Thomas' speech.

"All things are open to interpretation," Thomas replied. "Take the Laws of Juniper. Was Juniper a lawmaker, or a healer and teller of stories? I tell you, she was both. And in her stories, do we not find the secret of what we must yet do?"

"But you know the Laws prohibit it," Joseph interjected before the crowd could rally behind Thomas. "We have spoken of this many times, my brother. Why do you insist that it is so?"

"Because I believe that the Elders wish it for us," Thomas said.

Joseph shook his head. "I know the Tales of Juniper as well as anyone. I have heard since birth the legend of the horse that rode up to the forest, that there may very well be animals dwelling in the unknown reaches of this world, that we know not what the darkness holds. But this is not reason enough to believe that we should venture into it. Does not the First Law state, 'Do not go where it is dark?' And of the hunt you are so keen to propose, do we not read in the Third Law, 'No weapons, no harm?' If you think we are punished by the Elders now, what torments might yet be in store should we flout the Laws themselves?"

"That is your interpretation. I would keep my own. The prospect of creatures, to hunt the beasts that lurk in the dark — perhaps it is this danger which Cassia is forcing us towards. By driving us from this city, she may be preserving us from a greater threat which she has discovered, but we are yet to understand. If you disregard my interpretation of matters, then so be it."

"Interpretation is all we have, Thomas. While the Elders were here among us, they steered us. And were they here now, they would once more shine their light upon us. It is not my fault they are gone. Nor am I to blame that the devices which once held their thoughts and images so clearly have betrayed us, breaking beyond recovery and erasing all but their most scant notes. The parchments of Juniper's Sessions and her Laws – passed down from one generation to another – are all that we have, but we must interpret them with the wisdom of the Elders, or else we are naught but blind."

"Then open my eyes, Joseph. Please. Tell me . . . tell us all . . . what is to be done about this plague?"

Silence erupted in the great hall. The people were torn between the words of Thomas and the reasoning of Joseph.

"That is my question for the council," Joseph said. "Is there no-one else among us who knows what we must do?"

There was no answer. We could either listen to Thomas, and seek to leave the city, venturing into the darkness to hunt the Horses of Juniper, or listen to Joseph, remain where we were, hoping that our steadfastness and obedience might stave the dreaded weed. This made Thomas powerful indeed, for we had always done nothing, and the scourge had spread. Now was the time for action, and Thomas carried the favor of the many, although none would say it. I myself kept silent on the matter, despite my feelings, for the sake of my better judgment. Joseph must have sensed there were many who would be willing to pledge themselves to Thomas. But it was Joseph who spoke with the Voice of Maximus, and it was he alone who held the power to print, without which, no journey into the cold of darkness could succeed.

Joseph hung his head. "I hear your words, brother Thomas, and I do not ignore them. The way is not clear, and so if this scourge is indeed punishment from Cassia, then I must seek a sign from the Elders as to what should be done. I shall descend the cliff, and shelter in the solace of Cassia's Palace that sits upon Lake David. There, a sign shall be given, and when I return, I will know what must be done. What say you to this?"

The council stamped their feet, and so too did Thomas, whose face shimmered in a wry grin.

"I leave at the first crescent. This council has reached its end." Joseph stood and stamped his own foot, and the crowd dispersed into murmurs.

Dinah wove a path to the arm of Thomas, and kissed him on the cheek. Both smiled, considering the assembly a victory, and the most ardent of his supporters gathered around to congratulate him on his eloquence. Dinah was indeed the most beautiful of all the living. My eyes fixed upon her, and for a moment, she looked my way. Her glance carried the gift of Sonja, Bringer of Mirth, and my heart raced when her smile widened as our eyes met briefly across the great hall. But my gaze was distracted by the hand of Joseph, who clasped my shoulder, forcing me to look away from the beauty of Dinah.

"Come, Gerard. Let us away and make plans. I wish you to accompany me to Lake David."

"Of course, brother," I said.

I had no choice in the matter. Not only was I compelled to listen to the Voice of Maximus, but I could not refuse the wishes of my older brother.

II

In Joseph's dome, we spoke of what had been decided at the gathering of the council. Upon hearing it, Beatrice threw her arms in the air, disrupting her children as they played on the floor of the dome, too young to comprehend the peril at our door.

"Can you afford to wait for a sign?" Beatrice asked of Joseph with the skepticism only a wife can muster. "The weed is spreading so fast. I fear it will be too late if there is any more delay."

"We must trust the Elders, my love," Joseph said resolutely.

I admired his faith. I wished I had his same conviction. We had both been raised in the same house, listened to the same stories, and I knew the legends as much as he. I knew of Maximus, the Ruler of the Elders, who built the kingdom we inhabited. It was Maximus who governed this domain, possessing power over what may be printed and what may not. I knew of his bride, the Lady Sonja, Bringer of Mirth and Keeper of Beauty, and how their children were the most handsome of any, from which seed our own family had sprung. I knew of Juniper, the Healer and Lawgiver, who told such wonderful stories to soothe and calm the spirit. She was bride to Harold the Seer, who observed all, and left us the means to peer deep into the expanse above by his telescopes. And then, finally, there was Cassia the Red. She gave us food and the means to breathe, and she took such delight in the sons of men, that she wed them, becoming their bride.

Yes, I had heard stories of the Elders ever since I was a child. I knew that they had lived for generations among us, until their offspring was all that remained of them. We had the city, which proved their existence and ingenuity, and taught us much about them. But I could not overlook my doubts. Not like Joseph. He accepted the legends into his heart. He believed in the myths that belonged to history, whereas I concentrated on the mechanics of what remained.

"*Do you see this motor? It is exquisite in its design,*" I once confided in him when I was young.

"*Thank Maximus for its printing,*" he replied.

And that was the end of it. He did not seek to understand it more, but sufficed in being grateful for its existence. If only I could close my mind to questions, and learn to trust as he did.

'We must trust the Elders,' he had said. Beatrice was soothed by it, but his words brought me no comfort.

"Do you think it wise to be leaving us at so critical a time?" Jade asked. Trust our sister to find fault with his plan.

"I see no other choice," Joseph answered. "I know that something need be done, but I must see the path before I can walk it. I cannot see it here, and so I must leave."

"I am afraid, my love, of what might happen while you are away." Beatrice's lips trembled as she spoke. I had never seen her distraught over anything before. Not like this.

"I understand," Joseph whispered. "I know what I must do." He kissed her forehead and stood, walking to where his children played.

"Father!" they beamed.

"Come here, my loves. Let us play a game before I bid you farewell."

They threw their arms around him and wrestled him to the ground. He laughed. Even at a time like this, he could laugh. Yet another reason I envied Joseph. Truly, Sonja's mirth flowed in his veins.

Beatrice took me by the arm. "Gerard, dear Gerard. You must promise to bring him back to me as soon as you are able." She clasped tight hold of me.

"I promise it, Beatrice."

"I do not trust this Thomas," she continued. "His hair has always been too red for my liking. He believes himself Cassia reborn, I think. You must return Joseph before he is allowed to take hold of the people."

"What fear have you of that, dear Beatrice? Thomas wishes only to leave the city and hunt in the dark reaches of the world. He cannot do this unless my brother agrees to print him suit and weapon, for he cannot survive in the darkness without these things. Do not fret. Thomas is slave to my brother while ever he lives."

Beatrice could do nothing but agree. Yet, perturbation remained etched across her brow. "You speak truth, Gerard. But still, I do not trust this Thomas."

"Think no more of it," I assured her. "I will bring my brother back to you as contented as you see him now."

She smiled, and thanked me, standing to join her children as they wrestled Joseph merrily across the floor.

Jade took me to one side. "It is clear that our brother will not be free to make the broadcast to Orbicon this night. You must do so, brother."

I nodded, and left the room, stepping into the Chamber of Maximus, where I might communicate with Orbicon, the Realm of the Elders.

I sat opposite the sacred dials and switches on the gray altar, and pulled the talisman of speech close to my mouth.

"This is the voice of Gerard, dweller in the House of Maximus. Hear me, and receive this message well. My brother, our leader, Joseph, who speaks with the Voice of Maximus, has decreed that we shall sojourn to Cassia's Palace which sits upon Lake David. He does this to seek a sign from you as to what must yet be done. The scourge continues to grow wild and free, and it cannot be tamed."

I stopped speaking, and let out a sigh. I knew what I should say — that I should ask for a sign, and make petition to the Elders. Joseph would not have hesitated. I gripped my heart and shook my head.

"I did not speak my mind as light dwindled on the council," I whispered, "and so I must speak it now. I believe we should be studying this weed. I do not take it as a sign or an omen, but as a fascinating spectacle, yet to be understood by our finest minds. I know that there are many like me among the people, who seek to understand new things. But we have no voice, and no leader but Joseph. I held my tongue, for the love of my brother, but the love of the people compels me to speak thus. I should not wish so much to die by saying nothing, than to live by speaking out. I must have the strength to tell my brother of what I know to be true, that it is by the study of this weed that we shall conquer it — and it is the strength to speak which you must give me. I make my petition to you, asking that you give me a voice which will be heard. I am Gerard of the House of Maximus. Hear me, and respond."

I replaced the talisman on the table where it always rested, and released the switch that would cause Orbicon to hear my words. Then I sat back in the chair, and Joseph entered.

"I come to make petition to Orbicon," he said.

"I have already done it, brother," I told him. We stood together, and he placed his arm upon my shoulder, smiling at me.

"You are a wise man, and a truer brother," he said. "Did you ask for all that we shall need?"

I nodded.

"And were you heard?"

"I can but hope."

He slapped my arm. "Excellent. Now let us away to print the tools for our journey — the gifts that Maximus bestows."

"There is no need for you to join me, brother. This is the last night you will have with your wife and children until our return. You should be with them. I can arrange the printing."

He smiled. "Very well." He removed the medallion he wore around his neck, and lifted it over my head. "I give you the power to print as you wish. Print wisely, and return quickly. For I wish you to rejoice this night by my side. May Sonja smile on us both, and grant us joy before we leave. There is no finer omen than this."

"I shall not dally, brother." I left the room carrying the medallion around my neck.

I exited the dome and stepped into the plaza, wishing not to delay for even a moment, heading to the printer under the watch of Maximus, giver of all things.

III

The plaza was filled with people, but that was true of everywhere. Hot was the air and cramped was the room, and I was slow of foot in traversing the bustling bodies in the city streets. Even at night, the domes were so crammed, people had no choice but to spill into the streets. The younger children occupied beds inside their dome, while the older ones slept outside the doorways, unable to enter their own homes for lack of room. Too crowded had we become, and pushed even more for space now that the weed was growing upon the walls, creeping ever further into our domes. Nobody wished to be near the green moss, so they pressed together even tighter than normal. It was no wonder discontent spread among them as virulent as the weed itself.

"*We must expand,*" was the cry, and I could well understand it. But the sails that gave us power could not sustain the building of another dome. If they buckled under the strain, it would be the end of us all. Our vast city had reached its limit, and now its occupants were reaching theirs.

I hurried through the throngs, from one plaza to the next, until I reached the dome wherein the printer stood. Taking care that none might follow, I pressed the medallion into the door, and unlocked the barrier which prevented entry to the sacred chamber. I hurried inside, the medallion knocking against my chest as it hung beneath my robe. The door clicked behind me, locking me in, the gentle glow of the printer my only light.

When Joseph printed, he offered prayer before typing the sequence into a keypad. There was a lock, a combination, that must be entered first should one wish to make use of the machine, and this I had known for as long as I could remember. It was the secret of our family, to be passed on from generation to generation — the gift of Maximus.

I offered no prayer.

The keys clacked as I input the digits, and a screen lit up, asking me to configure the parameters for the printing. I scrolled through the oldest designs to see if there was already something in its memory from which I could draw. Before long, I found designs for a shelter, and tanks large enough to supply us with inhalation to last a while. These I printed, and they appeared before my eyes. Tools I fashioned also, from which we might repair any damage to Cassia's Palace, for I knew that none had made pilgrimage there in so long a time.

Once these were readied, I bundled them in my arms, but they spilled from my grip with every step I took. Balancing the many supplies, I shuffled ahead, exiting the chamber, careful to lock the door behind me. The procedure took longer than I had hoped, for I was forced to carry the equipment through the door and place it carefully at my feet before I could close it and lock it safely. When it was done, and I had secured the medallion beneath my robe once more, I stooped to gather the supplies in my arms, and heard a voice above me.

"Gerard of the House of Maximus. By the Elders, do you hope to carry all of that by yourself?"

I stretched my neck to glimpse a streak of red. "Thomas of the House of Cassia. I swear to you on my House that it is so."

"You cannot carry such a burden alone. Permit me to aid you," Thomas said.

"It is not so far a journey, and I am quite able."

"I do not doubt your strength, Gerard. But I insist on rendering you aid. To refuse me would be to argue, and does the Law not state, 'No arguing, no bickering'?"

I raised an eyebrow. "Since when were you one to quote the Law?"

"Come, Gerard, will you not thank me for my kindness?"

"Very well. You may carry the shelter. I shall take the tools and these tanks to refill the chalice of inhalation. And may the Elders reward your kindness."

"A chance to speak with you is all the reward one could hope for." He stooped with me and gathered his share of our burden. Flattery poured from his lips like water from a tap. It was easy to see why he was so popular.

I double-checked the lock on the door to the printer before I left. We made our way through the crowd, hampered by our load and the many who bombarded the streets.

"By the looks of these supplies, it seems that Joseph does not intend on making the pilgrimage alone," Thomas said. "Tell me, will you be joining him, Gerard?"

"I take the pilgrimage at first light." I would not lie, that was the Eighth Law of Juniper.

"That is good news, indeed," he said through a crooked smile.

"Why, Thomas, should it please you so?"

"Where one may fail, two may succeed. If the Elders frown upon Joseph, they may yet smile upon you."

"Do you think that they frown upon my brother?"

"Not at all. But I am certain that you are smiled upon."

Our progress seemed slower with two of us than it would have been had I carried it alone. And his chatter slowed us even more.

"I noticed you were silent at the gathering, Gerard. I cannot be the only one who has ideas how we might halt the scourge. You are intelligent. Tell me, now that we are just two, what would you propose to do about it?"

An urge possessed me, to confide my thoughts on the matter, but Beatrice's warning whispered in my mind. *I do not trust that Thomas,* she had said.

"My brother speaks with the Voice of Maximus," I replied, "and I would not question his words once they are spoken."

"Nor I. Your brother wears the robes of Maximus well. But do I not wear the robe of Cassia? Am I not entitled to think for myself, to use the intellect that my ancestors have passed on? Are you not entitled to the same?"

"I do possess thoughts, Thomas. But a fool thinks with his mouth, where a wise man keeps his own counsel."

"As I suspected. You *do* have an idea as to how we should proceed."

We moved from one plaza to the next, and I said nothing in reply. I had already said too much.

"I tell you this much," Thomas whispered so that the crowd around us would not hear. "If there is another way by which to halt the scourge, I would not hesitate to support it. As you know, I hold the ear of a great many, and my support for a sensible solution would carry much weight among the council. If ever one were to play the fool, and voice their thoughts aloud, I am certain that it would be well-received. Their words may even be regarded as spoken by Maximus himself. I must say that I spotted you wearing the medallion of your brother. May I say that it suits you, Gerard."

I understood his intent clearly enough, and his offer, but it did not entice me. I may have had ideas, and disagreed with Joseph about the Elders, but I would not betray my brother. Still, I did not want Thomas to know this. To reveal the truth to a mind like his was akin to opening oneself to attack. "And what price would your support incur?" I whispered.

"Let us say that any noble-minded son of Maximus would grant me provision enough to make the hunt. It is not so great a crime, to listen to the voice of Juniper, is it? For if that were so, then would adhering to her Law not also be a crime?"

"I think you presume too much. My brother would never grant you such a request."

"Yes, but Joseph is about to embark on a perilous journey. If he should not return, then you would speak for Maximus."

Was that a threat, or merely a seed he tried to plant, in case my ambitions were as detestable as his own? Did he really think that he might goad me into betraying my own kin? Perhaps Beatrice had been right.

Greed contorted his already twisted smile.

"Mark my lips, Thomas. My brother shall return."

He bowed his head, but the smile remained. "Of that I have no doubt. And when he does, if he is no wiser as to how we proceed, then someone must speak for Maximus.

Remember what I have said, should you choose a course that is not silent."

"Many say that you have a smooth tongue, Thomas of the House of Cassia. But now I know this for myself to be true, for I have heard your words, and they are slick as the mossy blight."

"I prefer smooth as the finest robes." Thomas snorted.

We made our way into the plaza where stood entry to my dome, and across the atrium, there too was the door of Thomas' own dome. Outside his doorway, Dinah spoke with a group of other women. I could not take my eyes from her. She radiated such beauty, that even in the darkness of the streets, she cast light. Dinah watched us carry our supplies, but I think she watched me more than Thomas, and I turned my face to the ground when her eyes lingered.

"Speaking of the finest robes," Thomas said, "do you see Dinah across the plaza?"

I looked up at her, and saw her laughing, which stirred me into a smile. "I do."

"Do you like her gown?"

A shapely robe hung from her shoulders to her feet, accentuating her curved physique in the most modest but elegant way. But any garment would have paled in comparison to her loveliness. "It is a very fine gown, Thomas."

"Indeed. And you should feel it in your hands. It is soft as her skin. That robe was Cassia's own. Worn on the night she would wed a man. I have inherited many of Cassia's possessions. I wonder, perhaps it may do you well to come and visit me while it is still dark, before you set out on your pilgrimage? I can show you many more wonders, and it may incur a good omen for your journey."

"I think a good night's rest would be the best of omens," I told him.

"Of course. But consider it. And if sleep escapes you, then I shall be waiting. Both I, and Dinah."

We reached my dome and he dropped the shelter that he carried to the ground.

"Thank you for your aid," I said.

"May the Elders guide you to my Dome, so that glad tidings we may share, and then in journey where you roam, the Elders' smile will find you there."

"Glad tidings be with you, Thomas."

"I'll be waiting." He stepped backwards, bowing as he did so, leaving me alone to enter through the door, dragging the equipment inside.

"You made good time," Joseph said as I entered.

"That I did." I rested the equipment on the table, and returned the medallion to him. "Where are the others?"

"They are at rest. Come, let us do the same. A long sleep will do much for us both."

"Very well. Goodnight, brother." I retired to my sleeping quarters, where I lay in the darkness, trying to forget the words of Thomas of the House of Cassia.

IV

Sleep escaped me. I could not rest. Perhaps this was an omen. But I did not believe in such things. It was Thomas' words that prevented me from sleep, for I had been foolish enough to swallow the poison of his mind.

Had he wished to dispose of Joseph, then his best chance would be in this pilgrimage. I had promised Beatrice that I would return with my brother, but now Thomas threatened that. What was his intent? Was he to play a scheme most foul?

I tried to think my way around it. I had carried the tanks of inhalation, so he could not have sabotaged those. The tools that we might need to scale the cliffs and fix the Palace had never left my arms, so he could not have played those false. It was only the shelter that he had carried, and of this I was glad. Certain, was I, that it would not be in his interest for us both to meet our end, for he had some need of me yet, otherwise he would not have offered to carry my voice through the council as if it were the Voice of Maximus.

What did he want of me? What was the purpose of his deceit?

I could not answer these questions from my bed, but I felt I must have an answer to them before the first crescent of light. To leave now, with so many riddles, would prove to undo the venture before we had even set out upon it. There was only one course of action open to me, and that was to confront Thomas about these matters directly.

Without a further hesitation, I rose and threw my robe across my shoulder, silently creeping out of the dome until I was safely in the plaza. I shuffled through the crowds, and found myself stood before his door, knocking upon it thrice.

"Enter," bade the voice from beyond, and I stepped through the threshold. The voice did not belong to Thomas, but to the one who had adorned Cassia's gown, and still wore it even now, as she stood before me.

Dinah looked even lovelier than she had done all but an hour before. Her hair was gathered high, pinned in the most wonderful design, and as I entered, she pulled at one of the pins. Her dark hair bloomed into an afro, making her cheeks even more shapely.

"Would you care for some refreshment, Gerard?" Her voice matched her beauty – that of the Lady Sonja herself.

"I would speak with Thomas," I told her, not wishing to be distracted from my purpose.

"I am sure that he will join us in good time." She brought me a drink and beckoned me to sit. "In the meantime, let us speak with one another. I've been expecting you this past hour. I was not certain you would come at all, but I am glad that you have. I have seen you many times in the plaza, but we have not had chance to speak."

Her words were like music, and, though it inconvenienced me, I did not resent Thomas' absence. She sat beside me on the large couch, and pulled her feet up beneath her, so that she might face me. Her look was as disarming as her smile, which lit her eyes with such joy that I was enchanted by them.

I sipped my drink. "We have been neighbors these past years, but you are right. It seems odd that we have never spoken until now."

"Why do you think that could be, Gerry? Do you mind if I call you Gerry?"

"You may call me what you wish." I blushed. "And I do not know the answer. I suppose the Elders do not wish us to meet."

"Until now, perhaps," she whispered, lifting her drink to her lips. She arched her neck and let the liquid fall down her throat. Her beauty was intoxicating, and I was becoming drunk on it.

Where was Thomas? He said that he would be waiting for me.

"The Elders smile upon us this night," Dinah said.

"As they smile upon Thomas. Where is he?"

She sighed. "He is too busy talking to the sun."

"What do you mean by this?" I asked.

"It is something that was passed down to him. He says that Cassia would speak with the sun once darkness fell in the city, and he has taken it upon himself to do the same. Perhaps he is in conference with her now, and is asking for her to show Joseph the way."

"In conference with Cassia?"

"Yes, he tells me that the sun listens to him when he speaks. But I do not pay much heed to his brash claims." She took the last of her drink in one swig.

"You do not believe that what he speaks of the Elders is true?"

"I am not sure what to believe when it comes to the Elders," she said.

"You are a doubter?" I tried to mask my surprise and elation, for I had never imagined that I would share anything in common with perfection, such as she.

"Perhaps. Are you going to scold me for it?"

"I would not scold you, Dinah. Not for anything."

She smiled. "I am thirsty. May I share your cup?" She moved closer. I offered it to her, but she did not take it. Instead, she wrapped her fingers over mine. Her soft skin tingled my rough hand as we gripped the cup together.

"It is your water. Who am I to withhold it from you?" I said.

I let her lift my hand to her mouth. She sipped, staring at me with those unfathomable eyes. I was caught in her glance, and after she finished, I was so mesmerized, that I didn't notice her pull my hand to her lips and gently kiss my fingers.

Realization stirred me. "Dinah, what is the meaning of this?" I pulled my hands away.

"I should think the meaning is quite clear." She forced her hands on mine, pulling her perfect form closer. "I've been watching you for so long, and waiting for this moment, Gerry. You don't know how many times I've asked the Elders for this."

"It cannot be." I shook my head, and caught her delicious scent.

"Why ever not?"

Here was the most beautiful of all breathing things on this world staring me in the eyes and telling me that she had dreamed of this. That we had shared the same dream all this time. But I could not allow it. "What of Thomas?"

"What of Thomas, indeed?"

"Are you not wed?" My jaw dropped, incredulous at her lack of interest in her husband's feelings on the matter.

"Even if I were, there is no Law of Juniper against the taking of another man, is there?"

I shook my head. "But never has it been done. Not one of the Elders was ever accused of such a thing."

"Very well. Then I ask you, did you see me and Thomas wed?"

I tried to remember, but could not. "Alas, no."

"Do you know of any who did see it?"

My mind raced, but came up short. "Not one."

She nodded her head. "Then what makes you so sure that we are wed?" she asked.

"It is known that you are."

"A scurrilous lie!" She balked, throwing her arms and standing, turning her back on me.

I stood too, and placed my palm on her elbow, beckoning her to stop. "A lie? Explain your meaning, Dinah, for I am at a loss to understand the plainness of your speech."

She turned towards me, and we stood so close, we were almost touching.

"I tell you truly that Thomas is no more than my brother. These past years, he has been too afraid that I would wed a man of unworthy heritage. So he has broken the Law, and told untruth so as to spare me from an ignoble union."

"You mean to say that you are his sister?"

"The same," she said.

"I can scarcely believe it. Lineage is a matter of record. Are you saying that the records are wrong?"

"There is no such thing as an entirely true record. You must know this."

"But . . . I can't . . ."

"Gerry. If Joseph, or anyone else knew of our father's sin – that we were born of different mothers but we share the same House – what would become of Thomas? Or of me? You don't want to see me disgraced, do you? I thought . . . I hoped I could trust you."

Impossible. A forged record. A false lineage. And yet, spoken from the lips of such an angel, how could I not believe her? In that moment, the clarity of the choice set before me sliced through my mind sharper than any blade.

I could believe the truth of this beauty before me, or deny it for the sake of a scribble in an archive.

My eyes steeled. Let the records keep their lies. She was his sister.

"You can trust me, Dinah. I shan't let you down."

"You must believe that Thomas is a good man. He is protective of me, but he is generous too. He is only too willing to share with you. His power, his friends, and his sister."

My mind worked fast, but not quickly enough to comprehend what she was proposing until she said the words.

"And so I make my vow, in all good conscience," she said. "As long as the sun is in the sky, I am yours and you are mine. If you will have me?"

The vow of marriage. "This is no wedding."

"Why not?" she asked. Determination possessed her eyes, drawing me towards her, and I was powerless to resist.

"We are but two."

"Is that not enough for a wedding?" Her hand found its way into mine, and her gentle fingers ran up my arm as she stepped even closer.

"And you would have me?" I was almost speechless at the thought of it.

"Have I not vowed it?" Her lips parted, ever closer.

"As long as the sun is in the sky–"

She pulled me to her, and our lips pressed together as one.

We were wed in her dome while she wore the betrothal gown of Cassia, and I, the robes of the House of Maximus. She tugged me into her chambers, and there we stayed as man and wife until first light approached. Thomas did not return for the full balance of the night.

V

"You must come back safely to me, my love," Dinah whispered as she stared at me with those wondrous eyes, while I held her in my arms.

"Of that, I promise you," I said. "Although, I hate to be leaving you when we are not yet one day married."

"I wish that you could stay, but I know why you must leave. May I ask one thing of you?" She slipped from my cradle.

"Anything."

"Do not make it known that we are wed until we are together again. I long to be at your side when the news is made."

"And I wish to be at your side always." I stood from where we lay and gathered my robe around me. "I shall keep our secret until I return, and we shall announce it together."

"Gerry. Think of me, won't you?" She covered herself with the bed linen.

"Ceaselessly," I whispered. I leaned down and kissed her before turning to leave.

"Gerry," she called, stopping me in her doorway.

"Yes, my wife?" I asked.

"Don't you want to know why I, a daughter of Cassia, picked you for a husband?"

"Very well. Why am I your chosen mate?"

She looked at me intently, as if her words were important. "Because you are as powerful as you are honorable. You are a son of Maximus, one of the heirs to the last son of the Ruler Elder and the Lady Sonja. Do not doubt your power, my love. Joseph may be the firstborn, but you are no less strong."

"Was it not for my handsomeness?" I chided.

She smiled. "May Cassia keep you safe for me."

"And may she watch over you." I left before the light first shone in a crescent through the spinning wall, giving the illusion of day. My footsteps were mute as I tiptoed across the plaza, and back into my dome, which was empty.

I had all but forgotten about Thomas and his machinations. Now that I and Dinah were in union, it would not profit him to harm Joseph, whether he realized it or not. And so Joseph's safety had been secured. A good omen indeed.

We ate a last breakfast with Beatrice and the children, as well as Jade and Simon, who joined us late. Why my sister had chosen a lout like Simon for a husband was a mystery not even the Elders could solve. Despite the heaviness of my eyes, I smiled almost as much as Joseph, for new love refreshed me far more than sleep. Beatrice was more settled, but still possessed an anxiousness that would not ease for anything.

"Farewell, my loves," Joseph said. He bestowed the medallion upon Jade to safeguard in our absence. "I leave to seek a sign from the Elders that will prove to be our salvation. Be merry, and may Maximus watch over you until I return."

We heaved the shelter and the tools between us. With packs on our backs, we took our first steps on the sun-drenched sward in the direction of the cliff's edge, and Lake David.

The plateaux stretched out, craggy and crusted, until we reached the cliffside.

"Shall we lower the shelter?" I asked.

"The lakeside is sacred. We shall carry it down so as not to invite the Elder's displeasure."

I tried not to roll my eyes. "Very well."

"Let us climb together, brother. We shall not fail if we remain united."

We moved with caution and care, but our burden was cumbersome and awkward, so that there was no easy means of descent. The cliff was steep, and the sun constant, and it was hot work.

Halfway through the climb, I paused to secure my footing upon a ledge, but Joseph did not see it, and threw the weight of the shelter towards me. I caught it, but was thrown off balance. My hands shot out for a ledge on the cliffside. I grabbed hold. Tensing. Gripping. But I could not keep the shelter fast in my hands. With deep breaths, I hung limply, watching the shelter fall into the vast depths below.

"Are you injured, brother?" Joseph yelled.

"Only my pride," I told him. "I have lost our cargo."

"There are worse things to lose." He climbed to render me aid. With a firm grip, he reached over and lifted me until I stood again with a solid foothold on the crimson cliffs.

It was impossible to know how long had passed, but eventually, we reached the ground. I collected the fragments of the shelter, which had shattered into pieces.

"It seems that we shall be sleeping outside, brother," I said.

"Perhaps. Let us make haste to the Palace and see if Cassia will not open her door to smile upon us yet."

We wandered along the shore of where Lake David rested, the red haze shimmering across its surface, as if the light were dancing and merry. Cassia's Palace was no grand structure, but a simple room, which held all things. Upon reaching it, I was amazed to find that a small hole in the roof was our only obstacle, for I had expected it to be inaccessible. Either that, or in a state of decay and collapse, without a hand to care for it.

"You see, brother. The Elders took our shelter, for they knew we had no need of it." Joseph tapped me on the back, adulated. "The home of Cassia." He gasped.

"I wonder what secrets it holds." I looked around with interest at the clever ways that so much could be contained in a room so small.

"It need hold only one. The secret of what should be done about the scourge." Joseph never forgot our reason for having come, even for a moment.

"True, brother. Let us not waste our good fortune. I shall make reparation without delay."

It took no more than an hour to weld together a patch for the hole in the roof, using the fragments of the shelter as a new shell. Once done, we lit the mechanism that would condition the air, and it hummed for a few minutes, before it settled, and we could breathe easily within the shelter.

"Excellent," Joseph said. "Rest easy, brother. I seek an answer, and there is no finer time to petition the Elders for a sign than this moment."

"How will you go about it?"

"I shall bathe in the water of Lake David and await a sign. Meantime, you rest. The climb will take its toll lest you sleep."

He left the dome, and I watched him through the window as he disrobed and stepped into the water, holding his palms skyward.

The motor did not spin the dome, and so, rather than taking to the bed and sleeping, I chose not to rest until I had discovered the reason. I knew what most would have said about the Palace, 'If Cassia willed for it to spin, then it would spin.' But Cassia's will and mine were at odds, for I had decided that it should spin, and so I would make it thus.

I stripped the floor of its slab covering, taking care not to damage the stones. Beneath the grates, I found the motor, lifeless and broken. It would require parts if I were to fix it. Parts printed. But I could not journey back alone to print them.

Still, I inspected the motor. Upon lifting the grated hatch, I stooped and lowered my head and arms into the gap below, wishing to peer closer at its design. I reached in, and toured the mechanism with my hands, but it benefited me not. Until my fingertips wisped against some other form behind it. Curious, I extended my arm and felt another metal shape, and so I grabbed hold and pulled it to the fore. It possessed all the properties of a power source, but for what, I could not fathom.

So I took it from where it had lay dormant, and then, with nothing more to be done, I replaced the hatch and the stone floor, so that Joseph might not scold me for disturbing them. Then I put the metal cylinder which I had found into the satchel that carried my inhalation tanks, and I took to my bed, basking wearily in red rays of sunlight.

For countless hours, Joseph and I waited in the Palace, making no further progress. Days passed — how many, I cannot be sure. But each day, he would bathe in the lake with his palms stretched up towards the sun, while I would spend my time inside the dome, examining the oddities ingeniously hidden within.

I discovered a great many clever compartments, housing utensils of one sort or another. The Palace felt like a home, and it made me think of Dinah, and the home we would build together someday. Perhaps I would bring her here, and we might take a pilgrimage together. She would surely enjoy the serenity of the lake, for it was beautiful, and things of great beauty are often drawn together. Each moment held the dancing light of the red sun, so that the clear water seemed enchanted. Fantastic to behold, though it still could not compare to the vision that was Dinah. After endless days of watching the red sun and the water's edge, I was not content to look at it without dreaming of her wondrous face.

I had all but exhausted the limits of curiosity within the dome, and thought I had discovered all its secrets, until I stumbled, quite by accident, upon a crease within the wall. I wondered if it was not a crack forming in the shell, and so I ran my hand along it. But it was no crack of nature. Rather, a carefully positioned seam with a hinge. I grasped it and opened it, and inside there rested the frame of a small 3D printer.

I startled at the sight of it, for I had only known of one printer in the entire city. Yet now, here was another, although it did not emit a glow, and I assumed it to be only a shell, for there was no sign of it being anything more than a scale-model. Perhaps a model of the printer in the city? But no, this was no idol, though idle it remained. The memory of the metal cylinder that I had found buried in the floor shot through my mind, and I retrieved it from my satchel, where my supply of inhalation was already running out — Joseph had used it to fill his chalice as he bathed incessantly in the lake. I fixed the power unit to the machine, and alive it came. Here was a means of printing which had hitherto eluded me.

I printed the parts to fix the motor, and got to work. Once the dome was spinning, I printed more inhalation tanks.

Joseph was incredulous as he rushed out of the water and back into the dome. "What has happened?"

"We have the means to print all we need so that we might stay here for as long as you would wish it." I was about to tell him what I had found, but he did not allow me the chance.

"This is surely a sign of the Elders' approval. We are in the right place, my brother. The shelter has been reborn, and so too will the Elders make our city. It bodes well for us. They wish for us to stay so as to send me a sign. Of this, I am sure."

I smiled at him, for I did not have the heart to tell him that it was me who had performed this 'rebirth,' as he had named it.

For three weeks, the shelter spun, and Joseph kept bathing in the lake. Each day, I thought of Dinah's words to me, and longed to be back in her arms. 'You are no less strong,' she had said. And surely, my fixing the shelter was proof of that.

This was no sign from the Elders, but a reminder of what I had spoken to them once before, that in study we shall save the city.

Every morning, I determined to speak to my brother of this, to tell him of what I knew to be true. But once he had woken, there was no stopping him from bathing, and once bathed, there was no talking to him, for he was in no mood for conversation. My desire to return to Dinah filled my beating heart with a passion I could hardly contain. Though it seemed I would never return to my beloved wife.

Until one day, when Joseph came into the dome with a look of sadness, and frustration.

"Why do they not answer me?" he cried through gritted teeth. "I ask them for a sign and yet, there is none. Do they not hear me?"

This was my chance. "Are you certain that they have not already answered you?" I asked.

"What mean you, brother? Speak," he beckoned.

I took a deep breath and swallowed. "The only thing that has happened since our arrival is that the Palace has spun, and a printer has been found. But I have yet to tell you how this came about."

He sat down and gave me a listening ear. I could tell that he would hear me out, and it settled me in no small measure.

"It was not Cassia or the Elders who caused the motor to spin, nor did they give life to the printer that produces the chalice of inhalation. While you were bathing, I lifted up the stones of the floor and examined the motor beneath the ground. It was there I found a metal cylinder, which I took. When I stumbled across the printer, it was lifeless, until I installed the cylinder, then printed off the things that would restore the motor. Since then you have been asking for a sign from the Elders, but I believe this is the sign you have been seeking all along."

His eyes widened. "You defiled the stonework of the floor? It is no wonder that Cassia has not answered me!"

"Calm yourself, brother. If, by your logic, Cassia was displeased, then would she not have prevented me from fixing the motor, or finding the printer?"

He did not answer, but could not argue.

"Hear me," I pleaded with him, recalling the words of Dinah, and found courage in them. "For a long time, I have known what must be done so as to lift the scourge, but I have not spoken of it, for in my love for you, I sought to preserve your will. Yet, before we left, I made petition to Orbicon that I find some means of speaking to you about this very thing. The Elders have been patient with me, but the moment is finally here. Brother, I know what must be done."

"Tell me, oh wise brother of mine, how is it that you would lift the scourge? For it seems to have been obvious to you all this time, where it has eluded all others. Indulge me in your great intellect, oh brother mine." It was as though another man sat before me, and not Joseph. Never had I seen him so upset. But I could not hold myself back, for he had wounded my pride, just as I had wounded his.

"I shall tell you bluntly," I said. "You are blind, brother. The solution is before your eyes, and yet, you fail to see it. I have fixed this shelter by means of study and examination. We must study the scourge – understand it better so as to find its weakness. It is only by understanding it that we can defeat it. Is that not obvious?"

He shook his head and cackled. "You accuse me of being blind, and yet, it is you who does not see. The city is our home, brother. A home is not to be studied and picked apart, for in doing so, you would make it a laboratory. Do you know of a laboratory? It is an ancient word, long banished to the past. Yet that is what you would propose to make our home. And where does it stop? In understanding it, you will defeat the scourge, and then what? If you understand all things, including yourself, will you not defeat yourself also? Is that not the very reason that the Elders sought this place out centuries ago? Where is your faith, brother?"

"What good is faith if it is blind? You speak of the Elders as if they are still here, but there has not been an Elder among us for over 400 years. Where are they now? Why do they not answer you? Perhaps it is because they have no ears to hear you with, for they are as we shall be if you do not act — with eyes closed and breath gone, vanquished by the truest scourge of all, death itself."

He clenched his fists. "Hold your tongue, lest you speak lies, and force my hand against you."

"You cannot punish me for speaking truth, brother."

"Truth!" he screamed. "What truth is there in falsehood? I suppose you will soon be telling me that the prophecy is nothing more than a wishful hope. If the Elders are no more, then how do you explain the prophecy?"

"I know what is written. You need not lecture me on the prophecy of the second crew."

"Do you?" Joseph rocked back and forth. "The Elders promised that they will come again, that they will return, and that Orbicon will send others to take the place of those

Elders who have fallen. More will come from Orbicon when the time is right. How can this be true, if what you say is anything but a lie?"

"How can you be sure that Orbicon is even real?" I asked.

He stopped his yelling, and I mine, and the fire in his eyes transformed into a pit of fear. They bore into my heart, and I could not stand to look at my brother any longer, for it was clear he felt I had betrayed him.

"I cannot listen to this treachery," he said. "You speak with the tongue of Thomas, ready to forget the Elders so as to please yourself. While you think in such falsehoods, you are no son of Maximus. But when you see the sign, you will regain your sense, and your faith. We shall speak no more of this until the sign is made."

He had spoken with the Voice of Maximus, and there was no more to be said.

***

I could not sleep that night. With a heavy heart, I lay waiting for the first crescent to shine through the spinning dome, so that Joseph would leave me to perform his ritual bathing. My head and heart were at war. I knew that I was right, that our only hope lay in the power of our hands. But my heart was grieved, for my words had injured my brother, and I could not help but feel that I was a traitor to his faith, perhaps the worst treachery of all. I remembered Dinah's words, and realized their terrible meaning, that I was not powerless, for I possessed the power to cause my brother pain.

When the sun came into the dome, Joseph took to his feet and left. As the window spun, he came into view, and he leaped around in the water. A great shout of joy echoed across the water.

"Come, my brother. Come and see the Elders' sign," he exulted.

I ran out of the dome to join him.

"Look!" He pointed at the water, which was no longer clear, but clouded in a strange murk around him. "It is the sign we have been waiting for."

His face beamed with a smile, and he looked like my brother once more. I did not have the courage to tell him that all I saw was murky water, where he saw the Elders' power.

"Let us not delay," he said, "but let us return to the city with joy in our hearts, for I know now what we must do."

VI

Beatrice's tears met us when we returned to the city. She and the children threw their arms around Joseph's neck, and filled his face with kisses.

"I am so happy that you have returned to me, my love," she said.

Jade and Simon helped me to carry our things into the dome.

"Did I not promise you that I would return?" Joseph asked with a smile across his lips.

"And you have your answer?" Beatrice looked hopefully into his eyes.

"I do. The Elders have smiled upon us."

Their faces spoke relief, although mine betrayed a sadness, for although Joseph had forgiven me, I could not help feeling at odds with my brother for the first time in my memory.

"And not a moment too soon," Jade said. "For the scourge has spread even further. It now reaches the motors of the city. I fear that we are only days away from losing power." She gave him the medallion and he placed it back around his neck.

"Fear not, my sister. For the Elders' will is clear." He placed a reassuring hand on her shoulder.

"And what is their will?" Beatrice asked.

He puffed his chest out, towering large as any dome. "I began to doubt that they would hear me," he said. "I waited without an answer for so long. My faith was tested, and I began to question the wisdom of the Elders, but Harold saw it all through his lofty telescope, and sent me a sign when I needed it most. I had bathed in Lake David each day, but when my faith was under its most crucial test, I entered the water to bathe, and around me, the pool clouded, as if Cassia herself were speaking with me."

They all stood aghast at this apparent display of the Elders' power.

Jade turned to me. "Did you see it?" she asked.

"I saw the water was clouded," I said.

"Just so," Joseph continued. "And here is the meaning of the sign. The path is not clear. The way is clouded, and we do not have an answer. But this is no more than a test of faith. We must continue to wait, no matter what happens, and trust in the Elders to rid us of the scourge."

They glanced at one another, their foreheads tarnished by creases of concern.

"So you mean to do nothing, brother?" Jade asked.

"I mean to trust the Elders to deliver us. That is hardly doing nothing," Joseph said. "And so must you. I announce it at first darkness this very night. Now, what else have I missed, my dear children?" He paced through the dome and into their room, and the sound of laughter drifted through the walls.

Beatrice approached me. "Did it really happen as he said?"

What could I tell her? A nod was my only answer.

She bit her lip, but forced a smile. "Thank you for returning him to me, as you promised," she said. "I discharge you of your oath."

And then she turned to Jade, to comfort her, for she had many worries as to whether doing nothing was really the best course to take.

I could not stand to listen to the discussion, and so I left. I journeyed across the plaza, and pounded Thomas' door, anxious to see my beloved wife.

He opened and bade me welcome, sitting me down in the same place where I had discovered Dinah's love for me all those weeks ago, and offered me a drink.

"All in good time, Thomas. First, I must see Dinah," I told him.

"There is, indeed, a time for everything," he said. "First, you must tell me of all that has occurred these past six weeks. Did your brother return with you?"

He looked at me through an accusatory eye, as if he cared not about the welfare of Joseph, but hoped that the answer may provide an opportunity for him.

"My brother is quite well, and will be calling the council to meet at first darkness," I said.

He tutted. "A pity."

"Pity, Thomas? Why should it be pitiful that Joseph be well?"

"I do not speak of his wellbeing, but of his delay in calling the council. I had hoped that we might learn of what his solution will be to the scourge."

"I do not think that it will please you, Thomas," I said before I could think, regretting it the moment it slipped from me.

He cocked an eyebrow. "You fear I may think it less than adequate?"

I shook my head. "I have said too much already."

"Perhaps you think I will be disappointed because that is how you feel yourself. Is that not so?"

It was true. I was disappointed in my brother. I had presented him the solution, which he had cast aside as if it were an affront. Yet, his own interpretation of a cloudy pool had caused him to condemn the lives of all in the city. Jade had said that the weed now threatened the power. If the city were to lose power, there would be no air circulating within the domes, and no means of printing, apart from the 3D printer that I had hidden in Cassia's Palace before we had left. But so small a printer could not be relied upon to fill the lungs of an entire city. Many would perish. Yet, that is what my brother decreed. And there was no way to change his mind.

Still, despite knowing the toll that Joseph's stubbornness would take upon the city, I had already betrayed him once, and the thought of doing so again overwhelmed my heart. He may have been wrong, but he was still my brother, and I loved him dearly. What sacrifice was I prepared to make for his love?

Thomas looked at me expectantly, assessing the turmoil I could not keep from my face.

"Patience, Thomas," I said, "and you will learn of his ruling soon enough."

"But it may not be soon enough. Tell me, will you remain silent at the council meeting tonight? Or does your brother leave you no choice but to speak out?"

I remembered his offer, to make my voice as the Voice of Maximus. But I could not rob my brother of his title. I could not do that to my kin.

"I shall not speak against my brother, Thomas."

He shook his head. "That is a pity. Come, I shall call Dinah." He rose and summoned her, and a moment later, my beautiful Dinah entered from another room. I ran to her with my arms outstretched, wanting to hold her more than anything else. It had been so long since she had been in my embrace, and I craved it now, caring not if Thomas saw us. But she cowered away from me.

"Why, sir, I think you too bold! My husband is watching," she said.

"What mean you by this, my love? Are you not Dinah, and am I not Gerard?"

"The same," she said.

"Then surely your husband will approve."

"I can assure you that he does not," Thomas spoke from across the room.

"You have no need to play false with me, Thomas. I know the truth. But perhaps you do not know. Have you not told your brother of our union, my love?"

Dinah stared at me through those beautiful eyes, and then laughed furiously, as did Thomas.

"Of course I am aware of your union, my dear Gerard," Thomas bellowed. "But that does not make it any the easier for a husband to bear."

My face reddened. "What mean you by this, Thomas?"

"It is not easy for a husband to address such a matter as this with anyone, let alone the man who has spent a night in his wife's bedchamber."

"But she is your sister."

"Perhaps," he said.

"Perhaps? What mean you by perhaps? Either she is your sister, or she is not."

"Well, that very much depends on you." A wicked grin spread like the weed across his face.

My mind hurried to fathom meaning in this, but I could not think quickly enough. "Explain yourself, Thomas," I charged him.

"I would be only too happy to oblige you." He paced towards us, slowly, with a predatory air. "The lady Dinah has a singular beauty, does she not? I have always admired it. But I am a generous man, only too happy to share that beauty with others. Some day, I may even give her to another. And this is where the conundrum becomes clear. If you were to aid me in my scheme, then Dinah may indeed be my sister, and I would be only too glad to give her to you. But if you were to refuse me, then Dinah would be my wife, and I am afraid that I could not prevent her debauchery from becoming known."

I understood well enough to see the mess I was in. "You aim to blackmail me by the use of Dinah, my own wife? What have you to say about this, my love?" I stared at her. Surely she was incapable of being party to such deceit.

"I am not thinking clearly, Gerry. These past six weeks, since the night you left, I have been unwell, for I am with child."

With child? The need for space overwhelmed my mind. I could not think inside this dome. What did she mean, with child?

"So you see, you cannot hide from this." Thomas cut through the mist that clouded my thoughts. "For either way, I have your brother in my hand. His reign cannot continue once your adultery is made known, and he will be forced to give his voice to another. Yet, if you speak against him, his voice will become yours. And not only that, but Dinah will become yours too. It is a simple decision, I think."

A fine trap they had set for me — for Joseph through me. How could I have been so foolish?

"Joseph would rather die than suffer shame," I said.

Thomas shrugged. "In which case, it really is a pity that he returned well." Thomas turned away.

But I could not let this be the end of it. I clutched my heart. "It is too painful to bear," I said. "Whatever I do, it will break his heart, and I could not live with myself for inflicting such pain upon my kin. There must be a way that I can spare my brother."

"It need not be painful," Thomas said.

"You have set this trap, Thomas. You know how to escape it. Is there a way to spare him?" I asked.

Thomas' crooked lips pursed as he basked in the moment, stretching the silence between us until he had soaked in it long enough. "Send Joseph to me," he said. "Allow me to share in a simple drink with him. That is not so much to ask, in order to gain a wife as beautiful as Dinah, is it?"

What new scheme was this? A simple drink had caught me in this snare. What manner of foul trickery did he plan for Joseph? But I refused to consider the answer. Here, he offered me a chance to save my brother. To spare him pain. I would not miss this chance for anything.

"What say you?" Thomas asked.

"If I agree, then the matter is settled? There is not another trap of yours waiting for me, is there, Thomas?"

"My dear Gerard, where is your trust? Should you agree, then I shall expect nothing more from you." He paused, as if that were an end to it. Yet, with Thomas, there was always more. "But," he continued, "to receive a prize as fair as Dinah, I am certain you would want to extend your gratitude. Her love is a priceless gift, is it not?"

"And what form would this gratitude take?"

"Let us just say that I would not expect you to repay my kindness until you hold the Voice of Maximus. And then, I think, you understand what you must do."

"The hunt? You wish for enough material to be printed so you can travel into the dark?" I asked.

"Precisely."

I pushed the menace of his threats out of my mind. Thomas could not be trusted, but a drink was not so much to ask, in return for keeping my poor brother's heart from breaking.

I hung my head before nodding. "I accept. He shall be with you soon enough."

"Good," Thomas said. "Until then, I shall leave you alone with your wife. You will have much to discuss with one another. Is that not so, dear sister?"

"Indeed it is so," Dinah said.

She rushed towards me, throwing her arms about my neck, and covering my face with kisses. I tried to block out the feelings surging through me. I tried to remember her part in this scheme, but with each kiss she bestowed upon me, the possibility of her deceit melted away, until I could do nothing but take her in my arms, and carry my wife into our bedchamber. For was she not the most beautiful thing in all the world?

VII

Joseph shook his head.

"A simple drink, brother. That is all he asks," I said.

With those words, I condemned him. Had I known it all along? Did I realize even then that he may never return from the dome of Thomas? Did he?

Joseph sighed. "Very well, brother. I will do as you suggest."

Did he see that I had betrayed him, the same way that I had betrayed him on Lake David? Was he forgiving me by walking to his death? It was too late to unspeak those few fateful words now. Once uttered, a mistake remains for all of time.

I watched him rise and leave the dome, despite the protestations of Beatrice. The door closed behind Joseph, and even then, I felt my heart break.

An hour passed and he did not return. Then a knock rattled the door. Jade answered.

The doctor stood in the threshold, downcast. "It is Joseph. We have pleaded with Juniper for healing, but in vain." Those words meant death, bringing tears to the eyes of all who heard them.

Beatrice erupted in a fit of wails, her whole body pierced by the news. She wept enough to fill the world with tears.

I grew numb. Had I been expecting it? Did I know then what I know now?

I replayed that scene in my mind over and over again, trying to convince myself that I had no share in it, or that my motives were pure. By my actions, I would save the city. I had spared my brother pain. But I had caused him pain enough by trusting that scheming Thomas and the beauty of his ward, my wife, the lady Dinah.

Every moment since then, I relived the memory. It was as though another person carried on with life around me, while I remained a prisoner to my decision. It was not me, but another man who left Joseph's dome and announced their marriage to Dinah. Another man who took the Seat of Maximus, with Dinah beside him, while the news of Joseph's death repeated in my head over and over.

The council gathered before me, and the crowds muttered as ever. But I did not hear their words, for all that I heard was the weeping of Beatrice, still plaguing my ears all these hours later.

I had tried to console her, but I feared Beatrice suspected me.

"Why did you bring him that message?" she had screamed. "Why did you invite him to the dome of Thomas?"

"I could not have prevented him from bathing in Lake David. It was the Elders who sent the cloud in the water. Is it so unreasonable to think that the lake poisoned him? You cannot blame me for what has happened," I pleaded, but with only half a heart.

"You think the Elders have taken him? I know better than that. I shall never forgive you, Gerard. You belong to Thomas now." She sent me away.

I had told her that I would return to take my place in the House of Maximus as its rightful heir. She told me to leave, but she knew she had no choice but to agree. Joseph's children were too young to take the title, and something must be done to halt the scourge.

Her tears had drifted from her chambers, which would soon become my chambers. Mine and Dinah's. Then the sound of Beatrice's weeping was replaced by the voice of Dinah, as my wife's whisper floated softly to my ears.

"Do you not think it time to call the meeting to order, my beloved?" Dinah urged me.

I nodded, staring blankly at the hundreds gathered before me. "My brothers, hear me," I shouted, and I held my hands aloft, the way Joseph had so many times before.

The din hushed at my voice. Thomas had kept his word. My voice fell on ears that were eager to listen.

"Joseph of the House of Maximus speaks no more," I said. "He is gone to Orbicon, to meet with Maximus. The lot now falls on me to bring an end to this scourge. And I know what must be done. Our finest minds must study the scourge so as to understand it. Were not the Elders students of the world? That same spirit must be ours. And so, I appeal to those of you who have the mind for it. Take this weed as an opportunity to follow in the footsteps of our forebears. If we understand it, only then will we defeat it."

A great stamping of feet rocked the walls of the dome.

Thomas approached, raising his voice above the others. "What of the many who sleep in the streets of the city's domes? What relief will you bring for them while we wait for this study of yours, Gerard, Son of Maximus?"

The crowd settled, just as Thomas knew they would. Just as we'd agreed. But I knew my part in this show.

From the Seat of Maximus, I loomed over the assembly. "I am not deaf to the plight of those who are without room among the city's domes, nor am I blind to the requests which have been made to the Seat of Maximus in times past. The scourge threatens our homes, and has taken many of them. But I am not without an answer for this."

"Let us hear it," Thomas said.

"We are too many here. Of that, there can only be one solution. Thomas of the House of Cassia, I charge you to lead an expedition into the unexplored regions of our world. To do so, you will need to print a great many things. So, Thomas, you must go to Cassia's Palace. If Cassia approves, then she will provide you a printer, her very own, which will not belong to the House of Maximus. She will bestow this printer upon her own House. With a printer of your own, all things are made possible. Any who would wish to join you, good Thomas, may do so. This is the decree." I looked up to the others. "What say you, my brothers?"

The whole assembly stamped in favor.

Thomas smiled.

Dinah leaned towards me, and placed her hand upon my arm, smiling warmly while she cradled our child within her.

A great rejoicing poured out with the prospect that we would end the scourge and save the city. But I could not rejoice.

"May the Elders smile upon us," rose the chanting of the crowd. I did not have faith enough to join them in the chant.

"The meeting is at an end," I decreed. The Voice of Maximus had spoken, but it was an empty voice, a voice that would mourn my brother Joseph as loudly as it had betrayed him.

"Come, let us away," whispered my wife with eyes aflame, and I could do nothing but obey.

As I stepped from the throne, I turned my head, and thought I caught a whisper of Joseph's shadow standing before the crowd. But when I blinked again, the shadow was no more.

My body left with Dinah that night, but my soul remained behind, at the foot of Joseph's vanished shadow, remembering him with outstretched hands, calming the crowd. I heard the echo of his voice imploring them to trust the Elders, to trust the prophecy, the same way they trusted him. The same way he had trusted me. Forever in my mind, my brother would rule this city, even while my body carried out Dinah's wishes. No beauty in all the world could take his presence from that great hall, nor silence his voice from ringing in my ears, the true Voice of Maximus.

Forgive me, brother. I had no choice. I did it for them. For the people. For your legacy, and the city you promised to protect.

I did it for you. Spare me your hatred.

Forgive me.

TYRELL

I

EARTH

My grandpa used to tell me this story. There's a man who wakes up one day without the faintest idea of anything. This man was about fifty years old, and there he was on the corner of a downtown street, with no memory of who he is, where he is, or anything else. That poor fool didn't even know his own name.

He takes a look around, sees the streets and the houses and the people, and he thinks, 'Say, I wonder if I live in one of these houses here.'

So he asks a lady for a room, and she says, 'Sure thing, mister, I'll give you a room.'

The next day, he's all ready for work and he says, 'I need a job to get some food.' So he sees a store on the corner and he asks the man running it for a job, and the man says, 'Sure thing, mister, I'll give you a job,' and before another minute passes by, he's got a broom in his hand and he's sweeping the floor.

The next evening, he gets his money, and he gets his food, and he gets home and cooks himself a beautiful meal. He sits down in his house and thinks, 'I've got it made. Life couldn't be any better.'

But when morning comes, this lady who's kinda familiar comes up to him and says, 'Geoffrey, what are you doing in a horrid little place like this?' At first, he thinks *who is this woman?* but she tells him that he should go with her, and he follows.

Well, she takes him to this expensive car and drives him to a mansion. There's all the bells and whistles in this place. Think of something – a diamond staircase, a crystal fountain, golden window panes — this guy's got it.

'What is this fancy place?' he asks the lady.

'This is where you live, Geoffrey. Don't you recognise it?'

Well, that man never went back to that little house he rented from that poor lady, and he never swept a broom in his life again. Why would he? What did he share in common with those vagrants back on that tiny street? Everybody struggled earning so much as a plate of food, while he had all the riches for himself. But you know what he used to wish for, late at night when he couldn't sleep? He wished that he could wake up one day knowing nothing at all, because true happiness is being free from where you came from. He had everything a man could dream of, and all the worry that came with it. Ain't nobody as happy as the man who lost his guilt.

My grandpa used to tell me that story before I'd go to sleep, and I always liked it. I liked the idea of living in a swanky mansion. That's why I remembered it. But grandpa would berate me and say I missed the point. He belonged to the last generation to believe that heritage could hold a person back. Things had changed. Maybe not for the better in a lot of ways, but when storms blew houses down almost every day, and earthquakes shook the

TV while you were watching your favorite box set, the upside was that everybody found themselves stuck in the same boat. There was no looking down on people just because of where they came from. But I guess that was hard for some people to imagine. I'd not been through what my grandparents went through. I ain't seen that life. I've just seen what's here, what little of it is left.

So it didn't come as a surprise to me when I was accepted to the Mars Mission at SpaceGen. But my grandpa — he was shocked.

"Look at this, our little Tyrell is gonna be a spaceman." He clapped his hands.

My parents didn't see me make it onto the Mars Mission. A hurricane when I was five took care of that. Death doesn't show partiality as to where a man's from. I guess the world just took a while to catch up. But I knew they'd be proud of me. I knew they'd want me to feel pride in myself.

SpaceGen. It was everything these days.

Everybody knew space travel was the only thing left if we were gonna survive. SpaceGen was the only place launching, and that meant revenue. They were huge. Most of those SpaceGen guys wound up with mansions like I'd never even heard in grandpa's stories. *That could be me one day*, I thought. I liked thinking that. Gave me drive. Got me where I needed to be — flight school with a physics degree, recruited for a scholarship program at the SpaceGen Institute for Education.

I remember walking through campus and thinking, *Tyrell, you've already made it.*

That was before the launch to Mars.

When they landed on the red planet, I'd just graduated and got put into the Astronaut Program, where I'd be trained to go up to Mars someday. I watched the first flight from my room on my broken down laptop. It all seemed to go smoothly enough. Landing gears fired, rockets ignited, parachutes blew. They'd done it. Touchdown. Watching the landing was like taking a glimpse into the future. We were finally gonna get off this planet, and have a chance at life somewhere that wasn't trying to kill us.

I was scheduled to leave on the ninth launch, sometime next year. But then, two days after the shuttle landed on Mars, the calendar for flights was postponed for no reason. I got messages coming through right from the top saying the future of the Mars Mission was in doubt. We'd seen them land, so what was the problem?

Mars suddenly seemed as far away as before we'd landed on it. Maybe even further.

That was when I got the call.

"Yeah, this is he," I said into the receiver.

"Good. Tyrell, can I call you Tyrell? We know that you were scheduled to launch to Mars on one of the canceled missions, but we'd like to meet with you to discuss another option. We're looking to put together a crew, and your name has been recommended to us by your tutors at SpaceGen. Would you be willing to meet with one of our representatives?"

I didn't need to think about it. "Where and when do you want to meet?"

We arranged the time and place. A little diner about a five minute drive away from HQ, the day after next. I called my grandpa and told him about it.

"Who called?" he said.

"I can't remember if they even said a name."

"Boy, you'd better be careful as to what they got to say. I remember scam artists back from when I was a young man. You just keep your head now. If I was you, I wouldn't go to that meeting. You hear me?"

"Sure thing, grandpa."

I knew he was warning me about something. He was looking out for me. But his worry only made me more curious.

The diner, day after next.

I'd be there.

II

The diner was a rundown little place, with grease dripping off the walls. The seats looked more like booths, and they'd drilled the tables to the floor. If a storm hit, the structure seemed too flimsy to hold up, but the windows were big, and I could have seen a storm coming from miles away. That's how I spotted the car in the distance.

It shimmered like it was brand new, not covered in the dust that gets everywhere out here. I watched it drive slowly across the road, kicking up a cloud of dust behind it, until it pulled outside the diner, and a short woman got out of the driver's side, alone. The weather was fine, but I didn't recognise the storm that was about to hit.

The lady walked into the diner, took a look around, strutted across to my table, and sat in my booth opposite me. She was maybe in her fifties, and she chewed gum. She had these big old sunglasses on, and when she took them off, her eyes were younger than her face.

"Fine morning," she said, between chewing her gum.

"Ma'am." I gave her a polite nod.

"Tyrell, I'm assuming?" she asked.

"That's me."

"Well, I figured it must be you. After all, we're the only ones here. Hardly rocket science."

"Rocket science ain't so hard," I said.

"No?"

"What's so difficult about it? Produce enough force and the rocket goes up. Simple, right?"

She laughed. "I'll take your word for it." Her t-shirt read 'Orbicon' beneath a thin jacket, and she pulled the sleeves up to expose her forearms. "How about we eat something? I always liked the waffles from this place."

She held her hand out, looking round for a waitress, who caught her eye and came to take our order. Her unwashed hair hung loose around her face – the same shade as the dust, except for the blue streaks she'd put through it – but she pushed it behind her ear as she ordered for me. Two plates of waffles with blueberries and cream.

"You think the cream's real?" I asked.

"I wouldn't like it as much if it was." She smiled a girlish grin again. "Why don't you tell me a bit about yourself while we're waiting?"

I couldn't see any harm in giving her the lowdown, so I told her all about the hurricane and my parents. About grandpa and his stories that made me want to do something for myself. My inspiration and my motivation. I told her everything I could think she'd want to know, and then the food came, and we tucked in.

"Delicious, am I wrong?" she slurred, with her mouth full.

I just nodded and smiled.

We didn't talk much as we ate. The food was too rich for me, but she finished hers, and then she finished mine. Where was she putting it all? Didn't seem like she had a scrap of fat on her. And yet, she powered her way through those plates the same way a rocket eats through fuel.

"Let me tell you a bit about me," she said at last, reclining happily enough. "My name is Halley. Me and my brother, Henry, took over a space exploration venture when our Mom died a few years back. We used to have the world's leading space exploration program. You ever heard of the space collider?"

I shook my head.

"It was long before you were born," she continued. "I'm talking about forty years ago. Anyway, we're the first and only organization to pioneer interstellar travel."

It twigged. "You're talking about gravitational wave propulsion?" I asked.

Her smile widened. "That's Orbicon."

"Wait. Orbicon?" That explained the t-shirt. "You're Halley *Rolands*!"

"Guilty as charged."

"Stars. Who hasn't heard of you? We learned about Orbicon on day one of the Astronaut Program back at university. Funny though. I ain't never heard the *grav-wave launch satellite* called a space collider before. Dr. Emily Rolands was the founder, right? She was once the greatest mind on the planet. And then, out of the blue, she just gave up on her work. What happened?"

It was the first time Halley stopped smiling. "Let's just say that after the launch of the Icarus One, Mum didn't want to put anyone else at risk. We never received a transmission from Trappist-1E — the planet we sent those people to, thirty-nine lightyears away. All we got was this weird static with blips and background radiation and a whole bunch of cosmic junk. We assumed the worst. So Mum decided to shut the program down and channel all of our energies into supporting the Mars Mission, and SpaceGen. Well, there's been a hitch at SpaceGen since they landed on Mars, something to do with time displacement and orbital locking. And now, my brother and I think it's about time we took another look at interstellar options."

"And that's why you wanted to see me?" I guessed.

She smiled wider. "I like you, Tyrell. You're sharp. So I'm not going to lie to you. I'm putting together a team of astronauts to send back to Trappist-1E. SpaceGen are fully supporting us. For the sake of the Mars Mission, we need to measure how people interact with an orbit that is less than Earth's, rather than one that's greater, like Mars. It's dangerous. The one time we tried this forty years ago, we never found out what happened to those people. Now we want to try again. And I'd like you to be on the crew."

Waffles churned in my stomach. Made it hard to think. "Why do we need to measure life on a planet with a lesser orbit?" I asked.

"You ever heard of 'Rolands theory of the orbital constant'?"

"Course I have."

"We always thought its application would make Mars the most viable option when it came to the future. But the astronauts on Mars aren't moving and interacting with spacetime in the way we predicted. They're moving almost twice as slowly as we are. We think it's an effect of the orbital constant. That's why we need to see what effect being on Trappist-1E has on people. Otherwise, we're likely never to leave Earth. And you know what that means?"

She picked up a spoon and scooped up the cream that had melted into the blueberries, sipping the liquid. She was talking about the future of humankind in between sips of synthetic cream. There was nothing quite as distracting as someone who doesn't seem stirred when they should be.

"So, let me get this straight," I said. "You want me to travel thirty-nine lightyears away on a ship that you can't say for sure won't kill me, to a planet where you don't know what will happen if I get there, all so that you can test a theory?"

She licked her lips. "You really should try this." She pointed at the plate with her spoon.

"What's in it for me?" I asked.

"Well, it tastes good for a start."

"No, not the waffles. I mean the mission. What do I get out of it?"

"What is it you want? A mansion? A fancy car? Fame? Money? You name it. But if you can't think of a better reason to do it than saving the human race from extinction, then do it for the waffles. We'll be sending you with plenty of waffle mix, blueberries, and cream."

I liked her honesty. I liked the idea of doing something important. But I couldn't help feeling like she was the lady in grandpa's story. 'Geoffrey, what are you doing in a horrid little place like this?' She was offering me another life, the implications of which I might live to regret. But I couldn't exactly *not* go with her. What she was proposing was crazy, just like the blue streaks in her hair, but she'd got me hooked, and it wasn't any less crazy than staying on Earth. Through the window, clouds loomed in the distance. They were storm clouds.

"Okay. I'm interested. On one condition."

"Name it," she said.

"I want to be the captain."

She laughed. "Eat up, Tyrell. We've got work to do."

III

How do you train to travel faster than light? Sounds like the start of a joke, right? There ain't a punch-line. There's no real answer. But that's the question we all asked ourselves once we'd got set up at Orbicon HQ.

"I think the other crew died," Janice, the pilot said. "I think their particles never realigned and they're still in millions of tiny pieces traveling so fast through space we can't see them." She flicked switches in the cockpit, turning the buttons from red to green.

"Don't be so morbid, Janice," Jamie said. Always the engineer, even now his eyes inspected the bolts fastening the craft together while his fingers double-checked his harness. "I don't wanna think about the odds of us flying through space forever in tiny pieces."

"Why not? It's not like it'll hurt or anything."

"You don't know that."

"Alright, you two," Barbara interrupted. "Settle down. There's no need to speculate on what happened to the other crew. We haven't got any data to extrapolate a hypothesis." Barbara was the Australian doctor, and the self-appointed mother of the crew.

"We do have data," Janice insisted. "The data is that they disappeared. So the logical conclusion—"

"You heard the doctor, Janice," I said at last. I couldn't stand watching the stomachs of the rest of them churn. Carlos, the biologist, had almost turned green. He'd have liked the color. It would have reminded him of the cytoplasm of some tropical leaf. "Now let's get this started." I thumbed at the comm-switch. "We are a go for launch," I said into the microphone.

"Roger that. Beginning matter collision in T-minus one minute." The voice crackled, but we all heard it.

Janice was about to start up again, but I defused her with a look.

"10 . . . 9 . . . 8 . . ." The countdown reached zero, and then we accelerated so fast that I lost my breath. The force of the motion against my suit was so powerful, I couldn't move. I sat pinned to my seat, shaking, wondering how long it would last before I blacked out.

"Yahoo!" shouted Sadie, the mathematician.

"I think I'm gonna be sick," Carlos screamed.

"Just hold on," I yelled. Then we started slowing down, and the giant crane that held our training cockpit spun out until it stopped. "Everyone okay?"

"Let's do that again!" Sadie yelped.

"Carlos, you good?"

"Just get me off this thing." His face washed over a sickly pale.

"Great job, people," a voice said over the tannoy.

Janice shrugged. "We'll be going a lot faster than that when our cells divide into tiny pieces and—"

"Pack it in, Janice," Barbara snapped as we climbed out of the seats. We walked back through the corridor into the sim-suite, where all the other mechanisms simulating our flight were kept.

But Janice was right. We weren't even close to the speed we'd be traveling on the crest of the gravitational wave.

"Same time tomorrow?" I asked, and everyone nodded.

I went straight to the observation room, where the doctors had been monitoring us. Henry Rolands peered over their shoulders.

"Henry, can we talk?"

He smiled at me, the wrinkles in his face transforming with his grin. "Of course, Tyrell. Gentlemen, if you'll excuse us."

The doctors stood and left the room until it was just the two of us.

"What's on your mind, Captain?" he asked.

"It's Janice, sir. I know I'm gonna have to speak with her about spooking the crew, but I ain't got the heart to. She's just scared."

He took a seat in one of the chairs. "You asked to be captain of this crew, Tyrell. That means making the big calls. If you haven't got the heart to tell Janice to button her mouth, then how will you cope when you have to make a real decision?"

"Sir?"

"Let's play out a scenario. You land, but there's an accident. Janice is stuck, pinned behind a console. If you move her, the communications array will explode, which means your mission fails. No communications array, no data, no point in you even being there. We've spent all of this time and money developing a brand new system of communications so that we can actually receive data this time, and if you move her, it's up in smoke. But if you don't move her, she'll die slowly and you'll have to listen and watch. What do you do?" He looked at me and smiled. He'd said it all through his smiling teeth.

"I don't see how that's relevant, sir."

"You don't? Listen, I'm not going to push you, Tyrell. Halley thinks you've got what it takes, and I trust my sister's judgment. But let's get this straight. You handle Janice, and it shows me you've got heart, so that when the time comes, you'll do the right thing. You catch my meaning?"

I nodded. "I'll speak to her right away."

"Good. Nice numbers, by the way. You're handling the G-force a lot better with each simulation."

"Thank you, sir."

"Same time tomorrow?"

"Goodnight, sir."

I left, climbing down to the changing rooms where the others were getting out of their flight suits, and I took Janice to one side.

"Listen, after this, let's grab a beer, you and me?" I said.

"Is that an order?"

"Only if you tell me you're busy."

"Yes, sir." She saluted.

***

Fifteen minutes later, Janice and I sat at a bar in the next building on the complex. We sipped our drinks in silence for a little while, and then she broke it.

"I know what you wanted to see me about Ty," she said. "I'll stop with the doom-mongering."

"We're all scared, Jan." I glugged the rest of the bottle.

"Even you?" she asked.

I held up my empty. "This is good stuff, isn't it?"

"Yeah, it's got a kick," she admitted.

"Maybe we shouldn't be doing those simulations, and we should be knocking this stuff back instead. You never know, faster-than-light travel might end up being more like ten of these than anything else."

"I'll drink to that." She knocked back the rest of hers and we clinked bottles.

I called the others and got them to join us. One of the perks of being Captain — I never had to drink alone.

Barbara was the last to arrive. "What's going on?" Her Aussie accent was thicker than usual. Although, that could have been the beer playing tricks on my ears.

"We're training for our flight," I said. "Now get this down your throat, you're already lightyears behind."

The following morning, the simulation was more raw and intense than ever. Not even daredevil Sadie saw the fun side of it. We stumbled out of the cockpit and almost collapsed straight away. Still, the real thing couldn't be any worse than this.

"Thanks, Captain," they all chimed, blaming me for our sorry state.

"Tyrell," Henry shouted from the doorway to the observation room, and I ran across to join him.

"Sir?"

"Good job, Captain," he said. "Janice never uttered so much as a peep. You chose the communications equipment after all." He smiled, and closed the door behind him.

I called my grandpa that night.

"So boy, how are you training for faster-than-light travel?" he eventually got round to asking.

"We say nothing, and drink beer," I said. It was as good an answer as any.

IV

No return. One way trip. Last goodbyes. I could call it what I wanted, but there was no way to put a label on what it felt like to know I'd never again see green grass, blue sky, birds, trees, a sunset.

The day we left Earth, I'd made peace with leaving, but I couldn't bring myself to say goodbye. A little bit of me still clung to the thought of coming back some day, though my head insisted it was impossible.

The rocket took us out of Earth's atmosphere and broke into pieces as we burnt out the engines' fuel. Our cockpit docked with the space collider as planned. Seeing the collider for the first time was like coming across some ancient tomb inside the pyramids and finding it was set up with Wifi. It resembled a museum piece as it drifted in space. I guessed technology had progressed these past forty years, so that everything looked different than it used to. But once we were on board, it had everything we needed.

My quarters were big compared to my room back at HQ. I could stream phone calls, so I talked a lot with grandpa.

"I wanna tell you this story," he said, the night before the launch was planned. "It's about this kid. Young, good-looking. He was always too clever for his own good. And then one day, the King told him that he'd been chosen to travel to a place miles away from anywhere else. So the kid told his folks about it, and his folks said, 'Boy, you're making a mistake.' Every day before he left, this kid would go to his folks and they would tell him, 'Boy, you're making a mistake.' But they couldn't change the King's mind, nor the kid's mind for that matter. And after the kid went away, his folks realized that he hadn't made no mistake, but they had. You see, they should have told him how proud they were of him. They should have told him to mind himself when he got there. And they should have told him that, no matter what anybody thinks, if he stays true to himself, well, it don't matter where he is. You hear me, boy?"

It was the last story he ever told me.

***

Launch day came too soon, and before I knew where I was, Earth hung below me like a tiny marble, and stretching out before me was the emptiness of space.

"I think the other crew survived just fine," Janice said to everyone. "They didn't all split apart into tiny atoms never to reassemble. It was fine."

"That's the spirit, Jan." Barbara winked.

"Everybody ready?" I asked.

"Let's get going before Carlos gets too sick," Jamie said.

"I can't wait for this." Sadie gripped her harness like a kid on a rollercoaster.

"Here goes nothing." I flicked the switch. "Mission control, this is Icarus Two. We are a go for launch. Repeat, we are a go for launch." I'd wanted to call the ship *Jonah*, after my grandpa. But I guess I could live with *Icarus Two*, for the sake of tradition.

"Roger that, Icarus Two. Matter collision in T-minus one minute."

That must have been the longest minute of my life. I had Janice next to me, closing her eyes, sweat staining her suit. Then I turned to the rest of my crew. They were all a little nervous, except for Sadie, who was about to pop with excitement. Then I turned back and looked ahead into the stars until the voice came through the speakers, counting down from Ten.

3 . . .2 . . . 1, and then everything went dark.

I remembered what it felt like to be in that simulation after our night of beers. I hadn't thought that anything could have been worse than that. Well, I was wrong.

I'd been in darkness before. Most darkness was dead, stale. When the lights went out, everything was still there. Darkness ain't got no power. But some kinds of darkness were alive. The kind that swallowed a person, chewed them up, and spat them back out. That kind of darkness was a creature — a beast I stared in the face of, and somehow survived.

First thing that returned when we reached the other side was light. Just a blur of light. That sweet, comforting blink, reminding me that I was still breathing. My head pounded so hard, it was a migraine and a hangover all at once. But worse than the pain was the numbness. I couldn't feel anything, but then everything was heavy, and everywhere was pounding. It was a jolt, but not a jolt that took us forwards, or even slowed us down. We were moving forwards and backwards at the same time, but we weren't moving at all. I could have drank ten beers and then got into a simulator that threw me into a spin, taking me from zero to five hundred in the space of ten seconds, and still had to multiply that feeling by a factor of 12,000 before I'd got some idea of what it felt like to open my eyes thirty-nine lightyears from home.

"Everyone alright?" I asked.

"Fine," Carlos said without even hesitating.

"I think I'm gonna die," Sadie groaned.

"We're in one piece. I don't believe it!" Jan's eyes sparkled like two glasses of soda.

Barbara gripped her head. "Not so loud, Jan."

"Where are we?" Jamie asked.

I looked out the window at the star in front of us. Dim and red. They'd told us it was a dwarf star, so I assumed it'd be small, but from where I looked, it was huge. I ain't never seen anything like it. Circling in an orbit around it, seven planets hung in the sky. Some were on one side of the sun, and others on its far side, but the whole thing fit together nicely, like the inside of a watch.

"We're looking at Trappist-1," I said.

"Wow. It's beautiful." Jan flipped the shield of her helmet and peered at it through an unfiltered visor.

"I can't open my eyes yet," Sadie complained.

Barbara reached over to her. "Are you alright?"

"Yeah, I'm just spinning a little. What does it look like?"

"It's amazing, Sadie," Jan started. "There's this huge ball of flaming red, and then there's all these jewels around it. It's like the prettiest dart board you've ever seen. Permission to take us into orbit of Trappist-1E?"

"All in good time, Jan. Let's give Sadie a chance to come around, and then we'll take the Icarus down."

I got on the radio to Mission Control and told them we'd arrived safely in the orbit of the Trappist-1 sun. My first report. No response.

A few minutes later, we made our approach. Thrusters fired, maneuvering us in increments. Progress was slow. The large sails which had carried us here billowed like the frills of a can-can skirt, totally useless to us now, as we'd ridden the gravitational wave as close as we were going to get to our new exoplanet.

The nearer we drew to Trappist-1E, the more we saw of it, and the more we saw, the more we were rendered speechless.

"Is that what I think it is?" Jan finally asked.

I couldn't believe my eyes.

Along the ridge where light met dark, we'd expected to see a barren planet made up of rock and some pools of water, if we were fortunate. But as we approached the planet, a huge city sprawled out across the surface. Buildings that looked like small domes stretched for miles across the ridge, shadows through the soft covering of mist.

Fragments of rock orbited the planet, too small to be moons, but still pretty huge. Tracing a path through them would be dangerous, so I took the throttle, and eased up until Jan could plot a course.

We stared at the city below. Parts of the domes were broken down, like they'd decayed, and other parts were newer. The city kept going as far as we could see into the distance, and we circled above the planet, spinning around it, to spy out a landing spot.

On the far side of Trappist-1E, a large building poked through the mist, different to the others, surrounded in a cloud of vapor. It guarded a flat plateau, and there was enough space around it for a good landing.

Jan plotted a safe course through the hurtling rocks trapped in the planet's atmosphere, and we hit the thrusters to start our approach. The force pinned us to our seats, but it passed after the initial burst, and every one of us leaned forwards, perched as close to the screen as we could get.

About a minute later, we broke the atmosphere and touched down on the surface opposite the large building, which had about a hundred chimneys. Clouds of smoke rose into the air. The chimneys were all connected by a large system of pipes and walkways, and then, from this strange factory, people rushed towards our ship.

People. Actual people.

They wore robes, but they looked human.

Impossible.

What were we seeing? It couldn't be real. If I rubbed my eyes, it would probably all disappear.

The people, six of them, stopped a little distance away, and fell down on their faces, bowing before the ship.

"Is this real?" Barbara said.

"You see them too?" I asked.

She nodded.

"Come on." I disengaged the engines and turned to my crew. "Let's go see if this is all some weird hallucination."

The others sat motionless, transfixed by the sight, all except for Barbara. She joined me as we unclipped our belts and stood, the weight of gravity compounded by the ridiculous layers of our suits.

I climbed the ladder from the cockpit down to the ground, stepping onto another world for the first time. I'd expected this moment to be special, for my heart to race and the impact strike me as significant. But instead, it reminded me more of the feeling I got after trying to solve complex equations after a few beers. Barbara followed me to the ground. She might as well have blindfolded me and spun me in circles. It probably would have counteracted the disorientation.

Carlos' voice filtered through our helmets. "Carlos to Tyrell," he said.

"I'm listening, Carlos. What is it?"

"I've just done a reading of the atmospheric gasses, and you'll never believe it, but you can take your helmet off."

"What?"

"You heard me. You can take your helmet off. I don't know how, but the atmosphere is made up of Earth gasses. It's breathable, non-toxic."

I shook my head. As if things weren't weird enough. "Have you confirmed the readings?" I asked.

"Twice."

I turned to Barbara. "What do you think?"

"The suit's heavy," she said.

I shrugged. "I'm gonna take it off and see what happens."

I unclipped my helmet and removed the clasps on my suit, stepping into the hot air. The radiant red sun touched my skin for the first time. It was like summer on Earth, only without the tornadoes.

The six people who'd emerged from the building all remained facing the ground. Their robes covered them, for the most part. I'd trained to encounter hostile aliens, but not modest ones. There ain't a manual for 'how to approach a modest alien.'

We traced a path towards them.

"Greetings," I called out. Not sure why. Could have been manners. Instinct. I had no reason to expect them to understand me.

One of them lifted their head and bowed. "They have come," he said.

"The Elders have returned," another piped up, and then they all yammered over one another, throwing their arms up and down as they bowed to the floor.

"They have heard our cries and sent relief," one called above the others. "Do not look at them, for we are not worthy."

They spoke our language perfectly. Leaving Earth had been surreal, but this was something else.

"Are they human?" I asked Barbara.

"Looks it from here," she replied.

I turned to them while they stayed prostrated in a heap, like slaves bowing before their masters. "You have no need to bow before us, and you're free to look me in the eye. My name is Tyrell. What's your name, and where are we?"

I stopped only a few feet from the nearest man, who tentatively raised his head, with tears in his eyes. "Thank Maximus for sending you, Tyrell. My name is Cobalt of the House of Cassia, and you are just in time."

"Just in time for what?" I asked.

He wiped the tear stains from his cheeks. "To save us. That is why you have come, is it not?"

V

I signaled to the others in the cockpit to join us, and we waited for them to clamber down. Once we were all together, we followed Cobalt through the doors beneath the nearest chimney, out of the sunlight.

We entered a dark corridor and the air was much cooler. The sterility of the hall reminded me of hospitals back on Earth. Then we entered a larger room, filled with switches and monitors floor to ceiling.

"What is this place?" I asked.

"This is the control center," Cobalt said.

"The control center for what?"

"For the atmospheric conditioning plant, of course."

I glanced across the faces of my crew, and they were as clueless as I was.

"Any ideas?" I asked. They all shrugged.

Cobalt looked afraid, as if he'd upset us somehow. "Forgive my ignorance," he said. "Have I answered poorly?"

"No, no, Cobalt. Not at all. But I think it's us who are ignorant. What is an atmospheric conditioning plant?"

"Ah, a test from the Elders. I shall not fail." He smiled, relieved. "The plant is made up of 117 chimneys that emit gasses into the atmosphere so as to fill it with breathable air. This means that any who wish to go outside no longer require use of their chalice of inhalation. Of course, we all still carry one, to honor the memory of Cassia, and in case anything were to happen to the plant." He took his necklace in hand. It looked like it held an inhaler on the end of it. "But for over a hundred cycles, these chimneys have breathed life into the surface of the world. We monitor the chimneys from here, adjusting the levels of the gasses they produce by these switches. Have I answered well?"

"You mean, the atmosphere of this planet is artificially controlled from here?" Carlos asked.

"Precisely so."

"Amazing." Carlos gawped. "But what effect is there on atmospheric pressure, or the greenhouse effect?"

Cobalt smiled. "Indeed, there can be no doubt of it. You are from Orbicon, the Realm of the Elders, and you have the eyes of Harold the Seer. Since the chimneys were installed, there have been changes on the planet's surface. We did not predict them. Is that why you chose to come here first, rather than the City of Maximus?" He looked so hopeful.

"Is that why you need saving?" I asked. "Because of these chimneys?"

"By the Elders, no. The impact of atmospheric conditioning is slight by comparison."

"Comparison to what?"

"Do you mean to test me again?" he asked.

"It's no test, Cobalt. We're just trying to understand what's happened here — where we are, and what this place is. We come from far away and weren't expecting to find anything here."

"Yes, you come from Orbicon. No-one knows where it is, but we know it is beyond our reach. Are you pleased with what you have found?"

There it was again. Orbicon. How in all the stars did he know that name unless he knew of Earth? Dr. Rolands had never mentioned anything like this in all her theories. Was it possible she could've got it wrong?

No.

That would be crazy to even think. Orbital locking was sound. It had to be.

Cobalt frowned in worry. I'd taken too long to answer. What was his question? Was I pleased with what I'd found?

"I don't know yet," I said. "It's all so much to take in."

"Then let me show you the City of Maximus." He bowed to each of us as he said it. "The city will surely please you."

"Sure. Yeah. Take us to the city." What else was I supposed to do? Refuse?

He relayed orders to the others who had come out to meet us, and I gathered the crew in a huddle.

"What do you make of it?" I asked.

"Lost for words, Ty. What is all this?" Barbara said.

"It's unbelievable." Carlos gasped, trying to take everything in.

"I say we try and make contact with whoever's in charge, and get some answers," Jamie suggested.

"Agreed," I said, and then Cobalt joined us.

"Follow me, and I will show you the way to the City of Maximus." He led us deeper into the atmospheric conditioning plant, through dark corridors. Eventually, we came to a platform and a shuttle that looked like a train carriage, which we boarded. Once inside, the doors closed automatically. We shot off through a tunnel until we emerged on the other side, on the planet's surface again.

Chimneys and domes stretched in all directions as far as the horizon, glistening red in the light of the sun.

This was crazy. Maybe we hadn't survived the thrust of the gravity wave? Perhaps the planet we stood on was no more than a hallucination we shared? Anything would make more sense than the other explanation — the one which throbbed behind my eyes — that this was somehow real.

Still, Orbicon hadn't trained us to just sit around and shake our heads when we saw something we didn't understand. We were here to save a planet, not question whether another world was even real.

"I know that there are many who deny the prophecy," Cobalt said. "But I want you to know that I have always been a believer." He placed a hand on his heart.

"Believer?" I asked.

"Yes. I have always believed the legends, despite the arguments of our higher minds."

"What legends?"

"The legends of the Elders, of course. The stories of Maximus and Cassia, Juniper, Harold, and the Lady Sonja. Ever since the reforms of Gerard the Wise, many lost their trust in the Elders, but I was never one of them."

"Gerard the Wise?" Sadie giggled. I shot her a look. Yes, it sounded odd, but was it any more strange than the rest of it?

"Yes, he was the leader of the reformation. Over two hundred years ago. The first to seek truth in the world around us, and his followers have done wonderful things. Without them, we would never have built the atmospheric conditioning plant, or the City of Maximus. But there are some who blame the followers of Gerard for the sorry state we are in."

"What do you mean by that?"

The carriage lurched to a stop and I was thrown across the floor, landing in Sadie's lap.

"Ahoy, Captain," she laughed.

"Sorry, Sadie." I picked myself up.

"Stay down, Tyrell," Cobalt warned. "A tremor comes."

It was too late. The tremor hit and the whole carriage shook hard. So hard, I landed right back where I'd fallen. The train shuddered with a terrifying force, and it went on for at least five minutes. We had no control over where we fell. I tried to grab hold of something, anything, but all I could find were Sadie's ankles. She held onto a seat, and I don't think she minded. I don't think she even noticed.

But eventually it passed, and the shaking stopped. The carriage sped off again in the direction we were headed as if nothing had happened.

I turned to Cobalt. "What was that?"

"It is a tremor. We have learnt to detect them so that we can prepare before they hit."

"What causes them?" Jamie asked.

"It is our proximity to Trappist-1F — the next planet in our system. The planets pass very closely, and the gravitational forces cause shakes. They were never a problem when the surface of the world was solid, unbroken. There was no room for disturbance, until the failed hunt of Thomas."

"What do you mean?"

Cobalt slumped as his cheeks reddened. "Gerard the Wise was a visionary, but he favored his wife's brother —

Thomas of the House of Cassia. Gerard granted him permission to hunt in the darkest tropics of the world. Thomas took a printer from Cassia's palace on Lake David, and concocted all manner of terrible weaponry, which he unleashed upon the surface, blowing it to pieces. He was so convinced that creatures hid below the surface, below the ice on the dark side of the world. But there were no creatures, and all that he achieved was to crack the rock."

"That's awful," Jamie said.

"Truly," Cobalt continued through a sigh. "Thomas tried to return, but Gerard's wife, Dinah, was killed in one of the first tremors – an act he could not forgive. So our people separated – most remained among us here, but others followed Thomas into the darkness. The nothingness. And to hunters, nothingness is the greatest threat of all, for without prey, a hunter turns to madness. And so it was. Thomas' descendants bred, spreading across the dark zone. Those who venture to the light still raid us from time to time on our borders. Look, you can see their devastation for yourself."

He pointed towards a dome that was breaking apart, half-decayed in the distance.

"Many lived there at one time," Cobalt mourned. "But not so now. Still, Thomas' horde will never take the City of Maximus."

"So, ever since the surface was cracked, you've been experiencing the tremors?" I asked.

"Yes. But I believe that we are as much to blame as Thomas."

"Go on," I prompted.

"We tried to fashion domes from stone. We drilled to extract the stone, but in the drilling, some of it broke away. You see it above you, drifting in the sky, casting its shadow as it spins above us. We were not deterred until the tremors worsened, and then we abandoned the project."

I craned my neck for a view through the window, and glanced up to where the field of asteroids circled the planet like clouds of rock. "Do you mean to tell me that those things in orbit are fragments of the planet?"

"Yes. The many moons are the injuries our world has sustained under the banner of understanding and progress."

"And is it these tremors that you need saving from?"

The carriage slowed and the door opened. The terrain ahead was rocky, climbing and disappearing all of a sudden.

"Come," Cobalt said. "We must travel on foot across the wilderness of rock." We left the shuttle to clamber across the peaks and troughs that stretched in stone for miles ahead.

Every answer Cobalt gave seemed to throw up two more questions. But maybe I'd get some real answers when we reached the city. Or maybe I'd wake up and find myself still in Earth's orbit, with mission control telling me something went wrong. Because something was very wrong here.

There were people on this exoplanet. *People!* I wasn't an ambassador. We were scientists, being led to a city on an alien world. And here I was, pondering the answers it might hold, when I should have been worried about the impression we made. Interstellar war, and all that kind of stuff.

Where were Henry's pop quiz no-win-scenario hypotheticals when I needed them? Back on Earth — that's where. Fat load of use they did us now.

Could I trust this Cobalt? If what he was saying turned out to be true, then that meant Dr. Rolands was wrong. Which was the first impossibility. But then again, how was any of this possible if she was right? None of this should exist. And yet . . .

No. I needed proof. The fate of at least one world was riding on us, and I wasn't about to let the first person we ran into send me for a loop. Not when decades of research by minds greater than my own rang like an alarm bell in my brain.

Something was unreal. And before I could say for certain what it was, I'd need concrete evidence. Not just a pretty story. Something solid to grasp hold of instead of simply questions.

In the distance, beyond the chasms and cliffs, a large dome rose, shimmering in the sunlight with a dozen smaller domes that surrounded it on all sides. Even from here, it loomed through the faint vapor of mist which made everything look transient. It had to be the City of Maximus. The city of answers.

Or so I hoped.

VI

I had no idea how long we climbed for. Cobalt didn't seem to be in any rush. He kept looking over his shoulder at us with an awestruck expression, as if we were movie stars.

It made my skin crawl worse than if a colony of mites had been stuck in my suit. But the others didn't seem to notice. We were all as confused as one another, and it showed on our faces. I hoped I didn't look as puzzled as they did.

In between the rocks, water pooled where the mist had condensed. I'd read about spelunking on an old website in my school library, from before the Earth's downturn, and the pictures uploaded with the article were eerily similar to these crevices and pools. Hardly what I'd expected from my first day on an alien planet. But there was nothing really alien about it. The people looked like us. The technology was like ours. Even the air was sweet to breathe.

Yet another riddle to add to the mix.

Jamie, our engineer, hung back and tapped me on the shoulder. "Hey, Ty. I've been studying the look of those domes we're heading for. I thought they looked familiar, but I didn't realize it until we got a little closer."

"Familiar? You mean you've seen them before?"

"We've all seen them before. Take a closer look at the way the panels slot together. You see the chrysalis of hexagons?"

My mouth gaped. "You're right."

"You see it?"

"I see it."

"What do you think it means?" he asked.

I didn't know, but it spooked me. I ain't one to get spooked easy, but seeing the solar panels slotted together in exactly the same way the Icarus Two was designed — how it was built to fold apart — sent a chill through me, even in the hot sun.

Next it was Barbara who slowed her walk to speak with me.

"I've been watching how Cobalt moves across these rocks," she said. "I can't figure it, Ty. He's an alien, but he moves just the same as we do. Every bone. Every sinew. I can't see a single thing about him that would suggest in his physiology that he's anything except a human being."

Even when he wasn't talking, our new guide was raising questions we couldn't answer. Not without turning our backs on the person who founded Orbicon in the first place. The one whose work had got us here.

But if they *were* humans, what did that mean for the rest of her theories? If thirty years were six months here, like we expected, then how could a colony sustain itself? How could it continue?

And yet, there had to be a way, because here it was.

On the far side of the 'wilderness,' as Cobalt had called it, another carriage sat on tracks, leading straight out to the dome in the distance. Cobalt didn't need to tell us to board. We all did by instinct, and then the doors closed and the shuttle sped off at an amazing speed.

The familiarity of everything around us bred uneasiness. One too many eyebrows raised as cautious glances bounced back and forth between us. I needed answers, and fast. We all did.

"Cobalt, when we arrive at the city, do you have a leader that we can meet with?" I asked.

"Of course. The heir to the Seat of Maximus."

"Will you arrange a meeting with them?"

"I shall do as you command." He bowed. "Although, when the people see you, I am not sure that we shall be able to reach the heir with ease."

"What do you mean?"

"Rumors spread across a world faster than light. If we arrive at the city and news of your arrival has beaten us to the dome, then every soul on Trappist will be waiting for us."

"Including this . . . heir?"

"Indeed."

Maybe *they* could give me some answers? Cobalt remained bowed, and I feared he wouldn't ever raise his head again.

"Thank you, Cobalt," I said.

He recoiled, glancing humbly at the floor.

The others watched, grinning. Sadie even did a curtsy at me, to join in with his deference, and they all giggled. All apart from Jan. I'd never seen her so quiet.

"Is everyone alright after the hike?" I asked.

"I don't like us being so far away from the ship," Jan said.

Despite the risks, how could I have left anyone behind? No way was I splitting us up. And the first rule of contact stated to agree to any offer of guidance. This wasn't exactly our world, was it? Or . . . no. I ain't starting down that rabbit hole until I'm sure there's a rabbit to begin with.

"Classic Jan. Always thinking the worst," Barbara said, and it put everyone at ease. Everyone but me.

"Take me to your leader," Sadie joked in a robotic voice.

The rest of them laughed.

"As you wish," Cobalt replied, which made Sadie laugh all the more.

The city we approached was impossibly huge. The dome must have been three or four hundred stories tall, at least, and miles wide. I'd hate to guess — maybe between fifteen and twenty Earth miles. And then there were all the other smaller domes adjacent to it, connected to one another. The surface was made entirely of solar panels, but they moved, slowly rotating all the time.

We left the carriage, and once the doors closed, it sped back off in the direction from where it had come. There was another carriage at this end, which I assumed worked the same, taking people away from the city before returning of its own volition.

Nobody stood waiting to meet us. No crowds. No clamor or frenzy.

At least something went right.

Cobalt led us to the entranceway, a small dome that didn't rotate like the rest of the colossal structure it was attached to. Through the doors, we stepped into darkness. Beyond the lobby, our eyes adjusted to the absence of the red sun.

"It is night in the city, but you can stay with me in my dome until first light," Cobalt offered.

"It would be better for us to speak with your leader as soon as possible," I said.

"Of course, Tyrell. I shall make haste." He guided us through the streets, lit by dim bulbs that stretched so high into the vast chamber, they might as well have been stars. We didn't have time to take everything in. It was too massive, and I didn't dare move my eyes off Cobalt, in case we should lose him, no matter how much I wanted to look around and observe this new city.

He made his way through the dome's stone-clad streets until he approached a doorway on the edge of the structure. We stood behind him while he knocked. People whispered, and a few gathered around where we stood, their eyes fixed on us.

"Who are they? Could it really be?"

Then one from the crowd raised their hands and called out, "That light in the sky was no asteroid! It is them! They have returned. We are saved!"

I turned around, and the crowd hushed in awe before they chanted, "Hail, Orbicon!" over and over.

Hands rushed at us as tens of people suddenly swarmed into hundreds.

Cobalt leaped in front of us and pushed us back towards the doorway. We grouped together as one, our bodies pressing against one another.

"I didn't realize you'd be so popular on an alien world, Captain." Sadie leaned to my ear. "I honestly think you could take your pick from any of the ladies, sir. Even the pretty ones." She chuckled. Her laughter grounded us. Made us feel human.

Then the door Cobalt had been banging on suddenly opened.

"State your business with the House of Maximus," a voice barked from its far side. I barely heard it over the noise of the crowd.

But Barbara was closest, and I heard her well enough as she shouted from my side. "Let us in!"

"State your business," the voice repeated.

Cobalt stepped back and called out over us. "It is Cobalt of the House of Cassia, and I bring news. The prophecy is true. The Elders have come. They seek an audience before the Seat of Maximus."

"Speak you truth?" the voice replied.

"I would not defile the Laws of Juniper and speak lies."

"Then enter, you and the Elders with you."

The door slid open and we fell into the entrance, leaving the madness of the streets. The interior was luxurious. I'd never seen anything so fancy. There was comfort wherever you looked, and we were shown into a room with furniture covered in the softest fabrics I'd ever felt.

A minute later, a man entered the room with robes loosely fastened around him. He wore a medallion around his neck, different to Cobalt's 'chalice of inhalation.'

"Are they of the sky?" the man asked Cobalt.

"With my eyes I saw it."

The man smiled in relief. "Cobalt, you may leave. I wish to speak with the Elders alone."

"If it pleases them," Cobalt said.

"It pleases me." The man crossed his arms.

Cobalt looked across at me, and I nodded. He scurried away and left us alone with this man.

"I am Tyrell," I said.

"And I am Onyx of the House of Maximus," he replied.

"We come in peace." I'd always wanted to say that, but I felt silly saying it now, and the rest of the crew smiled at hearing it.

"Of that I have no doubt," Onyx said. "Tell me, have you heard our petitions to Orbicon for aid, or have you always known you would come in our most desperate orbit?"

"I only know what Cobalt has told me."

"And did he tell you that we are in need of saving?"

"He did."

"Then he is wise, for that is so."

Here was another one who spoke in riddles.

"We have experienced a tremor," I said, "and we know of the people who live in the dark. 'Descendants of Thomas,' he called them, who raid your borders. But from what I have observed, you seem to have the technology to save yourselves from these things."

"You are wise," he said. "But the tremors are not the reason we need salvation. It is only a matter of time before the end comes for us. We have heard reports that Thomas' followers are mining in the dark tropics, and we see new cracks forming all the time. They cannot be stopped. And we cannot dissuade them." He bowed his head.

I looked at the others. Worry etched their faces. Where was the excitement of all this? A new race of humans on an alien world. We should've been giddy as charged particles. So why this aching pit in my stomach? Why these lines on the faces of my crew?

"When they first attacked us," Onyx continued, "we packed up our dome and set out to build another. Each time they came near, we withdrew, as we wished not to engage them in conflict. We have covered the ground with weakness where each new dome we built. Now, there is nowhere else to run. We have built for the last time, the last city — the City of Maximus — but we are not equipped to fight in the dark or make them stop. With the atmosphere bearing down on the planet, and the many moons that speak of our mistakes, there is already too much pressure on the ground. Even if they were not mining, it would only be a matter of time before the cracks we have made will split us in half."

I blew out a sigh. "Do you know how long?"

"We cannot be sure, but we sense it. The end is coming, just as it threatened us before. It is our fault as much as it is theirs. We gave no heed to the consequences of our discoveries. We only sought to understand. We did not seek what lay beyond our understanding. It is this which will mark our end. It is this which we need saving from — ourselves, as much as this ruined world."

The crew stared at me expectantly. I was the physicist. It was up to me to understand what he was talking about, and I understood enough to realize that he was right. On a planet made of rock, any crack could mean its end. Pressure exerted on the crack would weaken the entire structure. But worse than that would be the impact of mining.

On Earth, the ground was made of plates which moved, and oceans minimized the seismic activity. But here, if what he said was true, there were no oceans to absorb the shifting of plates. If the ground were split apart, and the shell broke into plates, tremors from the gravity of the nearby planet would be nothing compared to the quakes that the ground would produce.

In other words, they'd all be dead soon. And us with them.

I nodded at the others, trying not to make my expression too morbid, but they realized the risks of planet-wide destruction were real enough. I mean, it ain't exactly like I could hide that kind of realization from my face.

I turned to Onyx. "And what makes you think that we can save you?"

"It is said that you would. We have tried to follow your ways. We even sought to make the city able to escape the ground, just as it is fabled that you once did in the realm of Orbicon. But the crimson sun cannot give us the power we need to master the sky. That is why we have asked for you to save us. For it is known that the Elders hold the secret of all things."

"Who are these Elders you keep talking about?"

"Is this a test of my faith? I assure you, I am quite devout. I speak to the realm of Orbicon every night." He knelt and kissed his forefinger.

"Look, for the last time, this ain't a test. Get on your feet and tell me of these Elders, and how you know about Orbicon," I said.

He stood, puzzled. "It certainly sounds like a test."

Yeah, like the ones Henry Rolands used to pull on me. "Fine. It's a test. So what's the answer?"

He dipped his head, avoiding my eyes. "The Elders are our first ancestors, who traveled from the province of Earth, in the realm of Orbicon, over two thousand cycles ago. Their coming from Earth gave them power over the orbit of the sun, and so they did not age, but they lived for hundreds of years. They built our city on the foundation of their solar sails. They gave their children laws and when the last of them perished, it was prophesied that they would return one day. Ever since they vanished from our world, we have sought to follow in their ways, and now you have come again from the sky to save us. To show us what we must do with what we have learned. For we have finally come to understand the solution that Harold the Seer gave us after all this time. And this is why you are here, is it not?"

Disbelief slackened my jaw. *This is nuts. Where are the cameras? Whatever prank this is, let's just call time on it so we can all have a big laugh at my expense.*

After Onyx finished, he looked up. "Did I answer well?"

What he talked about seemed ridiculous, but I was hardly going to tell him that. "Onyx, may I discuss this with my crew for a moment?"

"You may do as you wish here, for we are all your children." He stepped back to give us space.

My head was still trying to recover from our journey. *Over two thousand cycles ago,* he'd said. People from Earth could never have traveled here two thousand cycles ago. But then, I wasn't exactly the expert. Sadie was the mathematician. She could work it out faster than me. "Sadie, how long is two thousand cycles here?"

She looked at me as if I was crazy. "It's roughly two thousand orbits of the sun," she replied.

"No, I mean two thousand orbits ain't the same as Earth years, is it? According to Rolands' Theory."

"I get you, boss. No, it works out at a little over thirty Earth years."

Thirty Earth years. None of this was possible in that time. Not the domes. Not the trains. Not the level of destruction. Which meant only one thing – evidence that something was wrong. And it wasn't our eyesight. But voicing the idea that Dr. Emily Rolands could've been mistaken – I couldn't even start to form the words.

"What are you thinking, boss?" Sadie asked.

I winced and rubbed my forehead. "How long ago did the Icarus One launch?"

"You can't be serious?" Barbara said.

"Why not?"

"Are you suggesting the Icarus One landed on this planet and colonized it, and this is the result? Do you know how insane that sounds?"

Jamie stepped forward. "Is it any less crazy than traveling thirty-nine lightyears to a planet which we thought was just rock, and instead, we find it inhabited with humans that bow down to us and ask us to save them? It doesn't make any sense."

"I think you want to believe it because you like the attention." Sadie rolled her eyes at Jamie.

Jan piped up. "Listen. Let's assume that all of this is real for a minute. What are we going to do? Our mission is to report back to Orbicon what it's like to live on a planet that has a lesser orbit to that of Earth. Are we gonna jeopardize that because of what's already here?"

I remembered being in that observation room on the simulation deck, and the scenario Henry had given me. Was it the people or the mission? That was the choice here. I'd been trained to put the mission above all other things. But could we really just ignore these people?

"Didn't he say that he talks to Orbicon?" Carlos asked.

Barbara scowled. "What do you mean?"

"I mean, our mission is about communication, but he says he's in communication with Orbicon already."

Carlos was right.

"Onyx," I called out. "Show us how you speak with Orbicon."

He bowed. "Gladly. Follow me."

He led us to another room that was locked. He swiped his medallion over a panel, and the door swooshed open. He shepherded us through.

Inside, an older model of the same communicators we'd brought aboard the Icarus Two filled the space. I couldn't take in what my eyes were seeing.

And then it hit me. "You remember the names of the crew in the Icarus One?" I asked.

"Sure," Barbara said. "There was Captain Shelby—"

"No, first names," I interrupted.

"Erm, give me a moment." She counted them off on her fingers. "Max, Harold, and Kirk. June, Sonja, and Cassandra."

"The City of Maximus. Harold the Seer. The Laws of Juniper. The House of Cassia. And the Lady Sonja," I said.

Whatever the effects of orbital locking on this planet, these people — these humans — were our responsibility.

A memory struck like a thunderclap. Back from Earth. It was that old story my grandpa used to tell me, about the man who woke up one day and didn't know a thing about himself. Then, when he learned who he was, he wished he could go back and be oblivious again. In this moment, I'd become that man. I wished I could go back somehow and not know where these people came from, because it changed everything. It meant we were responsible for the state they were in. They were following the pattern we set, and it had nearly torn them to pieces. Literally.

Knowing where they came from changed the mission, and there was no going back. No choice. Just duty. And the guilt of knowing that whatever had happened here was all our fault.

My legs shook. "We'll help you and your people, Onyx. Right, everyone?"

They all nodded, even Jan.

Grandpa was right. There ain't nobody as happy as the man with no guilt.

"Okay. So we're saving two races from extinction now. Anyone got any ideas?"

HALLEY

I

November 2047

Dr. Emily Rolands. 'Mother of modern science.' I think science was her favorite child. I know I certainly wasn't.

Discovery is everything, she always said. *Life is discovery.* There were days when I was convinced she was more interested in what she could discover *about* me, than she actually was *in* me. Being a daughter wasn't easy, but especially was that true when I had scientist extraordinaire Dr. Emily Rolands for a Mom.

Even as a kid, I had an inkling she was a big deal (much bigger than me), and she always would be. Everyone expected me to be the same as her. To grow up and find some new thing that would change everything about our understanding of the universe.

If that's what people thought, then I couldn't have been more disappointing.

It wasn't that I found science tough. It was just the opposite. Science was too easy, so I couldn't have been less interested in it.

#scienceisboring

But I don't think I ever considered it might have been my fault why Mom was so distant. I mean, I always blamed her. But if science was her favorite child, then I wasn't exactly a good sibling. I didn't play nice.

I wasn't like Henry. Ever since I could remember, he was always fawning over Mom. It was no wonder she gave him a job.

But then the launch happened.

The big Orbicon venture into space was trending everywhere I looked. Every station showed it, which meant that for the first time since I was a kid, I was actually interested in what was going on. I thought Mom would be pleased. But she wasn't.

She and Henry had been on some late night chat show to promote the launch. Henry's idea, of course. And we were watching them on air, waiting for the countdown. But Mom didn't want anything to do with it. She turned the TV off before the interview was even finished.

"Ugh." That's what I said. I think. I mean, I was mad. I was allowed that much.

For all my life she'd been on a pedestal, never around, always distant and unreachable. Always on the project. Always too busy. It wasn't like she'd meant it to be that way, but she was committed to the mission, so us kids always came second to the 'needs of humanity.' I remember when I was fifteen, we had this huge row, and I told her that she couldn't love real people, only the theory of people, and she'd said that it was her love for every person that made her do what she did. *Where's your love for me?* I'd yelled at her. She just walked away.

Anyway, I thought she'd be happy to watch her life's work taking shape. She'd never had a problem listening to her own voice before. So when I said 'Ugh,' and she reacted (she said she didn't want to be anywhere near

Orbicon for the launch), I admit it, I was surprised. And now that she was turning the channel over, I sat with my jaw practically hanging off.

Henry was upset too, which was funny.

Then her phone rang and she left the room.

"What's up with Mom?" I asked.

"I don't know, but I'm turning the TV back on."

I didn't stop him.

She was in the kitchen by herself. I shuffled to the edge of the sofa, ready to get up and see if she was alright, but the launch was happening, and it distracted me back into a slouch.

What would it be like for those people to find themselves on another world? Taking their first steps into a place that nobody else has ever been.

#firststepsontrappist1e

The camera showed the ship disappear, swallowed by this blackness that shot out like the path of a bullet, without end. The black line made all the stars vanish, and it looked different to the blackness of space. Darker, somehow. It was awesome. I mean, no special effects. No dodgy CGI. It was real. Like, actually real.

I finally shuffled through to the kitchen when it was all over, and found Mom opening a new bottle of wine.

"Are you celebrating?" I asked.

"Something like that." She tried to twist the corkscrew in, but struggled to hold it straight.

"Let me help you, Mom." I took the bottle from her hands. She didn't resist. The lid was off in no time, and I'd poured her a small glass. I didn't want her to suffer too much in the morning.

"Hey, Mom, what do you think it's like for those people up there, walking on a planet for the first time in history? Do you think they're nervous?"

"Whatever they are, they won't experience it for long," she said. "They're gone now. There's no stopping it."

She burst into a rant, and I didn't understand anything about what she was saying. Then tears filled her eyes, and she held her arms out. She'd done the same thing a few months back.

Out of the blue, she'd come into my room and hadn't said anything, but just cried, and I did the same thing then that I did now. I let her.

Before, I'd kind of enjoyed seeing Mom in such a state. It proved she was human after all. But now, I felt sorry for her.

"It's all over, Halley. Promise me it's all over."

"Sure thing, Mom. Whatever you want."

What would the world think if they saw Dr. Emily Rolands in such a mess? Capable of real feelings! It might've been the greatest discovery of the modern age!

***

The next day, Henry woke me up, pounding on Mom's door. He was so loud, I thought it was an earthquake or something.

"Turn your phone on," he kept yelling in between pounds.

I staggered out of bed and put on a jumper. "Quiet. She's sleeping," I barked at him.

"Halley, you don't understand. If you did, you'd be helping me. So just go back to bed and play on your phone, or whatever it is you do."

Rude. "Just chill, Henry. Before you hurt yourself."

"Chill? Chill! At a time like this? I don't think so."

I hadn't seen Henry this stressed in years. "It can't be all that bad, can it?" I yawned, bleary eyed. "What time is it anyway?"

He ignored me and pounded on the door.

"Go away, Henry," Mom's voice called through the door.

"This is urgent, Mom," he said. "It's about the launch."

"Not interested."

He looked at me as if he couldn't believe his ears. The look was mutual.

"Listen, we've not received anything from the Icarus – just the usual static and background noises of space – and the press are hounding us for a statement. We can't hold them back much longer, but we can't tell them that we've not heard from the crew. Otherwise they'll assume the worst and our stocks will plummet. I need to know what you want me to say to them. HQ has been trying to reach you all morning."

The door swung open and Mom stood there with the coldest expression in her eyes, it was like she'd opened the freezer door and absorbed its chill.

"Read my lips," she said. "Not . . . interested," she mouthed.

"But Mom—"

"What did I just tell you?"

I liked this new Mom.

Henry shook his head. "You can't be—"

"Henry, last night I watched six people travel to an early grave, and I put them there. Now you're telling me that our stocks might lose their value? That is the least of my headaches today."

"But what do you—"

"If you want a statement, you can release this: we are waiting on communication from Icarus One, the first and last ship to travel lightyears."

"Last ship? What do you mean *last ship*?"

"I won't send anyone else to die just to prove me right. Forget about Trappist-1. From now on, we focus on Mars. End of discussion."

"But—"

"What did I tell you? *Not . . . interested!*"

She wafted him away like he was an insect. He didn't know what to do, so he took out his phone and started making calls. I walked over to Mom, put my arms around her, and just hugged her.

She squeezed hold of me. "There are more important things in life than science and discovery, Halley."

Dr. Emily Rolands – mother of modern science – held me. Told me, after all these years, that discovery doesn't matter. What had happened to my Mother? Who had slipped up at the lab and replaced her with a human being?

II

May 2048

My phone blared for the third time. I swiped to answer.

"Mom. Do you know what time it is?"

"Halley. It's ten o'clock."

I rubbed my eyes. "In the morning. Yeah. You know I'm no good until after twelve."

"Get up. We're going for a drive."

"Mom. Do we have to? I thought we could–"

"I'll be there in twenty minutes. And wear something nice." She hung up.

I sighed and slumped out of bed. It wasn't like I could complain. How many years had I begged her to be more attentive? And now, since the launch, that's all she'd been. It was nice. I took lots of pictures, just in case this personality switch ever wore off. But it was also exhausting.

No human being should be forced out of bed before noon. It's practically torture.

I pieced together the plainest outfit I could rustle up. I mean, Mom telling me to wear something nice was basic code for *something that won't embarrass me.* How many meetings had she insisted I come to where she stood her ground and refused to send another ship to Trappist-1, only to roll her eyes at what I was wearing? It didn't matter how many times she got told the bigwigs needed more data because the readings from the Icarus never changed. She would just shake her head and complain about how I didn't own a top that wasn't too ripped or revealing.

Gotta admit, the biggest puzzle was why she wanted me there at all. What could I add to her conversations with scientists? I wasn't exactly an expert on the frequencies of static, or those noises from space that came through so fast you could hardly hear them. It was weird – the sound of space that scientists wrote off as background chatter. There was no pattern to it. Just a garbled bunch of blips and bloops that made the machine sound like it was broken or something. I assumed Mom would've been much more interested, but she didn't give it a second thought. And despite everybody expecting she'd eventually change her mind, she never did.

Maybe she just needed me with her as a 'get-out' option? An infallible plan b, to use in case of emergency? All those times she'd called me *a walking disaster* – perhaps that wasn't such a bad thing after all. And it worked, too. So many execs tried to convince her we were making a mistake by abandoning the Trappist-1 mission, and without positive proof of her theory, we'd never get the revenue back. Mom didn't care. She just said *Halley, what on Earth are you wearing? How many times have I told you? I'm sorry to cut our meeting short, but I have to deal with this.* Then she'd shake their hand and bid them goodbye, and after they left, she'd just kiss me on the forehead.

Eventually, they let her make a statement to say that Orbicon was changing its focus to aid SpaceGen in reaching Mars. We never saw the execs much after that. Which meant I could finally wear what I wanted again, without worrying about it being pointed out to the richest people in the world how much of a tramp I looked.

#wardrobefreedomfeelssogood

Mom pulled up in her armor-plated 4x4. She looked me up and down and nodded. "Come on, get in."

I climbed into the passenger seat and buckled up. "Where are we going?"

"To pay our respects."

Was that a tear in Mom's eye? If I'd known it was a funeral, I'd have worn a hat. "Will Henry be there?"

She shook her head.

Mom and Henry hadn't talked in months. After the announcement about Orbicon's switch to support the Mars landing, the press made a big deal of it, favoring the move. But the investors treated it like a betrayal. Henry entertained them with reassurances. Smoothed things over with that winning smile of his. He was good with people. He didn't get that from Mom.

But the animosity between them, which started as a breeze, had grown more powerful than a hurricane. I saw it on the news every day. The rumors of a Rolands family feud. Nobody cared about politics anymore. Climate change was so common, it didn't class as news. People tuned in for a half-hour debate about reality TV stars who lost their dogs to cheating ex-spouses in court, or the future of the planet courtesy of The Rolands. It's a wonder Henry managed to keep the cameras out. I couldn't login to social media without being featured on another trending opinion poll.

"Let's not talk about your brother," Mom said.

"Fine. Have you checked the route for storms?"

"I'm not an idiot, Halley."

"I know, Mom. I just . . . I feel better to ask."

"Well, I have. Feeling happy now?"

"Overjoyed."

"Good."

I let the pause hang between us too long, trying to muster the courage to tell her that talking was good, and she should think about trying it with Henry sometime. But instead, the awkwardness stretched into an easy silence as she drove off across the sandy roads in the direction of

SpaceGen HQ. There was a weird smell in the car, but I ignored it.

After an hour, she pulled up next to a really big piece of scaffolding, like an oil rig, but in the middle of the desert.

"What is this place?" I asked.

She opened the back door and picked up a bunch of flowers. They were pretty, but pungent. It explained the smell, at least. "Come on," she said.

I held her arm as we marched towards the base of the scaffold. "Where are we going?"

"We're climbing those steps to the top of this launchpad." She pointed up. "My first day at SpaceGen, when I was barely out of college, someone promised me a trip to this launchpad. Back then, it sounded magical. But this is all that's left of it. A heap of junk. That's what promises are, Halley. Broken. Always broken."

The sun scorched as it broke through a cloud. I doubled the intensity on my shades, but still squinted and scrunched up my face. Mom did the same. I guess we had that much in common.

Climbing the steps and ladders to reach the top of the concrete platform burned my fingers. A tall crane rose high into the sky. I panted, breathless. But I got to the top of the platform eventually, and stared across the desert.

"Here." Mom handed me six of the flowers she'd brought.

"What do I do with these?"

She smiled. "One flower for one life. Today's the day the crew of the Icarus One breathed their last on that distant world. This is the least they deserve."

She walked to the center of the launchpad and knelt to place a flower on the concrete. I copied her, and we did the same thing six times until there were no more flowers to lay.

Then she stood up and put her arm around me and the ceremony was over.

#launchpadmemorial

"Oh, Halley." Her tears soaked my shoulder, and the fabric creased where she rested her head.

"It's okay, Mom. Everything's okay." Well, besides the fact the Earth was, you know, almost dead.

"Forgive me, Halley. Can you ever forgive me?"

"For what? For trying to save us? I'm pretty sure you don't need to be forgiven for that."

She pulled back and rubbed at the creases in my top where her head had rested. "Your outfit. You should've worn a different top," she said.

If she'd been kidding, it would've been hilarious. But no. I guess Mom was the ultimate proof of the biggest truth in the universe: there was no winning when it came to clothes.

"Let's go," I said.

I should've taken a picture. Why didn't I take a picture? Of all the days we spent together, why was this the one that slipped away?

III

July 2081

I stood on top of the broken launchpad and laid a flower on it for Mom.

Same spot. Same kind of rose. It had cost a fortune to get a real flower engineered. Maybe that's why Henry had agreed to come? To get his money's worth.

He couldn't have made it more obvious that he didn't want to be there. Huffing. Puffing. Sighing. Groaning. Not taking his hands out of his stupid pockets. But maybe it was too much to expect him to show her some respect? He'd hated going back to SpaceGen. Getting involved with the Mars Mission was worse for him than anyone else at Orbicon. He'd been good at selling interstellar travel. After Mom refused to send another crew to Trappist-1, he had nothing to sell.

Before the launch, Henry had never minded being in Mom's shadow. He knew that one day, it would be his turn in the light. But ever since Mom pulled the plug, he'd had to share it with SpaceGen. And he hated her for that.

Families were weird. I mean, Mom regretted the launch so much that she made sure it would never happen again, but in doing so, she would become the cause of Henry's regret for years. Figure that one out. Henry had cast his lot in with science, and when Mom turned her back on the project, she turned her back on him with it. He was always a better sibling to science than me.

By the time she passed, they hadn't spoken in so long. But there was hardly a day when me and Mom didn't talk. That launch was the best thing that ever happened for us. And I understood why she changed so much, why she lost her faith in science. It was grief and guilt that did it for her. Grief and guilt — that was me and Henry when she died. I was the grief, and Henry was the guilt.

"Let's get this over with." Henry checked his watch as we stood on the launchpad. "I'm already late for a meeting with the CEO of SpaceGen. Booster tests are going well. He thinks we could be close to a solution for landing on Mars."

I brushed a tear out of my eye. "You sound just like her, Henry."

"Just like how she used to be."

"I won't stop you. Let's go."

We'd stayed up there long enough. The wind was wild, blowing the flowers we'd laid right off the platform almost as soon as we'd put them to rest.

"You know she was proud of you, Henry," I said.

"Not proud enough."

We climbed down the ladder, and into the car, buckling our seatbelts. Before he turned the engine on, he turned to me and did his best not to smile.

"Now that the company's in our names, and we have joint control, we'll need to sit down and talk about the future, Halley. Where we want to take Orbicon."

Future? What kind of future was there on this ball of rock? We were one big storm away from the apocalypse, and Henry wanted to talk about the future! "Sure, Henry. Whatever you think."

He'd already booked a board meeting for the following week.

#saynotoboardmeetings

There was nothing on Earth as drab as a board meeting.

I walked in late and Henry was already waiting. The room was gross. Designed to be dull on purpose. Like it knew how boring the meetings taking place inside it would be, and wanted in on the action, or lack thereof.

Board meetings — more like bored meetings. And there were no exceptions to that rule. None.

But Henry thrived inside the squalid gray panels and the fake wooden tables. He filled the meeting-room somehow. Like a bad stench. Dressed up smart. A proper businessman.

He kissed my cheek and asked me to sit across from him. He'd moved into his own place years before, and because I'd stayed with Mom right up to the end, I only ever saw him at restaurants, so I was used to sitting across from him.

"Halley, welcome to the future," he said.

"Is that how you start all your meetings?"

"Usually. But I don't normally get heckled for it."

I played with my split ends. "Don't you think it's a bit cheesy?"

"I've never had any complaints."

"You must be meeting with a lot of dishonest people then."

He raised an eyebrow. "I think you're stalling because you don't want to be here."

"You know me so well, Henry."

"Are you ready to do this, or should we make another appointment?"

A sigh escaped from my chest. "No, I'm ready. I just never thought we'd be here, you know?"

"What do you mean?"

"I don't know. Still alive. Talking about Orbicon as if it was ours."

"It *is* ours."

"Yeah, but it's Mom's too."

"Mom's gone, Halley."

I fought back the ache in my chest. "I know."

"This business is her legacy. So what do you want to do with it? Make it soar, or watch it die?" He was always a good salesman.

"I said I'm ready, didn't I?"

He handed me some folders. Mammoth files. Too big for me to just sit and read. He explained that the dossier held all the different departments of Orbicon, as well as an index for archived research materials. Mom's name was all over the place. Henry was right — this was her legacy. I'd only known Mom after she'd walked away from Orbicon. I never really understood her before then, always at a distance. But here was a chance to get to see her work, to get to know her as the most celebrated scientist of her generation. It was like a window into Mom that I never knew existed until now.

Henry talked me through the folder for the best part of an hour. After the first ten minutes, I'd wished for him to just get to the point. After an hour, I was ready to do anything to get out of that room.

"So the question we have to decide an answer to is this," he said. *Finally*. "Now that you know what Orbicon does, do we divide this up between us, or retain joint control over the whole thing?"

"What in heaven's name are you talking about?"

"Well, if there's an area of study you wanted to take control of, we could negotiate over it. You could take oversight of some projects, while I took over others. We'd keep our own profits, effectively splitting the company in half. Or there's the other option. We could retain joint oversight over all departments and run this together. I'm in favor of the first option. But if you want to go with the second, I'm happy to agree. Only, you'd have to pull your weight. You'd have to make Orbicon your life, just like Mom did before she cracked. It's the only way for it to work. That's why I'm leaving the decision to you. It's your life on the line."

Right now, I didn't want to imagine my final breaths on this doomed Earth being taken in boardrooms, on a treadmill of endless meetings over trivial matters until *wallop* and we were toast. That was how he'd pitched it to me. But I also didn't want to lose this chance to find Mom in these files. To get to know her like I'd never known her before. That was worth every painstaking minute of board meetings in itself. Besides, I'd been lucky to make it into my forties. How many people my age wouldn't kill for the chance to get paid for sitting down all day, away from the ash-storms and silt-slides?

"Halley? I need an answ–"

"Option two. We do this together. It's what Mom would have wanted."

He froze, caught in whatever headlights I'd cast his way. "Are you sure?"

"Have you ever known me do anything I'm not sure of?"

"Very well. Welcome to Orbicon, Director Rolands." He extended his hand to me and I shook it. "We'll get you set up with a pass and everything you need. You'll want to hire an assistant. I can have potentials waiting for you in the morning."

"Thanks, Henry. Can I keep this?" I pointed at the dossier.

"Sure. It's as much yours as it is mine."

"Thanks." I hugged the files to my chest, like I was holding onto Mom.

As far as Henry was concerned, these pages were just the way the company was run. But to me, they were a secret map that led to her, hidden and cryptic. And I was determined to crack whatever secrets it held.

Watch out Mom, here I come.

IV

August 2081

#interviewsaretheworst

Project Get-Halley-An-Assistant was fully underway. How many days had I been forced to sit through parade after parade of girls, one by one, no older than twenty-two?

They entered the room and took a chair across the table, decorated in their perfect make-up and sky-high heels, despite the fact they'd probably had to wade through a blizzard and flood to get here. They all gave perfect answers, and they all had perfect teeth. How was I supposed to choose between them? Close my eyes and point to a name? I had no idea which of them would be best for the job, but I did have this one question up my sleeve, which I asked each of them: "How much longer do you think we've got left on Earth, before it wipes us out?"

Most of them answered the same through their gleaming smiles. "That depends on the work we do here at Orbicon, which is why I feel that this job is the perfect role for me."

Ugh.

Or the other response they'd give was, "I don't know." I guess people didn't like to think about time running out.

But when tomorrow is finite, there's only one way of facing it, and that's head on. No point turning your neck and ignoring the collision. Might as well see it through, all the way to the bitter end.

And then one girl came along who said something different to the rest.

She looked just as perfect as the others. But where everyone else had worn their outfits effortlessly, her perfection looked like something she'd worked for years trying to get right.

I asked her the question. How long until Earth kills us?

"I give it forty years," she answered.

"Forty years? Why?"

She shrugged. "By that time, I'll be in my sixties, and I'd like to think I'll make it to be that old."

"You don't think that it depends on the work we do here at Orbicon?"

"To be honest with you, Ma'am, Orbicon isn't about saving the Earth, it's about saving humanity from extinction. I think we gave up on the Earth a long time ago. If anybody says different, they just haven't accepted the true state of things." She said it all with a scratch in her voice that knocked the sheen off her polished demeanor, her bright eyes never leaving mine.

"Tell me honestly," I said. "How long did it take you to get into that dress this morning?"

She smiled. "The dress was no problem, but the hair took me forever and the make-up even longer."

"So you were up at what time to get ready for this interview?"

"About three o'clock this morning."

My eyebrow lifted. "And what would you normally be dressed in?"

"Honestly?"

I nodded.

"A t-shirt and some jeans," she admitted. "And I wear my hair in a ponytail. It isn't attractive, but it stops it from getting in my face all day."

I leaned forward. "Interviews are the worst, aren't they?"

"I was going to post on that later." She smiled.

"Tell me. How many other girls out there look like they'd be more comfortable in jeans and a t-shirt, rather than their best dresses?"

"There are five more girls out there, all of them pristine."

"That's what I thought. The first thing I'm gonna need you to do is get rid of them."

"Get rid, as in . . ." She put her finger to her neck and swiped it in a line, miming a death signal.

"Oh, no! Not as in, get rid of them, as in, kill them or anything — just . . ."

She laughed. "I know what you mean. And thank you, Ma'am."

"And you can stop calling me *Ma'am*. After you've dismissed them, you can clear my schedule for lunch. I'm taking you out to celebrate."

"I don't know how to clear your schedule."

"It's okay. I don't have a schedule." I smiled. She returned it in kind. "There's a great waffle place I know of. You can get changed in your office. I'll let you borrow a t-shirt if you want. Remind me of your name again?"

"Roxanne, but please call me Roxy."

"Okay, Roxy. Waffles sound okay for you?"

She nodded, pulling her hair out of its perfect mold. "Whatever you say, Ma'am."

IV

November 2081

The Mars Mission should have been renamed *The Constant Standstill.* Henry screamed about it every time we were alone. SpaceGen made him promises of launch dates, and he was holding onto clients by the thinnest of threads. But I couldn't have been happier about it. It gave me and Roxy plenty of time to work through the dossier.

"I want to start today with the work my Mom did back when she first came here," I said. "Can you fetch me the files, Roxy, and put off my meetings until I've had a chance to read them thoroughly?"

"Sure thing, Miss Rolands. Do you have a copy of Rolands' thesis?"

"Is it in here?"

"No, the original is in the Smithsonian Bunker. I'll email you a copy. You'll want to make a start with that."

Roxy was great, not just for her relaxed attitude and cool t-shirts, but for the way she always held off Henry for just long enough for me to catch a break.

#rolandstheory

The first thing I read from the files was the 'Rolands Theory of the Orbital Constant,' or the 'Rolands thesis.' Of course, I knew what it said in principle. After all, science was easy. But I'd never read the paper itself.

Mom was so young when she wrote this. Every sentence dripped with invention and promise. I loved how she wrote back then. You could tell it was before the climate collapsed, back when hope still meant something. *'Life on Mars will extend the human lifespan.'* That was how it concluded. Life on Mars. That was what Mom had wanted all along.

Henry blustered through the door, having finally made it past Roxy's evasive maneuvers. "Halley, we can't keep on with this Mars Mission indefinitely. We have to explore other options."

"No, Henry. We stick with Mars. It's what Mom would have wanted."

"But Mars? Halley. How long have we been going to Mars? It's never going to happen."

"I eat 'never' for breakfast. This is for Mom, Henry. Let me give her this."

He shrieked and stormed out the room. Every day, he came to me with the same complaint, but the more I read Mom's writing, the more adamant I grew.

Mars was where our future was always meant to be. Mom believed it. And the Trappist-1 Mission was all in aid of getting us onto that red spot in the stars.

I was looking for Mom. Maybe Mars was where I'd find her?

March 2082

"Roxy. Can you get me data on the space collider?"

"Sure, Miss Rolands. What do you need?"

"Schematics. Reports. Proposals. Drafts. Dates. Whatever you can find."

December 2082

"Is this all there is on the Orbicon Launch?"

"That's everything, Miss Rolands."

"But there has to be more."

"There isn't. I've scrubbed all the archives."

"Well . . . can you look again? If I go through these notes any more times, I'll be able to recite them by heart."

May 2083

"Are you alright, Roxy? I heard about what happened."

"It's just a broken arm. Nothing that won't heal."

"But that storm. The bunker. I didn't think you were going to make it out ali–"

"It was nothing compared to what happened in Chile."

"I know. But, Roxy. You could've been–"

"I'm fine. Honest. I wouldn't be back at work if I wasn't."

"Alright. Okay. You know you can talk to me about it, right? Let me get you a coffee, at least. And you'll move your stuff into the main complex. No more going back and forth. It's too dangerous to risk you on the surface."

"I thought the main complex was reserved for–"

"For essential personnel. That's right."

"But I'm not a scientist, Miss Rolands. I'm just a–"

"You're *essential*. Understand? And for heaven's sake. How many times do I have to tell you to call me Halley?"

"Thank you. Halley. What are you working through today?"

"The space collider. It's unmanned now, right?"

"Right."

"But it's still monitoring for changes?"

"As far as I know."

"Then I guess it's back to the drawing board for the millionth time."

"You'll find something, Halley. I know it."

January 2084

New Year's Eve. How many of these did we have left?

For years, I'd absorbed her words. Scoured file after file after file. But all those binders I analyzed looking for Mom, looking for answers, brought her no closer. If I heard her voice, it was always just a lecture on the page. She never broke through the ink and let me in.

This year would be different. It was time to get out of the dossier and into the real world, while it was still here. I mean, sure, I'd toured the facility. But had I really looked? If I couldn't find her in the paperwork, maybe I could find her in what she'd built. Like, literally.

My resolve was set. Find her. While there was still time.

March 2086

Henry called me into his office.

"Halley. Look. How many times have we been over this? You were the one who told me to push for Mars."

"And I still think we should push for Mars. But–"

"There's no but." He used his condescending *I'm the big brother* tone that buried his words so far under my skin that I felt them crawling. "We don't have the resources to split our efforts. Either we launch for Mars. Or we launch for somewhere else. You can't have both."

I slammed my knuckles on his desk. "You said we were partners. Remember? That was the choice you gave me. An even split. I'm Director of Operations, just as much as you are. How many requests have I made in all these years? Name one."

"Well. You wanted Roxy moving into the main complex."

My nostrils flared, cheeks flushing red as two blood moons. "Henry. I've stayed out of your business. I haven't shown up to meetings with the investors. Haven't questioned your funding proposals. Haven't ever asked about where the grapes for that bottle of wine you keep in your bottom drawer come from. But if you *really* insist that we can't send an astronaut to man the space collider, then I may start wondering where the answers to all these questions might be found. Am I making myself clear?"

Henry froze. His eyes were like scales, weighing up the options as he searched my face. The lines on his face stretched taut and then he heaved a sigh. "Can you just answer one thing for me? Why, Halley? Why is this so important to you?"

Because after five years of searching everywhere I could think, I was still no closer to understanding Mom than when I'd started out. Because unless we got a person manning the collider, there would be no way I could ever go and see it for myself. Because if Mom wasn't down here, maybe I'd find her up there? "Please, Henry. This matters to me. Isn't that reason enough? Besides, you want to preserve a legacy here. Right? Make it soar? Isn't that the deal you sold me? This is how."

His shoulders slumped. "Okay, Halley. You can restart the collider project. I'll give you one astronaut to monitor the station. But don't push it. I know you're using this company to take a nostalgia trip. Just don't let it trip you over too hard, understand?"

"Thank you."

I left his office and called Roxy. "You know that box of chocolates you were saving for a special occasion which you didn't want me to know about?"

"How did you–"

"Break them open. Henry gave us the go-ahead." Something was finally looking up.

"Let's just hope nothing goes wrong between now and the launch date."

I snorted. "Oh, Roxy. What could possibly go wrong?"

V

April 2086

One month after I'd decided to kickstart a project which was deader than dead, the impossible happened. We landed on Mars.

#marslanding

Henry and I watched the landing from HQ. Roxy was with us, too. We didn't say anything, but I'd hardly call the room silent. It was like the air hummed in a giddy nervousness. We were taking one giant collective breath, sucking in the atmosphere.

When they touched down on the surface, we didn't cheer – we breathed a sigh of relief. Celebratory banners waved as our fists unclenched, our fingers aching.

After half-an-hour, we had to call it an early night and cram into the bunkers. A tornado whipped through the compound and didn't dissipate until it was almost light again.

The next day, we emerged from the bunker and checked in with the crew. Transmissions filtered through slowly. We thought it was a problem at our end to begin with. Diagnostics revealed nothing. Was it their end?

"Do you read?" the technician asked.

"I'm . . . so . . . rry . . . mis . . . sion . . . con . . . trol . . . but . . . can . . . you . . . re . . . peat . . . .?"

They spoke in slow motion. Weird. A problem with the equipment? Couldn't be. It all checked out. But nothing we said at this end seemed to make sense to them, and unless you could tune your ears to half-speed, it was the same vice versa. Just a garbled mess of noise.

Henry's phone was constantly at his ear, his sighs growing heavier with every call.

SpaceGen had spent all that money on equipment to get people to Mars, and now they were there, it was proving impossible to communicate with them. Their transmissions covered a vast distance, and there could have been any one of a hundred different things going wrong, but it took the best part of a day before Henry turned his phone off and called me to one side.

"Board meeting," he whispered.

"Now?"

He nodded, and we left the hub of scientists staring at consoles with their heads in their hands, not knowing what to do or how to fix it.

We huddled down in a drab sideroom, closed the door behind us, and spoke in whispers.

"You don't think Mom could have been wrong, do you?" he asked.

"What do you mean?"

"Rolands' theory? You don't think her conclusion's wrong?"

I thought about it for a moment. "Could be. You think it's orbital locking that's causing this?"

"I don't know. But if it is, then we're in trouble."

I frowned. "What do you mean?"

He glanced over his shoulder, despite us being the only two in here. "They'll make us the scapegoats."

"So what?"

"Do you know how bad this will be for us?"

"Listen." I rubbed my forehead. "I'm halfway through my sixties, and you're an old man. We spent last night trapped in a bunker because the wind got up. You've got no wife. I've got no husband. It couldn't get any worse for us than it already is."

Now it was his turn to frown. "Alright, Halley. Forget about the way this will hurt us. In the grand scheme of things, we hardly matter, right? But think of what will happen to Mom's legacy if it turns out she was wrong."

Understanding crept into my pores, tingling them with sweat. "What do you suggest?"

"Listen, what if we launch another Icarus mission?"

"Are you serious? Mom would never agree to such a thing."

"Mom's not here. Look, what if she was wrong? What if there's hope for the crew she sent to Trappist-1? Don't you think she'd want to explore every option, every chance, however slight it might be?" He was still a good salesman.

"You think now is the best time for it? We just bungled Mars. How many people do you think will get behind another push for Trappist-1?"

"Who said it has to be public?" He raised an eyebrow.

I opened my mouth to object, but actually managed to think before speaking for once. Off the books was the only way to go. We still had a budget, our pittance from SpaceGen, for 'research.' If anybody else knew what we were doing, they'd pull even that measly bit of funding and it'd be curtains for Orbicon. I couldn't do that to Mom.

"Okay," I said. "But let me be the one to do this. You'll be busy enough with SpaceGen. I'll get things ready. Nobody else has to know what we're doing until we're ready."

"Agreed. Looks like you'll get that trip to the space collider after all." Henry smiled and left.

I called Roxy into the room.

"Yes, Miss Rolands?" She poked her head around the door.

"Roxy, come on in. Shut the door behind you. I'm gonna ask you a question, but you can't speak to anyone about it. Understand?"

"Perfectly." She flicked the latch behind her, locking us in.

"Good. How quickly could we be ready to launch another Icarus mission?"

"Icarus? You mean, with everything going on out there, you want to send people to Trappist-1?"

"How long, Roxy?"

She flicked her hair out of her eyes. "Couple of years. Maybe less, if you're serious about it."

I nodded. "Let's see if we can do it in a year, shall we?"

February 2087

Henry sat across from me, his suit matching that dismal gray carpet. Even the tornado warnings on the news were less dreary.

"All the years I put into convincing SpaceGen to go to Mars – who would've thought they might actually pay off?" He raised his glass and tossed the wine back.

"They've approved the mission?"

"They approved another Icarus flight this morning."

"Oh, Henry. Mom would be so proud."

"Proud that we're doing the thing she told us expressly not to? Sending more people to die on Trappist-1E."

"That's not what we're doing, Henry. And you know it."

"Perhaps." His perfected smugness might have irritated some, but I always just thought he looked happy. And he deserved to look that way. He'd earned it.

Ever since the Mars landing fiasco, Henry had launched his own little mission — a private charm-offensive. I'd never seen him so slick, rubbing shoulders with the big boys and burning a hole in his pocket with how many cigars he smuggled across the border. Every luxury for the higher-ups was one step closer to another shuttle being launched. And finally, through a careful series of hints and suggestions, he'd somehow managed to bring SpaceGen on board.

"What made them change their mind and approve the launch?" I asked.

"Mars. Of all the things."

"Because of the aging?"

"Bingo." He winked.

The astronauts on the Mars colony were aging at the same rate as they would on Earth, which was faster than we'd anticipated, but they moved in slow motion. Nobody could explain why, except that it must have had something to do with orbital locking. People needed more data. And that's where Orbicon came in.

"Well, whatever strings you pulled, you deserve to celebrate, Henry. We're doing a great thing here."

"We'll be busy. I won't be around much, with all the funding yet to source."

"I expect not." A giddy smile swept my cheeks. "Does that mean we won't have any more of these meetings?"

"Don't sound too happy about it."

"Sorry. It's just. You know how I feel about board meetings."

He laughed. "It's been fun, sis."

"Same."

He extended his hand, and I shook it. It felt final, somehow. The end of an era. Or the start of a new one. Maybe both.

The next day, Roxy arranged my meeting with the first recruit. She made sure it was miles away from the board rooms. I didn't want to interview astronauts surrounded by gray wallpaper and tacky, sticky chairs. If I wanted something tacky and sticky, I wanted it on a waffle, and that's exactly what Roxy arranged. I would interview each of them at that old waffle place where I'd taken her years ago, and still went whenever I could, for a quick pastry fix. Their toppings were just about the only thing worth risking your life for by visiting the surface these days.

It had been forty years since Mom had recruited people to man the mission to Trappist-1. Only now did I really understand what it was she went through, coming to terms with sending people into the unknown, perhaps even to their death. The difference between her and me was that I didn't kid myself into thinking it was for the sake of the human race. I knew we were sending them into oblivion to prove a theory. To save her. Not us.

Maybe that's where she went wrong. She'd tried to save everyone, but maybe all I needed to do was save one person, and it would be enough.

Those diner waffles were great. Totally the opposite of the interviews I'd held to get Roxy. I picked my crew on the basis of how they ate. After all, I could tell everything about a person by the way they ate a waffle.

January 2088

#icarus2launch

It was nothing like the Mars launch. Or the first launch of Icarus One forty years ago.

I remembered watching the Icarus One take-off on that old TV with Henry. Now I was in space on the matter collider, watching it happen for real. Space was weird. But not without its perks. Sure, adjusting to zero gravity had left my butt with more bruises than a peach in a blizzard, but I got great reception on my phone, and there was no hurricane or storm or flood that threatened to wipe me out every ten minutes up here. It was almost peaceful.

I think Mom would have liked it in space.

The craft disappeared on a gravity wave, and I watched the same thing happen as I'd seen on the TV all that time ago. A streak of blackness swallowed it, and the ship vanished in a line of nothingness that shot forever through the stars.

Roxy gripped my arm as tears welled in my eyes.

"This one's for you Mom," I whispered as the Icarus Two disappeared into the abyss.

VI

January 2088

After the Icarus Two vanished, it took all of five minutes before every single person on the space collider barrelled into a frenzy.

We watched the screens with increasing panic as the person at the communication relay repeated over and over – 'Icarus Two, this is Collider Control. Do you copy?' But all that came back was static. Where were the crew? Why didn't they answer? History repeated, and we were left with the receiver to our ears listening to a dead line, left wondering what just happened.

And then my phone rang.

"What do you mean *we haven't heard from them?*" Henry spat through my earpiece.

I wished he'd just calm down. It wasn't my fault, was it? "Take a breath, Henry."

"Halley. What's going on up there?"

I sighed. "Everything is the same as it was forty years ago. We knew the risks."

"But we repaired the communication unit. It's foolproof. We should be receiving *something.*"

"There's no change to the transmissions we've been receiving. It's that same background noise. Same static. Those same weird noises we've been receiving since forever. Cosmic radiation or whatever it's supposed to be."

"But you assured me the upgrades would work."

"And they will. Just give it time. It's only been five minutes."

"Five minutes. A day. Forty years. It's the same old story. What do you think is going to happen when the press gets hold of this?"

"Probably the same thing that happened last time."

"We're ruined." Classic Henry. Too dramatic for his own good.

"We're not ruined just yet. The suppression order applies to us as well as to SpaceGen. We've got five years before we need to release anything to the press."

"That's if we last another five years." From the timbre of his voice, things Earth-side hadn't gone particularly smoothly.

I stared at the planet, shrouded by a tornado of swirling black passing across the ocean. "Was the storm bad?" I asked.

"It wiped out half the coastline."

I closed my eyes. When I opened them, I turned to the mass of space where minutes before, the Icarus Two had plummeted. "Then let's hope this works."

#itsalwaysworseonthewayback

Landing on Earth again was rough with a capital R - O - U - G - *and* H. Mom used to talk about jetlag, but planes hadn't been able to take off safely for decades with the sky being so hazardous and unpredictable. The last time I'd flown had been when I was still young enough not to care about the aftereffects. But now, I knew what she meant when she'd get back from a flight, complain about how tired she was, and spend the next month dozing in the daytime.

My whole body ached, but I just laughed through it. It had been worth it, and it got me out of about a month's worth of stressful meetings with Henry and our communication 'experts.'

By the time I'd got turned around and was ready to attend the meetings, there were already three teams assigned to the problem. No communication had been received thus far. People were already bandying the word 'failure' around. So I didn't really pay it much attention.

Instead of thinking about the missing crew, I rooted myself in the bunker and returned to my dossier. The one I'd been working from for all these years, trying to get closer to Mom. I knew all the good it would do – another waste of months analyzing gravitational wave theory. How many times had I delved into her mind, only for her words to reveal absolutely nothing new since the last time I tried it? But on the plus side, at least wave theory wasn't as boring as other scientific studies I'd done since working through the folder. If this was a map to Mom, then these detours into areas of study were necessary.

Nothing was irrelevant. Not Mom. Not Henry. Not me. Not those little blips of background radiation. Or the Mars colony moving in slow motion.

The slow motion.

Ugh. Another brain-ache.

All we'd ever achieved in the history of our travel beyond Earth was to land humans on a world just as inhospitable as our own. Oh, and to subject them to a time displacement anomaly that had no effect on their aging, but slowed them down. Life on Mars didn't extend the lifespan of humanity, like we'd hoped. And now we'd lost another six astronauts to the void of space, probably never knowing what had happened, or whether mankind stood any more of a chance lightyears away than it did right now, right here, on a savage Earth that grew deadlier with each passing day.

I flipped a page of the folder and my bunker door slid open. Henry appeared looking beaten. Disheveled. Like a guy who'd just bet the bunker and lost.

He collapsed to the floor. "SpaceGen are riding me harder than a demented jockey."

"It's going that well?"

"I've stalled them for as long as I can. But I can't hold them back any longer. I had to tell them we weren't getting any data. They're talking about making it public. The failed Mars Mission. The second Trappist-1 launch. Everything."

"That explains your new look."

"What's that supposed to mean?"

I plonked Mom's file on the concrete and cast a glare up at him. "Henry. In all the years I've known you, I've never seen one hair out of place. But look at you. Tie skewed. Shirt untucked. It's okay to admit it when you're struggling. It's not a sign of weakness."

He raked his hands through his scruffy locks. "What if they release the information to the press? What if this all comes down on our heads? Things up on the surface are barely holding together. If we take away the people's hope, who knows what they'll do?"

"You think this is the first time people have felt hopeless? Just because it's a first for you, doesn't mean it's a first for everybody else."

He shrugged. "What does it matter, Halley? What does anything matter if the planet's doomed anyway? What if . . . Mom really was wrong about everything?"

"Of course she was wrong. Haven't you worked that out yet? The Mars Mission proves it. The question is — how was she wrong?" I picked up the folder again. "I've been over this so many times. Mom's equations are sound. Her principles hold up to scrutiny. So what's the flaw?"

"Is that what you're looking for?"

"Maybe." That's what I said. But we both knew it wasn't true. I just didn't want to admit that I'd failed. I didn't understand Mom any better now than when I was seventeen.

Where are you, Mom?

"Have you got a copy of everything in there?" Henry asked.

"Yep."

"Including her thesis?"

I opened the file and flicked to the document. "Uh huh. Wanna read it?"

"It's the foundation of all of this. You think I'd understand it?"

I shrugged. "It's worth a try."

He took the dossier and his eyes scanned left to right, slowing and slowing until they dragged to a standstill. He passed it back to me. "You read it to me, sis. You always were the smart one."

I sighed. "Sure you wanna hear it?"

He nodded and closed his eyes.

I began reading, my voice reciting the paragraphs by rote while my mind darted off on tangents too crazy to name. It was the first time I'd looked at Rolands' Thesis since I knew it was wrong. But maybe the problem wasn't with the thesis. Maybe the problem was with me?

I'd been trying to see Mom in her work. But what if there was a better way of looking at this? I'd been staring back at Mom from a distance for so long, I'd forgotten what it must have been like to see things from her perspective. What was Mom doing when she started out on this? She was wanting to discover something. 'Discovery is life,' she'd said when I was a girl, and I was finally getting it. I was hoping to discover something too. But what?

I got to the end and closed the folder. "What did you think?" I asked.

"That you read beautifully."

My phone pinged. As did Henry's.

"What's the bet that this is about the mission?" I asked.

"Don't look at it."

But I couldn't just ignore it. I picked it up.

Message from Roxy.

Halley, news from comms. Background static has stopped. All readings ceased. Roxy.

The static had stopped? Did she mean the static we'd been receiving since the Icarus One mission?

Roxy, what do you mean stopped? Halley. Reply sent.

One new message. *Stopped means stopped. Do you want me to arrange a meeting for you with comms? Roxy.*

Tell them I'm on my way. Halley.

I pocketed the phone. "Duty calls."

"If anybody's looking for me, tell them I'm not here," Henry said.

Twenty minutes later, I hunkered down in the communications room with the technicians, each of them in a fluster.

"It just stopped, Director Rolands. There's no other way of describing it. One minute we were getting the signal, like always. And then the next minute, it went."

"Have you any recordings?" I asked the wiry looking man.

"We've been recording continually since first receiving the signal over four decades ago."

"I want all those recordings sent to me at once."

"Yes, Director Rolands."

***

By the time I got home, the comms boys had sent me the lot. I sat with the recordings playing. It was a fuzzy static, like an old radio. And beeps emitted so fast and high-pitched, I could hardly hear them, but the readings on the computer screen registered them. It's why they'd always been called 'blips' as long as I could remember. It sounded more like some awful jazz band from the 2040s than a scientific anomaly — 'dead static and the blips.'

I listened for a pattern. Everybody had written it off as just irrelevant, right from day one. After all, space was full of strange noises nobody could explain. It was why we had technicians for this sort of stuff – to filter out the important things from the same, droll, mundane, garbled hiss of space. And this had always been classified as the latter. By who? Some technician who specialized in headphone tech?

Why had I never questioned this before?

I pulled up the research on the static. Every report signing it off as routine. There was so much reading to be done. It was boring, but I did it.

One guy – in forty years, only guy – had ever concluded it could be faulty machines. That was the same thing they'd said about the slow motion on Mars. Faulty machines. But a systems check ruled that out.

What if it was connected? What if it was all part of the same puzzle?

I had an old file of Mom's thesis open on another tab of my phone.

My fingers operated on automatic, opening it every now and then, and every time, it was just there, staring at me, as if it was trying to tell me something.

"What is it, Mom?" I said out loud. Talking to an equation. I knew I was stressed, but not *that* much. "What would you do?"

I laid back with the fuzz and the beeps constantly droning on and on and on through the speaker. Then, after an hour of the same mind-numbing ffffffft, I flicked forward to the last recording and listened to it stop.

There was no reason for it to stop.

So I rewound the recording and played the last minute again.

It stopped.

Nothing new.

So I rewound it slower.

Played it again, and it stopped.

Rewound it slower.

Played it again.

Rewound it slower.

#stuckonaloop

Every time I rewound it, I did so a little slower, until eventually, the beep sounded like a different type of sound. It was like a voice.

I brought up Mom's thesis.

I played back the recording.

Orbital locking. Of course, it was so simple.

If a greater orbit to Earth slowed down a transmission, like on Mars, then a lesser orbit would speed it up. By how much? I could determine the rate through Mom's workings. Orbital locking was just a math problem, after all. Trappist-1E made one orbit in six days, which was about sixty times quicker than on Earth. So if I slowed it down by sixty times, then it should make up for the time difference.

The last five seconds would equate to about five minutes worth of speech.

I rewound it by ten seconds, and fiddled with the computer settings until I'd adjusted the playback speed. Then I hit play.

" . . . so if we're fortunate, then the raid last night will be the last one they make. But I ain't holding my breath. We've tried everything to make them see sense, but they just call us heretics and throw us out. I've made my last trip to the dark side of the planet. If they won't listen to sense, then it'll be their own fault when we leave without them. I ain't waiting around anymore for them. The ark leaves tomorrow. Everyone in the city is ready. They're calling it the *City of Tyrell* now. The others think I'm foolish for allowing them to treat us like this, but I stopped arguing with them a long time ago. People will do what they want to. There ain't nothing we can do to stop them. Now as for the rocks that are surrounding the planet, they're the biggest challenge we've got. Tomorrow, we'll have no problem lifting off. But to break orbit, we're going to have to get through that shell. Jan thinks we can blow a hole big enough to get through, but I don't want to risk it. So we'll take the ark closer to where the sun is hottest in the center of the planet, and lift off from there. The debris ain't as bad there. Jan's getting the course plotted now. The atmospheric conditioning plant will continue to operate – give Thomas' followers on the dark side as much time as possible. The telescopes that Doctor Wang left have given us the coordinates of the planet we think will be best suited to life. It's orbiting another dwarf star, but it'll be about a ten year journey from here, traveling at the speed of light. We can't travel faster because we've got no matter collider. Thankfully the people here worked out 'solar travel' a long time ago, they just had no way of getting off-planet to put it to use. And they're the ones who think *we* have all the answers. So this will be my final transmission. T-minus eight hours and twenty-seven minutes to lift-off. I've already given you the coordinates for where we'll be landing in ten lightyears. This is Captain Tyrell signing off for the last time, hoping someone can hear me. Over and out."

#mindblown
I burst into tears.
I did it, Mom. I found you.

The phone fell out of my shaking hands, but I somehow managed to call Henry.

"Halley, is everything okay?"

"Everything's great, Henry. We need to call a press conference straight away."

"Listen, I know it's hard keeping people in the dark, but I've reached a decision. We can't afford for the press to find out the truth. People would tear each other apart. No matter what you say, Halley, even the risk of hysteria is too much of a threat. I couldn't be responsible for that. Could you?"

"No, Henry. You don't understand. It's not bad news."

"What? You think us failing twice over isn't bad news?"

"Just . . . ugh. Listen to this." I played back the speech I'd just heard through the phone.

"What is it?" Henry asked.

I sniffed, rubbing my nose on my sleeve and pulling back my blue-dyed fringe. "It's the future," I said.

VII

November 2088

"So you're telling us that the astronauts from the Icarus Two are traveling at the speed of light towards a planet that we can't see through our own telescopes, and have transmitted the coordinates to us?"

"Precisely," I told the late night chat show host.

"But how is that possible?"

"It's like I already explained. The transmission we've been receiving from Trappist-1E since the first Icarus mission has been coming through to us for decades, but in actuality, it's centuries' worth of information. We'll be listening to the history of a new race of humans living on an alien world, detecting the development of a new culture for generations yet. These transmissions have changed the way we understand Rolands' theory, and they give us hope that this new exoplanet will not just sustain our life as a species, but will mean we can look forward to hundreds, if not thousands of years of life once we arrive."

"So I'm gonna keep my good looks after all?" the host said. "Mother will be pleased."

The audience clapped and cheered.

"This new exoplanet orbits its sun once every four days," I said, "so even those traveling from Trappist-1E will live longer than they would have done on their own exoplanet."

"But you think we can beat them to it? Squatters' rights?"

#lame

I remembered not to roll my eyes on camera, just like Henry had prepped me. "Not how I would have put it, but if it takes them ten years to cross that distance, then we should be an active, thriving colony by the time they arrive."

"So when are we going?"

"A preliminary shuttle is leaving immediately, and the first passenger shuttles will be setting off within the year."

The applause thundered the studio louder than the storm outside. Henry would have been proud. Mom might even have kept watching.

"But," the host said, bringing everyone back to Earth, "if we haven't been able to see this new exoplanet because . . . explain to me why again?"

"There's a nebula blocking our view. A giant cloud of gas and radiation and light and particles and all manner of other things that's like a mask when it comes to our view of space from here on Earth. But they can see it from Trappist-1E clear as day."

"Right. So if we can't see it from Earth, then isn't this just all a great big shot in the dark?"

"A shot in the dark is better than no shot at all, wouldn't you agree?"

"You heard it here first, folks. Thank you to Halley Rolands. We'll be right back with some music. Don't go anywhere."

When I walked through my bunker door, I had messages from Henry and Roxy telling me how great it came over. We'd have to employ three hundred new people just to answer the phones at Orbicon over the next month. Everybody wanted answers.

There was never a question in my mind as to whether or not I'd be going on the next Icarus mission. Not even the anti-Trappist groups chanting 'give Earth a chance' could've stopped me.

"Do you think your body will handle the stress of gravitational wave propulsion?" Henry asked, concerned that I was making some rash mistake.

"Henry, if I can stand to listen to you whining, then I'll have no problem with it."

"Well, take care of yourself up there won't you."

"I'll see you soon enough."

"Call it a couple of hundred years."

He'd be one of the last to leave. He'd stay to make sure that Earth's evacuation went as planned. But he'd come eventually.

"Be good, sis."

I gave him a hug, and then left for the launch bay. We were heading up to the collider that day to make the preparations on Icarus Three.

***

#byeee

Strapped into the cockpit with five others waiting to leave, I felt like I'd gone back in time. I was five years old again, being crammed into a bunker to escape some catastrophe on the surface. It was all a bit claustrophobic. Nobody expected to feel claustrophobic in space. But the waiting made everything stale. We just wanted to get going.

Roxy sat across from me, and then there were four others who had been chosen. I was the captain of the crew, although I wasn't qualified, but it meant I got to say those eponymous words — 'we are a go for launch.'

"Roger that, Icarus Three. Prepare for matter collision in T-minus one minute."

"Did we approve those designs on the larger passenger transports?" I asked Roxy.

"Yes, Miss Rolands."

"And we programmed the fluctuation in orbital gravity into the communication equipment?"

"Yes, Miss Rolands."

"Good. I just feel like I'm forgetting something."

"Don't worry. I took care of everything."

"Did you close the office windows?"

"Does it matter if I didn't?"

"10 . . . 9 . . . 8 . . ."

"Any last words?" I asked the crew.

"No, Miss Rolands," they all said in unison, which meant I'd reduced the brightest minds on Earth to, effectively, a pack of naughty school children.

"7 . . . 6 . . . 5 . . ."

"Goodbye, Earth," I whispered, wishing I could make it into a hashtag and post something about it before I left.

"4 . . . 3 . . . 2 . . . 1 . . ."

VIII

Year 1, Day 1

I opened my eyes upon the most beautiful sight I'd ever beheld. The light from the star was a deep red, and two mauve planets orbited around it, performing a cosmic dance. The sky was a ballet, and I could have sat in the theater of the heavens watching it forever.

"Is everybody alright?" I asked.

"Fine, Miss Rolands."

"How about you, Roxy?"

"Apart from being a bit queasy, I'm fine," she said.

In her flight suit, she reminded me of the first time I'd met her, dolled up in her finest, and hating every minute of it.

"Halley, can I ask a really stupid question?"

"Sure, Roxy."

"Is space meant to be purple here?"

In the distance, a blue star fired its light across space like a giant candle might warm an entire room. The hot red of a smaller sun and the aura of the distant blue star mingled together to create a lilac haze, banishing the black void of space and replacing it with the most gorgeous royal purple.

The only spots to mar this stellar canvas were the planets in orbit of that red sun. Our new homes.

"Pretty, isn't it?" I said.

"Yeah." Roxy smiled.

"When you're ready, Sanchez, take us down."

Sanchez moved us slowly forwards and I reveled in the slow approach to the planet's surface. It steadily loomed larger and larger until we were close enough to glimpse the ocean.

The planet had only one ocean, and it was on the border where light met dark. From what we understood of the description Tyrell had given of the planet through his broadcasts, the sea was frozen on the dark side of the planet, but liquified where the sun reached it. This massive ocean covered a third of the surface. But seeing it before us was too surreal. No description could have done it justice.

The closer we flew to the ground, the clearer the crystalline mountains became, and the purple foliage of trees growing on crystal rocks dazzled through the viewport. The sky's purple haze was reflected by the ground, and the whole planet shimmered.

We landed near the ocean, and transformed our vessel into the first dome that would soon become a city.

The planet was much bigger than Earth. Our new ocean could have fit the entirety of Earth into its depths. And the sun was warm, even through the suits.

Year 1, Day 5

The dome was up and spinning fine. I made our first communication back to Orbicon to confirm we'd arrived, and it was safe to send the next transport as soon as it was ready.

Year 10, Day 17

"Halley! Look!" Roxy pointed up.

Two giant tails of light streaked across the heavens, and at their head, a massive and familiar shadow.

"The next transport vessel! It's here!"

Finally. Others from Earth had come to join us. And not one moment too soon.

Year 607, Day 109

I'd almost forgotten Henry's face. How many hundreds of years have I lived in my little dome? Watched Roxy's children grow and have children of their own? How many generations? Is it eight or nine? But when Henry stepped off the transport, there was no mistaking him, no matter how old he looked.

"What news from Earth?" I asked, after we'd cried on each other's shoulders and practically hugged each other to death.

"Nothing much to tell. The only ones left behind are the ones who didn't want to come."

"How many?"

"I think the number is 2.3 billion."

"Over two billion people refusing to leave? I don't believe it."

"Let's not think of it. Earth's history now. What are we calling this place?"

"Planet Orbicon, of course."

Year 952, Day 65

No more transports had filled our skies since Henry had brought the last one. Not until today.

"What is it? More people from Earth. How did they make it off the surface?"

Chatter murmured through the crowds who gawped up at the strange craft looming through the mist.

"That's not an Earth-ship," I said. I bounded through the fray and couldn't hold back the grin which vanished my wrinkles. "It's the Ark. The Ark of Trappist-1E."

The vessel was a huge dome, and it set down nearby on the far side of the sea. When we reached it, Tyrell could scarcely believe his eyes.

"Care for some waffles?" I asked.

"You got our message."

"Thank you, Tyrell. You saved us all. Welcome to the planet Orbicon."

"It is the Realm of Orbicon," uttered the cries of thousands whom Tyrell had delivered safely.

He facepalmed himself so hard. "I've spent the past ten years trying to knock that out of them."

"Like I said — you're welcome." I smirked.

Year 1,208, Day 42

Discovery is life, Mom used to say. Some discoveries are accidental, and some are made on purpose. In leaving Earth, we had discovered a new home. My discovering the transmissions hidden for all those years had meant literal life for billions on Orbicon.

But discovery has its price. In the space of my lifetime, man had ruined two worlds in its name. Now, in my twelve hundredth year, alone atop a purple crystal hill, I sat awestruck by the beauty of the valley's trough, and I couldn't help but wonder how long it might be before some accident of discovery ruined this one.

I suppose it doesn't matter. After all, time flows through us as much as we do through it.

So when it's time to go, I know we'll be ready.

#sameasalways

ACKNOWLEDGMENTS

This book couldn't exist without some very special people. First of all, my wife and son. Thank you for the inspiration, patience, and smiles which have fuelled this story.

To my critique partner, EA Carroway — TCH4L. This story reads so much better now that your brain has demolished it and pieced it back together again. Thank you.

My beta readers are the greatest. EL Strife — you were the first to help me shape *Time's Ellipse* into its final form. Davene Le Grange — your tireless support and insightful feedback is invaluable. You're a treasure. Dawn Ross — your belief in me and fantastic input spurs me on. Thank you all.

To my writing family who have listened to me go on about this story way too much: Emily, Ren, the whole FFA crew, Ai, Richard, Nadine (who has the eyes of an eagle when it comes to spotting spelling errors!), Mum and Dad, and everyone else who I'm forgetting — thank you.

Adrian, the cover is 1,000% cooler because of you. You rock!

Books soar on the wings of those who carry them in their imaginations. Thank you for letting this story take a spin around your mind. Thank you for letting it take flight. And thank you for every review you write, whether it's good or bad, which lets me know a small tale of mine has reached someone.

And finally, to Keanu Reeves — like my beta readers, you, sir, are the greatest. Now when are you going to pick up this story and make it into a vehicle for your peerless acting skills? Huh?

ABOUT FRASIER

Frasier Armitage is a part-time robot and full-time nerd. He's an award-winning audio-dramatist and novelist who spends far too much time alone in a room scribbling about things which are impossible, AKA writing science-fiction. When he's not writing, you'll find him watching Keanu Reeves movies with his wife and son, noodling on his guitar, or trying to dig his way out of the mountain of books on his TBR pile.

To find out more about Frasier, visit https://frasierarmitage.com

Connect with him on social media using @FrasierArmitage

NEW YESTERDAY

FIND YOUR PAST

SAVE YOUR FUTURE

What if you could change everything in your life you wish you'd done differently? Fix regret? Unlock the potential of your past?

That's what Adam Swann did in New Yesterday, a city where events in the present can alter history. He's living the life of his dreams, yet he can't shake a name from his mind – the memory of a woman from a past he left behind. Who is she? And despite the dangers that remembering his former life would pose, why can't he bring himself to forget her?

Adam will unearth long-buried secrets as he searches the city for clues to the woman woven through his memory, haunting his every thought. As the truth of his past drags him into a conspiracy that threatens everything he knows, he'll be forced to choose between the life of his dreams or facing the man he used to be.

Keep reading for a sample . . .

NEW YESTERDAY

'THERE'S NO CURE for regret. Until now! How would you like to erase those troublesome past mistakes? Have you ever wondered what your life would look like if you'd done things different? Well, what are you waiting for? Pop on down to your local "Anderson Whitman" and see what's available in New Yesterday! That's right! If you're sick of the same old routine, now's the time to escape it. Explore limitless possibilities in the world's only city where time is as flexible as you want. With a wide range of lifestyle packages to choose from, changing your history has never been easier. So stop living in the past — make the past live for you. Wave goodbye to "if only." Don't delay. Start your new life today! Because, if your future's what you make it, why shouldn't your past be too?'

— Anderson Whitman Real Estate,
broadcast circa 2029.

ONE

IT WASN'T THE THREAT of a bullet through my head that forced my sweat to boil and bones to freeze. Locked in the elevator, floors ticked by like years. Cold steel dug into my vertebrae. But none of that caused the chaos hammering my brain, shredding my stomach, pumping ice through my veins.

No, my every nerve hung on one word —

Adam.

How did he know my name?

"Don't worry." The gunman tightened his grip on my collar. "This'll be over soon." I could only guess how.

Gears whirred, the soundtrack of my pounding head. From my pocket, the phone buzzed, blasting at my heart, jerking me into the wall.

"Don't answer it," he said.

His pistol jutted deeper into my back — a marionette's string tugging me any way he wanted. He slammed me against the mirror and emptied my pockets. The phone clattered to the floor, reverberating around the boxed walls of my descending coffin.

Celia's name lit up the screen.

Two seconds was all I'd need. Two seconds to answer and tell her where I was. She'd sort this out, retrograde the morning so I'd been nowhere near the 27th floor when this lunatic showed up. One phone call and none of this would've ever happened.

"Look," I said, my mouth dry as ash, "I don't know who you think I am, but you've got the wrong guy."

"I know exactly who you are." His eyes flashed, face twisted in the warp of the mirrored panel.

How many times had I glossed over that same face in warning bulletins and news reports? On pop-up alerts telling me to 'tap here if you've seen this man'? In black and white grains beneath the headlines. 'Linear Offender Still At Large,' 'Manhunt Continues,' 'Police Say No New Leads.' The most famous face in the city, and now it was preying on me, scolding me with its silent threat.

The lift steadied.

"Don't get any ideas."

Doors churned open to the underground parking lot. He dragged me to a battered minivan abandoned in the visitor's bay.

"Get in." As if I had a choice.

Empty packets of Doritos littered the passenger seat, a no-man's-land of leftovers reeking of booze and BO.

My abductor slid behind the wheel and dropped the gun in his lap. The engine wheezed as we pulled from the curb and filtered into traffic, melding with a parade of brake lights. The seat thrummed to the rhythm of the tires bumping over crumbs of tarmac.

"This is all your fault, Adam. You know that?"

"I don't—" I started but caught my tongue before it led me straight into a bullet. "Listen, whatever you think I did, I'm sorry."

"*You're* sorry? If you'd never found me, none of this would've happened."

Either he'd got a terrible sense of humor or he was a few records short of a jukebox. *Found him?* It wasn't me that had snatched him from *his* office. Maybe going linear really did make you as crazy as they said?

Outside the window, high-rises crammed us into narrow lanes, silver blurs pressing us in. Steam hissed out of vents to mingle with exhaust fumes. The street was a pressure cooker, boiling us in concrete. My skin prickled. Where was he taking me?

"Are . . . are you . . ." I stuttered.

"Spit it out!"

"Are you going to kill me?"

His hand hovered over the gear stick, reluctant to shift. "Only if I have to."

I clutched the seat while it jabbed against my shaking legs.

"It's nothing personal," he said. "I didn't plan for this. But it's the only way. Do you understand?"

What was there to understand about this guy? I sat stiff, the belt drilling into my chest.

"Just forget it," he huffed as the car sped faster down the boulevard.

Maybe if I closed my eyes, it'd all go away? I'd be back in my office going over the mall plans with Jeff, getting ready to dine clients at the gala ball later tonight, instead of being kidnapped by this madman. 'It was the only way,' he'd said. What did a person *need* a hostage for exactly?

Just breathe. Don't think about it. But the stench of stale sweat and the tap, tap, tap of his gun on the seat choked the air like two hands around my throat. There was no escape, no matter how tight I squeezed my eyes shut.

"What do you want?" I asked.

"I want my *life* back."

"Your what?"

"Are you deaf? You took it from me, Adam. And I want it back."

"But I . . . we've never—"

"Not you too?" He shook his head and tensed the wheel. "I was getting on just fine before you showed up, y'know? But then you came with your questions and your papers and your annoying little whine going on and on and on. You changed everything. And now you don't even remember it. This city's really done a number on you."

I could've said the same to him. Why was I even trying to talk to this psycho? Everyone knows better than to get involved with a nut job who's gone linear. I'd never met the guy until he'd strolled into my office and jammed a gun in my face. But then how did he know my name? "Where are we going?"

"To make things right."

We turned a corner and the car skirted the curb, screeching to a halt. Over the road, the Anderson Whitman logo decorated a steamed glass front. Screens filtered through properties on a slideshow, advertising apartments and houses across the city.

"Now when we go inside, you'll tell them this is your fault," he said. "You'll say you came to see me, and everything that followed has all been just a huge mistake. And then they're going to fix it so none of this ever happened. Okay?"

Okay? What was okay about any of this? "Do I have a choice?"

"There's always a choice, Adam. A right one . . ." He grabbed the gun. "And a wrong one."

Its harsh metal split the space between us like lightning. "You've got your gun. Why do you need me?" The circle of its barrel was a vortex, a black hole that swallowed my vision.

"Just do your part and nobody gets hurt," he said.

Gets hurt? I shook my head. "This is crazy. I can't . . . this isn't going to work."

"Of course it is," he said. "They'll listen to you."

"What if they don't?"

"They will. They *have* to."

What was he trying to do? Force Anderson Whitman to retrograde his past by feeding me the history he wanted? Blackmail them into changing his life by taking me hostage?

"Now what are you going to tell them, Adam?"

"That this is my fault."

"Good. And . . .?"

"And they need to fix it."

"Now just calm down. Everything'll be okay, as long as you stick to the script. You ready?"

Ready for what? Ready to lie for him so he could get a new past, or ready to have my head blown off?

I nodded.

He stuffed the gun inside his belt and tucked it beneath his trousers. "Come on. Let's get this over with."

TWO

THE GUNMAN POCKETED his keys and lifted the hood of his coat to shield his face. In a flash, he was at my window, holding my door open. His cologne stalked me through a queue of cars and we entered the Anderson Whitman storefront.

Across the room, desks staggered towards a screened-off area where chairs surrounded a TV. Along the back wall, glass cubicles partitioned the offices in a row. Everything shimmered white. From her desk, a receptionist in a blue blazer and matching neck scarf waved us forwards.

"Welcome to Anderson Whitman Real Estate. How can I be of service?" She pasted an empty smile across her alabaster skin.

"We need to see someone about retrograding," my kidnapper said from behind me, close enough to be my shadow.

She squinted at him. Recognition flashed across her expression like a photographer's bulb, before it dissipated into nothing. She shrugged and swiveled to her screen. "Have you got an appointment?"

How could she not recognize his face? What were the press calling him — The City's Houdini?

"Didn't think we'd need one," Houdini said.

She tapped at her monitor. "I'm sorry, but all our agents are busy with other clients at the moment."

My eyes widened, flicking between her face and the gap in his open jacket, where the outline of the gun bulged beneath his shirt. She stared at me, masking her disinterest with a veil of courtesy. *Just follow my eyes.*

He caught me glancing at the gun. "Pssst." Our gaze met and he shook his head.

"You can take a seat in the waiting area, if you like?" She nodded to the group of chairs on the far side of the room.

He paced to the desk. "You *sure* we can't see someone now?" His hand caressed its rim, toying with the wooden edge as his fingers crept closer to his waist. "Couldn't you rearrange their appointments to make them free, or something?"

"I'm sorry, but you'll have to wait."

He reached for his belt. His muscles twitched as he untucked his shirt. I glanced at the girl behind the counter and her ceramic, doll-like eyes. Was he so desperate that he'd draw his gun on her? Or worse?

"You're not giving us many options," he said.

"That's the way things are, sir."

His face galvanized into a murderous scowl. Static charged the gulf between them. Another moment and he'd blast her all over the walls. A broken doll.

"Alright, then. If you say so." He gritted his teeth. His wrist snapped for the gun.

"I'm Adam Swann," I said, stepping forwards.

He stiffened.

"Yes?" she said.

"Premium package member. SSA. Swann Sinclair Accounts. It really is urgent that we see someone." Cold sweat dampened my shirt. My entire body coiled, taut as a runner on their marks, waiting for the starting pistol, the one he'd shoved beneath his buckle.

She sighed and tapped her screen again. Her face buffered along with the database until the monitor bleeped. "Oh. Sorry, Mr. Swann. I didn't realize who you were. Julie . . ." A girl at the neighboring desk lifted her head. "Julie, will you show these gentlemen to the waiting area?"

"Follow me, please." Julie strutted to the chairs, heels clacking.

Houdini's hands dropped to his sides. Away from the gun. He raised an eyebrow at me, motioning us towards the girl.

The desk clerks watched their computer screens without giving us a second look. Hadn't any of them seen the news? Didn't anyone recognize this guy?

Beyond the desks, Julie turned and dawdled by the waiting chairs. On the TV monitor, the Anderson Whitman advert played over and over. She clasped her hands together. "We'll amend the schedule and a salesman will be right with you. Shan't be a moment."

Her feet pattered back to her desk and she took a seat as if everything was fine. No problem. She wouldn't have been so carefree if she'd known how close she was to getting mowed down by this madman.

His eyes scoured the room and he fiddled with his belt. *Don't think about what he would've done to those women. What he might still do.*

On the TV, smiling faces filled the screen as the voiceover repeated the AW slogan. 'If your future's what you make it, why shouldn't your past be too?'

Inside the cubicles on the back wall, estate agents propped themselves behind desks, with their clients in front of them nodding along in time. At the nearest desk, a lone agent stood and straightened his cufflinks.

The salesman was a chameleon in Armani pinstripes, changing his skin from person to person. He pushed the glass door open and it shivered on its hinges, smeared with a legacy of fingerprints.

"Come on in," he said through a disingenuous, toothy smirk. "I'm sorry to keep you, but I've not had two spare minutes to rub together today. You're here about a lifestyle package, I take it?"

I glanced at the gunman. *What now?*

"After you, Adam," Houdini whispered, inching backwards to let me through.

"Don't be shy." The salesman shepherded us into his office. "Won't you sit down?" He pointed to the smooth leather tub-chairs across from his desk. I sank into the soft beige, and Houdini perched beside me, wrists in his lap.

"Can I get you anything?" The salesman lounged in his seat. His suit's navy lines crumpled in zigzags. "Coffee? Tea?"

I shook my head.

Houdini sat still and silent as a mannequin.

"So." A smile slithered across the face of our host. "What can I do for you, gentlemen?"

Houdini's eyes flashed at me. His fingers rubbed together as if he were polishing a coin. He glanced down at the concealed weapon and then back towards me. *Just do your part, and nobody gets hurt.*

"This is all my fault," I said.

"Please, Mr . . .?"

"Swann."

". . . Mr. Swann. Let's not get ahead of ourselves. Whatever's happened, I'm sure we can work it out. It says here you're a premium member, with a full lifestyle package. Is that right?"

"I'm joint CEO of Swann Sinclair Accounts."

"Congratulations, Mr. Swann. That must be nice for you. You got anything we could use to confirm that?"

"What do you mean 'confirm'?"

He removed a tablet from his top drawer, tapping the screen to life. "Well, we need some proof that you are who you say you are. You wouldn't believe how many people come in here claiming their lives have changed and asking for them back. Some of the stories we hear, you could write a book."

"Is that so?" Houdini said.

"In fact, just the other day, I had a man trying to convince me he was a Maharaja. All because he was sick of stacking shelves at Gracy's and thought we could alter things for him. These poor interlopers who come into the city without a lifestyle package, hoping their lives might change, and then not being happy when it does. Makes you feel sorry for them."

My captor's eyes burned into me. "I'll bet."

"What proof do you need?" I said. "ID? Driver's license?"

"ID?" The salesman shook his head. "I'm afraid fabrications are far too easy to come by these days. People

11

losing themselves in retrogrades gone wrong. A list of clients we can check your details with should suffice."

"Our biggest client is actually Anderson Whitman."

"Wait. You don't mean Swann Sinclair Accounts, as in *SSA*?"

"That's it."

"Well, that makes things simple, at least. If you're in the AWG, running your details through the database shouldn't be too difficult." The salesman checked his Rolex. "Aren't you supposed to be hosting this big gala event at the Phoenix Hotel?"

"I was just getting ready to head out of the office when . . ." My voice trailed off and the gunman straightened in his seat. *What was I going to say? 'When I was forced at gunpoint into all this'?*

"When . . . what?" the salesman asked.

"When . . . when I . . . realized what a mistake I'd made."

"Ah. So you came straight here. I understand. Don't worry. You're in the right place." He set the tablet down on the desk and a ceaseless swirling circle spiraled across it.

"How long will this take?" Houdini asked.

"Once we've done the confirmations, amending a package shouldn't be too much trouble. What is it we need to clear up for you, that you've not been able to retrograde for yourselves?"

"Everything," I said.

"Can you be more specific?"

"It's hard to say. Nothing's been right since I met this man." At least that part was true.

"I see."

"Can we change the past so I never met him?"

"Of course." The salesman's fingers brushed across his tablet like oil on canvas. "When did you meet?"

My spine jolted upright. *When? Five minutes before we marched in. But I doubt that's what Captain Blackmail wants to hear.*

Houdini arched forwards, perched on the lip of his seat. "What does it matter?" he said. "Can't you go back and fix it?"

"Go back where? What do you think we do here? Time travel?"

"Isn't that how it works?"

The salesman rolled his eyes. "You think we've got a machine hidden away in a storage cupboard that takes us back in time?"

"You're supposed to change the past, aren't you? How else do you explain retrograding?" Houdini reddened, fidgeting with a frayed strand of thread dangling from a loose button.

I blushed the same shade of crimson as the salesman's tie as he straightened its knot and rubbed his hands together.

"I'm sorry to burst your bubble, gents, but time travel isn't possible. Not for human beings. We exist in the present. That's the *being* part of it. But we can change your present. And fortunately for us, here in New Yesterday, any changes we make today don't just ripple forwards, but backwards too."

"Are you saying things can't go back to how they were before?" Houdini said.

"Once we change a past, it's gone. You don't remember any of the histories you lived before the one you've got now, do you? It'd be ridiculous, wouldn't it? Carrying around all those versions of the past. All those tweaks and retrogrades. Drive you mad." The salesman's eyes rested on the gunman for a second too long.

Wait a minute. Does he know?

"But just because one past has vanished," the salesman said, picking up from where he left off without the hint of a seam, "doesn't mean it's hopeless. I'll bet we can get you something better than before. Think of it like a blanket. If you're unhappy with the way the fabric creases, we'll iron out the kinks. Make you more comfortable. Why would you ever want those creases back?"

"Some people might." Houdini's head shook faster and faster, like a broken metronome.

"Here, take a look at these." The salesman splayed folders from his drawers across the desk. On their fronts, photos of expensive manors or penthouse suites were all stamped with the Anderson Whitman logo. "If you want to build a house anywhere else in the world, you're stuck as far as time is concerned. But here, we don't just trade in three dimensions, we trade in four. You could build one of these houses twenty years ago. Longer even. You could have been born in an apartment that isn't even built yet. There are no limits in this city. We can give you anything."

"Anything but what's real." Houdini rocked back and forth on the fringe of his seat. He was a time-bomb, ticking down.

"Reality is so subjective, don't you think? If you're worried about keeping your past, a lifestyle package is just the ticket. It guarantees you the life you want to lead. We can always revert your history back to one of these. Why not flick through them? It's never too late to upgrade your package. We've got an excellent offer on—"

Time was up.

Houdini exploded out of his chair. His hands reached for his pocket and he slammed a sheet of paper on the desk. Its laminated folds blossomed, opening like the petals of a flower.

"This is what I want." He pointed at the paper.

The salesman sloped his spectacles down his nose and examined the document. "I see." He nodded. "Where did you come by this?"

"*He* gave it to me." Houdini pointed to where I sat.

"Is that true, Mr. Swann?"

Houdini turned to face me. His hand rested on his hips, tapping towards his weapon.

"What is it?" I asked.

The salesman tilted the page towards me. It was a planning document proposing that a shop move from one location to another. Except, the move would have happened six years before the date they'd signed it. There was no forwarding address, no alternative site for the previous business. But that can't have been right? They wouldn't have approved the old store to just vanish. Like it had never been there. Six years of profits disappeared in an instant. Retrograded into nothing.

Fever broke across my forehead. Sweat dripped into my eyes, stinging them raw and blurring my vision.

Why do I recognize that page?

I know that slip of paper. I've seen it before. Pored hours over it, trying to find something.

But what?

A name sprang into my head, clear as the glass walls of this office.

Lottie.

. . . Lottie?

I shook the memory away. The room spun, flexing in and out of focus.

"Mr. Swann?" The salesman's voice.

That single page jolted me like a defibrillator thunking two hundred volts through my brain. *How can I make this stop?*

"Look," I said. "I can't . . . do this."

"*Adam!*" the gunman yelled.

"I've . . . I've never seen this man before." My head fell into my hands.

The salesman dropped the laminated page and tapped his screen. "That's good. Very good. Excellent, in fact. Just what I'd hoped to hear."

The gunman reached into his belt and plucked his pistol. Its scuffed metal chamber seemed to fill the room. His hand quivered, aimed between the salesman's eyes.

"I want my life back! *Right. Now.*"

I pinned myself to the back of the chair, trying to push my way through it so I could run, but its leather frame forced me to remain.

The salesman's elastic grin stretched wide. "Won't you take a seat?" He didn't even blink. He looked at the man with such indifference. Just another customer. As if this was normal. *Is the gun invisible or something? Am I the only one who cares about getting shot?*

The gunman charged at the desk. "You're not *listening,*" he said. "That store was my life and I want it back! D'you hear?" He cocked his pistol and the bullet snapped into the chamber, the crackle before the thunder.

Unruffled, the salesman eased back into his chair. "My dear boy, what do you expect is going to happen here? Do you think you can threaten me? Who do you think is really holding the gun?"

"What?"

He raised the tablet from his lap. "In my hand, I have all the changes to your histories ready and waiting. With a swipe of this screen, we'll retrograde all of this. In less than a second, you'll have been in custody for a week, and our friend, Mr. Swann, will be preparing for his gala, measuring out the champagne like none of this ever happened."

"No! That store is mine! It belongs to *me*."

"Be careful," the salesman warned. "With the way things stand, I've got it worked out for you to be arrested for your linear infraction. We can't have you roaming the streets with memories of two different pasts, can we? But it'd be a terrible shame if you got knocked down in traffic before the police found you."

"Are you threatening me?"

"Accidents happen. Even in the past."

The gunman's finger rattled over the trigger. Houdini turned his crazed, frightened eyes on me. "No, he's bluffing," he muttered below his breath. He lurched towards me and grabbed my collar, wrenching me to my feet. The gun scraped against my scalp. "You're in this together, aren't you? You set me up. Don't think you can bluff me out of what's mine."

"Are you okay there, Mr. Swann?" the salesman asked.

"I . . . I just want to forget all this," I said.

"That shouldn't be a problem." The salesman smiled. His tablet chimed. "Oh, good. Confirmation's just in. Congratulations, Mr. Swann. Checks have come back normal. Give it a minute and your new past will replace all this. I'm so sorry for the inconvenience."

"You can't do this to me!" the gunman shrieked. "I'll kill him! Do you understand? I'll *kill* him!"

"You know, it's such a shame you didn't look through our lifestyle packages. They really are rather good."

The gunman's fist clenched around my collar. His arms strained into rungs of steel, hardened by mania. I was in the middle of a standoff, caught between two men about to draw. One man's metal barrel clawed at my skin. The other sat poised with his finger ready to undo all this. And why? Because of a piece of paper? A laminated sheet. The memory of a past that disappeared.

Lottie.

Time flickered like a broken TV screen. The curtain was coming down. And all I could think was 'Lottie'? *Who is she? What does 'Lottie' even mean?*

"Pleasure doing business with you," the salesman said, his finger pressed against the tablet.

Death's whisper escaped from the barrel as the gunman squeezed the trigger.

The salesman swiped.

Printed in Great Britain
by Amazon